CARRI

These are the stories of the Carrier including a supercarrier, amphibious destroyer. And these are the novels of international combat. Exciting. Authentic. Explosive.

CARRIER . . . The smash debut thriller about the ultimate military nightmare: the takeover of a U.S. Intelligence ship.

VIPER STRIKE . . . A renegade Chinese fighter group penetrates Thai airspace—and launches a full-scale invasion.

ARMAGEDDON MODE . . . With India and Pakistan on the verge of nuclear destruction, the Carrier Battle Group Fourteen must prevent a final showdown.

FLAME-OUT . . . The Soviet Union is reborn in a military take-over—and their strike force shows no mercy.

MAELSTROM . . . The Soviet occupation of Scandanavia leads the Carrier Battle Group Fourteen into conventional weapons combat—and possibly all-out war.

COUNTDOWN . . . Carrier Battle Group Fourteen must prevent the deployment of Russian submarines. The problem is: They have nukes.

AFTERBURN . . . Carrier Battle Group Fourteen receives orders to enter the Black Sea—in the middle of a Russian civil war.

ALPHA STRIKE . . . When American and Chinese interests collide in the South China Sea, the superpowers risk waging a third World War.

ARCTIC FIRE . . . A Russian splinter group has occupied the Aleutian Islands off the coast of Alaska—in the ultimate invasion on U.S. soil.

ARSENAL . . . Magruder and his crew are trapped between Cuban revolutionaries . . . and a U.S. power play that's spun wildly out of control.

NUKE ZONE . . . When a nuclear missile is launched against the U.S. Sixth Fleet, Magruder must face a frightening question: In an age of computer warfare, how do you tell friends from enemies?

Don't miss these CARRIER novels—available in paperback.

book twelve

CARRIER

Chain of Command

KEITH DOUGLASS

JOVE BOOKS, NEW YORK

CARRIER 12: CHAIN OF COMMAND

A Jove Book / published by arrangement with
the author

PRINTING HISTORY
Jove edition / January 1999

All rights reserved.
Copyright © 1999 by Jove Publications, Inc.
This book may not be reproduced in whole or in part,
by mimeograph or any other means, without permission.
For information address: The Berkley Publishing Group,
a member of Penguin Putnam Inc.,
375 Hudson Street, New York, New York 10014.

The Penguin Putnam Inc. World Wide Web site address is
http://www.penguinputnam.com

ISBN: 0-515-12431-1

A JOVE BOOK®
Jove Books are published by The Berkley Publishing Group,
a member of Penguin Putnam Inc.,
375 Hudson Street, New York, New York 10014.
JOVE and the "J" design
are trademarks belonging to Jove Publications, Inc.

PRINTED IN THE UNITED STATES OF AMERICA

10 9 8 7 6 5 4 3 2 1

ONE
Vice Admiral Matthew "Tombstone" Magruder

22 September

I didn't intend to kill the first one. Not really.

It was fifteen years ago, almost to the day. The Soviet MiG had a hard-on for me and my ass was nailed into the cockpit of an F-14A Tomcat by a four-point ejection harness. The conclusion was intuitively obvious. One of us was going to make an uncontrolled descent to the ground and impact at an angle completely outside of our aircraft's performance envelope.

The second that I heard the ESM warble telling me the MiG had me illuminated, I knew it wasn't going to be me.

U.S. Navy fighter-pilot training is as realistic as it can get. By the time I met my first real live MiG, I had two peacetime cruises under my belt, as well as Top Gun training. But ten weeks playing laser tag with adversary aircraft isn't the real thing. It isn't until you get cockpit-to-cockpit with someone who wants to kill you that you know what you're made of. Then the training kicks in, the reflexes they build into you. In my case, I killed the MiG before I ever really thought about it.

Something about seeing the coastline of Vietnam now materializing green-brown out of a swath of fog and clouds brought back the memories of my first kill as an F-14 pilot.

The coastline—or maybe remembering just what else that canopy of green hid underneath it. And how it must have been for my father during his final mission over it. The one he never came back from.

Sunlight glinted off metal to my right. I jerked the Tomcat left by reflex, opening the gap between my Tomcat and my too-eager wingman. What the hell was he doing so close in anyway? You fly as my wingman, I want two hundred feet of vertical and forty-five degrees of separation.

The Vietnamese MiG honor escort knew that. I'd briefed them before we left the ship, actually talked to the pilot in slow, precise English, making sure he understood. He rogered up for the entire formation brief, assured me that his flight of two was experienced in formation flying, and damned near promised me he could build one of those sleek babies from the ground up.

Not that I'd believed him. I've flown with foreign air forces often enough over the past twenty-four years to know that nothing equals U.S. Navy aviation training—nothing.

But I at least thought I'd made it clear that he was to stay out of my way.

The MiGs just off either wing knew that too. For an escort service, they remained a respectable distance off my wings, within visual but politely outside of my immediate envelope. I appreciated that, although God knows what they thought I'd do if they got too close.

That first kill: We were over Norway, on a routine patrol off USS *Jefferson*. Lieutenant j.g. Dwight "Snowball" New-combe was in the backseat, a brand-new fresh-caught Radar

Intercept Officer, or RIO. He started off shaky that day, but I never could figure out whether it was because he was flying with his skipper or because he was new. Hell, I hadn't been in command much longer than he'd been on board, and I'd been fast-tracked into the CO slot at that. Knowing that, I was probably just as nervous as he was.

Fortunately, my old buddy Batman was on my wing to keep me straightened out. He's two years behind me and it seems like he's been following me around my entire career. Right now, in his final months as Commander, Carrier Group 14, embarked on *Jefferson,* he's finishing up his tour just as I did—with one last foray into harm's way before he's relieved. With the reputation he's making for himself, I wouldn't be surprised if he puts on that third star before I do.

Every man needs somebody like Batman around. He's more outgoing than I am, with a quick, easy laugh and an even faster temper. You always know where you stand with him—there's never any guessing, although a few tours in D.C. shepherding the Joint Aviation Strike Technology—JAST—birds through the acquisition and purchasing cycles seem to have taught him a hell of a poker face. I doubt that it'll ever rival mine, but he's running a close second.

Batman. Rear Admiral (upper half) Edward Everett Wayne, if you want to get official. It was that "upper half" that was about to really screw him, just as it had me. Batman was getting promoted and the slot of CarGru 14 was a (lower half) billet.

This has always struck me as one of the oddest facets of the Navy advancement system. You start off doing what you love, practicing it, living it every day until you know the envelope of your aircraft and fighter tactics so well that they're more reflex than conscious thought. You get better and better at it until they send you to Top Gun school—then you really get good. You go back to the squadrons, fly your ass off, and move on up the promotion ladder, getting more and more responsibility until you end up damn near tied to a desk managing other pilots more often than you're airborne with a Tomcat strapped to your ass.

You get good enough and you never get to fly again. A hell of a good deal, right?

The second and third kills are easier. I remember them too. At least I think I do. After that, the details run into a blur of technical details—altitude, fuel state, the weather that day.

Maybe when you can't remember that first kill anymore, it's time to retire from the military. In the last two years, I'd had plenty of job offers from the Beltway Bandits that have the Pentagon surrounded. I knew enough people, still drew enough water with them to be a hell of a defense contractor. But I wasn't ready to retire, not just yet. There was something I still had left to do in the Navy—and for the life of me, I couldn't figure out what it was.

Tomboy was the one who finally nailed me on it. I had unfinished business with the Russians and with my dad.

A couple of years ago, during one of the innumerable conflicts that seem to spring up around the world, I learned something that shook me to my very core. A Cuban radical told me that there was a very good chance that my father had not died on a bombing run over Vietnam. Before he left, he as much as said that Dad had been captured alive but seriously injured, and taken to Russia for further interrogation.

Russia. The very thought of it made my blood run cold.

I have a few memories of my dad—nothing very specific, just fragments of memories, more like quick snapshots than specific sequences of events. I remember a pair of cowboy boots, my first attempts to hit a foam softball with a plastic bat, a birthday party here and there. He was gone so much during the early years, deployed with his squadron and doing what he knew was important to do for the country—fighting the war that no one was very sure we were winning.

For thirty years plus, I've believed he died over that godforsaken land. Even though he was officially listed as MIA—Missing in Action—we knew he was gone. When the word finally came changing his status to KIA—Killed in Action—it was more a confirmation of something we'd tacitly accepted for years rather than any real change. It wasn't until I married Tomboy that I realized how very much I missed him.

My uncle, Dad's brother, did what he could. A damned fine job, most of the time, filling in for his younger brother as the father figure in his only nephew's life. Mom seemed to appreciate it. I did too, but not to the extent that I do now.

Uncle Thomas thought I was getting suckered on this. He believed with all his heart that his younger brother died over that bridge. He tried to talk me out of this mission, but in the end, when all else had failed, he came through with the goods.

Not that it was that tough. When you're Chief of Naval Operations and a front-line candidate for the Chairman of the Joint Chiefs of Staff, you draw a lot of water. If once in a while you use it to do something for your family, how wrong can that be?

It's not like the *Jefferson* wasn't going to be here anyway. This cruise was billed as part of a new strategy in U.S. international relations, a mission of building strong military forces in new democracies in Asia. Maybe it's a good idea—maybe not. Too far above my pay grade for me to say. Uncle Thomas says it will just make them stronger allies. I worry that it makes them stronger enemies.

At any rate, while I was deciding whether to finally retire or to accept another assignment, Uncle Thomas held out the ultimate carrot—a chance to fly off a carrier through one more cruise. He knew I couldn't refuse the offer. He was right.

I ended up attached to *Jefferson* as sort of an admiral without portfolio, ostensibly a military liaison officer en route to work with the Vietnamese government in transitioning to an all-volunteer military service. I would end up doing just that, I knew, but along the way I would have the opportunity to develop the contacts and resources that might help me to track down the rumors that were now starting to float about my father.

By March, the argument was OBE—overtaken by events. Tomboy went on cruise, now the Commanding Officer of VF-95 on board *Jefferson,* and I went to Vietnam to look for him. My father, I mean. Dad—the one and only that I'd been hearing about for so many years. Odd, this strong connection I felt to a man I barely even remembered.

Below me the Gulf of Tonkin, just as my father must have seen it so many years ago when he was flying off the USS *Saratoga*. Dark blue shading to almost white along the coast, and shortly past the unsightly jungle of the city, the real jungle. Green, overwhelmingly so, from the air seeming to impinge on the city as though to reclaim the land man had settled. Aside from the fresh color to it, there were few signs of the war that had raged there for so many years. Land defoliated by Agent Orange, craters gashed in the fertile soil by thousand-pound bombs, all that absorbed back into the ecosystem of this thriving jungle. There was little that man could do to make a permanent mark on this land, not when all the forces of nature were arrayed against him.

"Want to run through the missed-approach procedures again?" a tinny voice in my ear said.

"Do you know something I don't?"

"Not at all, Admiral." My RIO was pointedly respectful. Far be it for a mere junior lieutenant commander to remind the famous Admiral Magruder of standard in-flight procedures.

Not unless he needed it. I took quiet pride in the fact that she'd mentioned it, performed one of the vital functions of any RIO on board a Tomcat—keeping the guy up front honest.

"Roger," I said, letting her know by the tone of my voice that she'd done the right thing. I began reading from the checklist, avoiding the temptation to try to do it from memory. I could, after this many years flying this airframe, but no doubt my ever-vigilant GIB—guy in back, except that he was a she this time—would call me on it.

Her responses were quick, professional as she read down her own list. Finally satisfied that we were prepared for final, I heard her snap her checklist shut and the small rasping sounds as she inserted it in the side pocket.

"You volunteer for this mission?" I asked, more out of curiosity than any real need to know. Put her on the spot a bit, maybe, as she'd done me by reminding me of the missed-approach checklist. It was an opportunity many junior officers would welcome, the chance to fly with a senior admiral. A little face time, a good first impression, and some sharp airmanship skills might stick in a powerful admiral's mind, sufficiently so to bless the RIO's career in carrier aviation.

"No, Admiral," she replied, her voice cool and incurious. "Skipper asked me to take it. We're in workups right now, and aren't even scheduled to go out for carrier quals for another two months."

Now that set me back a bit. If she hadn't asked for it, then there was some reason her captain wanted her in this backseat?

I thought I knew the answer.

"My wife have anything to do with that?"

A small hesitation, then a slightly warmer tone of voice. "I wouldn't know anything about that, Admiral. They schedule them, I fly them."

I nodded, now trying not to laugh. As big as the Navy was, the Tomcat community was a small, elite part of it. The best part, as far as I was concerned. And my wife, as CO of VF-95, now stationed on board USS *Jefferson,* undoubtedly knew well the skippers of every other squadron around, including the CO of VF-125, my backseater's home turf. A little quiet, off-the-record conversation—maybe a small discussion over the characteristics she desired in the RIO that flew with her husband—and bingo. One female lieutenant commander slated for my backseat.

I suspected Lieutenant Commander Karnes was probably a damned fine RIO. Smart, almost telepathic with her pilots, and so competent that she didn't need the long-standing partnership that arose in regular pilot-RIO pairs in order to be impressive.

That, and she was probably married. I doubt that was a conscious factor that played into Tomboy's decision, but I'd bet my right nut on it.

And Tomboy also knew for a certainty that I wouldn't ask my RIO about her marital status. No, that would have been entirely inappropriate. If it had been a guy, I probably would have, but in the paranoid atmosphere of political correctness that now permeated every portion of the combat Navy, such a question would be entirely out of line for a female RIO.

I checked in with the area air-control facility on the listed frequency, and two minutes later got a handoff to ground control. The MiGs on my wings were now glued into position as though connected to my airframe by metal straps. Good formation flying—like Tomboy, the Vietnamese would have sent only the best. I forgave them their earlier crowding.

I had the runway now, the cold, white strip of concrete stretching through the outskirts of the city. If there'd been any real benefit to the war, it was this—we'd left them with some damn fine airfields.

Overconfidence is a factor that will kill a Tomcat pilot faster than any mechanical malfunction. Being sure you can catch the three-wire if you just tweak it a bit more, wanting to look good in front of your tower flower and just plain ego. And though a landing aboard the carrier at night in bad weather was far and above the most challenging feat of airmanship one could attempt, making the same approach on a fixed, unmoving airfield posed a different kind of threat—just as deadly, but far more subtle. Out on the carrier, you knew what the possibilities were, had seen too many of your mates crash and burn, juggernauting down the floating airfield in a ball of flame. Or seen them hit the ramp, coming in too low and ignoring the frantic pleas of the LSO—Landing Signals Officer—to pull up, up, up.

Ashore, overconfidence was the real danger. Just because it didn't move didn't mean it wasn't dangerous.

I trimmed the aircraft carefully, quite aware of the fact that I didn't do this every day for a living anymore. I'd just come out of the RAG—the Replacement Air Group—after a quick one-month refresher course, requalified on carriers, but that didn't mean I had the reflexes I did when I was twenty-two and just starting to fly this magnificent bird. Experience may win out over reflexes most of the time, but it's better if you have both.

We touched down gently, right where the three-wires would be at the field if it were configured for carrier landing practices. I let her run out a little, slowly applying the speed breaks until our forward speed had decreased to a gentle taxi roll. The landing signals fellow was already out there, fanning the air with slow movements like a bird trying to take off, attracting my attention. I waved, turned the aircraft toward him, and decreased my speed even more.

We followed him in to the VIP ramp, and I slid the Tomcat onto her spot. Karnes and I went through our shutdown checklist, and the last noises of the engines faded away as they spooled down.

I popped the canopy, and eased myself over the side of the bird, climbing down the handholds. Karnes followed a few seconds behind me. It was a seniority thing—last in, first out.

A small delegation awaited me on the ground. I returned the salutes politely, and held out my hand to shake hands with the guy who looked like the most senior.

"Welcome to Vietnam, Admiral Magruder." The English was clear and fluent, only a slight trace of accent tingeing the vowels. I felt my hand tighten around his.

"I appreciate your cooperation," I said. It had taken me a long time to decide on those words, to figure out how to phrase my gratitude for what the Vietnamese were evidently willing to do.

That is, what they said they were willing to do.

"I am Bien Than, chairman of the Military Affairs

Committee. I will be your primary contact during your time in our country for these matters." He glanced from side to side at the rest of the delegation and the reporters, and his face took on a slightly guarded expression. "We should talk. Perhaps I can assist you in refining your plans."

Now, this was curious. What was it that Than evidently wanted to say to me that he didn't want to advertise to the members of the media crowding around us?

"It would be my pleasure." I started to elaborate on that, but then followed his lead and fell silent.

After we posed for a few pictures, Than led us away from the gabbling horde. I heard a few voices call out, some almost unintelligible and others were clear American accents. I smiled, waved, and followed Than off, repeating the magic phrase "No comment" as though it were a mantra that would carry me through their midst.

"Tombstone." That one particular voice stopped me dead in my tracks. Karnes, following close on my heels, bumped into me, and I heard her mutter a quick apology.

I turned to scan the crowd. There she was, at the forefront of the mass of media now being held back by security forces. As stunning as ever, with the years adding a patina of grace and confidence that was missing in her younger counterparts. She held the microphone down low, an indication that she knew her viewers would be at least as interested in her words as anything I'd have to say. This was in sharp contrast to the others, who thrust the foam-covered mikes at me in some sort of phallic symbolism.

Pamela Drake, star reporter for ACN News. She'd dogged my path for the last twenty years, first as a news reporter, later as friend and lover, then as an adversarial representative of the media that refused to admit that there was any reason that they should not be present for every

second of every military maneuver. Our disagreements over
the First Amendment versus the safety of my people had
escalated to the point where we'd broken off our engagement.

Lucky break, that. After being married to Tomboy for one
and a half years, I knew that there was no way that Pamela
and I could have ever had a life together.

Pamela had always insisted that I give up my career in the
military. Tomboy, with her own career skyrocketing, would
never even have considered such a thing. She knew how
important flying was to me—almost as important as it was
to her.

"Hello, Tombstone," Pamela said. Her voice reached me
even over the clamor of the rest of the crowd. It was an odd,
deadly sensation starting at her. Like watching sharks circle
your underwater cage. Dangerous, deadly dangerous, both
for me and my people—but somehow still so compelling,
so hard to look away from.

I don't know how long I would have stood there. I felt a
sudden, sharp pain in my back. A jab, an elbow if I weren't
mistaken. The momentary pain, not to say the sheer shock
that a junior lieutenant commander would attempt such a
thing, broke the spell. I looked away from Pamela and back
at Lieutenant Commander Karnes. She just stood there, her
eyes calm and staring. "Sorry, Admiral. I slipped." The
expression on her face bore no trace of guilt.

Pamela faded back from a foreground figure into just one
of the reporters, yapping like baying hounds after the stories
that were their life's blood.

Pamela had intruded too often in my military operations
for me to believe her presence here was anything but an
extremely well-planned example of her almost psychic nose
for news. She'd capitalized on our relationship several times

in the recent past, most notably during the last conflict in the Mediterranean. There she'd counted on my good graces to provide access to the story, and had gone so far as to throw herself into the ocean from the deck of an old fishing vessel nearing the carrier, knowing that the sea-air-rescue helicopters would undoubtedly pick her up.

That had been a mistake. A big one. She hadn't realized how much of one until I'd placed her under armed guard in a stateroom. How her lawyer had ever managed to finagle her out of the criminal charges that had been pending, I'll never know.

"Let's get going," I said to Than, who had stopped to watch this side play with an expression as inscrutable as Karnes's. I swore silently to myself, uncomfortable at being on the receiving end of a stone-faced expression.

That's how I got my nickname, of course. It had had nothing to do with the fight at the OK Corral. No, my orderly squadron mates had decided that my face was so expressionless that it reminded them of a tombstone. It had stuck all these years, as first call signs usually do. My friends abbreviated it to "Stoney."

It was a short walk into the icy air of the terminal building. Than led us around Customs, through a few side passageways that were luxuriously carpeted and decorated. A moment later, we were at the VIP Conference Room located immediately in the front of the airport terminal building. Than opened the door, and stepped aside to let me precede him in.

I stepped into a conference room much like any other. There was a certain ineffable sameness to these rooms, characterized by heavily draped windows—when windows were even allowed—gleaming wooden tables, and relatively comfortable chairs. The obligatory water pitcher and coffee urn stood in the center of the table, and a stack of brown folders at the head of it.

I slung my flight bag onto the table, not worried about how out of place the battered green canvas satchel would look amongst the trappings of power. I wasn't in the mood for courtesies, formalities, and the other rituals that had been handed to me along with my first set of stars. Then, I had not been senior enough to reject them. Now I was. I turned to Than. "It's been a long flight, sir."

Than nodded, and a grave smile crossed his face. "And a long time. I am hoping that the material I have for you will make it seem that much more worthwhile."

He picked up the top folder, and handed it to me without comment. I opened it, started to take a deep breath, and felt the air catch in my lungs. It was as if all power to make even the slightest voluntary motion had left me, like a deep sucker punch to the gut. I stared down until basic instinct took over and I found myself sucking in another deep, shuddering breath. I looked up at Than. He was concerned now, more than he had a right to be. He must have known how it would affect me.

"Where did you get this?" I asked.

"From a resistance fighter, a very old one. He says he has more—hard evidence, he says. Not just photos."

I glanced back at the photo, a face I thought I'd forgotten. It was so like my own, even more so now that the passing years had carved their marks on me. Was this how I would look in later years?

The photo showed three men in cut-off shorts and T-shirts, standing comfortably together. The man in the middle had his arms slung over the two on either side, and was grinning for the camera. The man to the left held up a newspaper, printed in English, with the words "Clinton Wins Second Term" emblazoned across the front of it.

There was no mistaking that face, not even after all these years. The skin was darkly burnished by the sun, rough and shiny on the nose as though peeling from a recent sunburn. The eyes were dark, maybe gray—I couldn't tell from the photo. Even with a smile for the camera, there was a sense that deep secrets hid behind those eyes, more eons of experience than any one man could have had. The eyes were alert, keen, confident without being arrogant.

It was my father.

TWO
Lieutenant Commander Curt "Bird Dog" Robinson

23 September

The E-2C Hawkeye off to my left was an ungainly-looking bird. Slap a huge rotating radar dome on the Navy's all-purpose -2 series airframe, add a weird cross-framed tail assembly, and you've got a bird that maxes out at 450 knots. And that's downhill with a tail wind.

I pitied the poor bastards riding sidesaddle in the E-2C Hawkeye. Bad enough that it's a prop plane instead of a jet, but the danged consoles are mounted along the fuselage. The aviators—yeah, we call them that even though they're really scope dopes—get to sit face-forward during takeoffs and landings. That's about it. The rest of the time, they've got the seats swiveled ninety degrees to the side and they're staring at tiny little blips on radar screens instead of all this big blue sky.

No jet engines, no missiles. What's the point of being an aviator?

About five minutes after we went feet dry over Vietnam, one of the Hawkeye Radar Intercept Operators answered that question.

"Viper 201, Snoopy 1. We're getting prelaunched emissions, probable SAM site." The RIO on tactical rattled off some range-bearing info, the sort of stuff my backseater, Gator Cummings, just loves.

"We holding it?" I asked Gator.

"Nope. But they've got better gear. If Frank says it's there, it's there."

"What the hell's an active SAM site doing down there?" That worried the shit out of me.

"Probably the reason we're taking Snoopy out for a look-see," Gator said calmly.

That's one of the things I like about Gator. He stays cool, stays loose, when other RIOs would get all bothered about a minor detail like SAMs.

"How close can I get?" I asked Gator. I still wasn't convinced we had an active SAM site down below.

"Thirty miles—no closer," Gator warned. "We're almost at the edge of the envelope now."

I mulled that over for a moment, trying to decide how serious he was about that. Gator always builds in a safety factor when he's talking to me, one that he says gives him time to punch out. Yeah, right. Like I've ever had a backseater punch out on me. While Gator's my usual RIO, I've flown with others. Never lost one.

Still, there had been moments when I knew he'd come damn close to jerking down on that orange-and-black-striped lever and departing the aircraft prior to landing. Probably the last time he'd been serious about it was when we were over the Arctic, and then only the fact that the weather would probably kill him faster than I could had kept him in the aircraft.

I knew there were still some long-range bastards down in that foliage below. But why would they be targeting us?

Vietnam was at peace as much as it had ever been in its shattered last century, and there was no reason to believe that we were wandering into hostile territory.

"Probably just normal maintenance," I suggested, wondering if I could get Gator to agree to that.

"You want to take that chance?"

I had my answer. Gator believes that serious paranoia is the beginning of sound operational planning, and I have to admit that he's usually right. Still, I wasn't within range just yet, and I hadn't done formation flying in a long time.

"Bet it goes off-line in three minutes," I said, with more confidence than I felt. Some of Gator's paranoia was starting to affect me, slithering down my backbone and creeping into the ends of my fingers. If there were bad guys down there, then the problem wasn't ours. Hell, I thought I could probably outrun anything they could shoot at us. However, the unarmed E-2C still in position off my right wing was another matter.

As capable and competent as it is at what it does, there's a reason they send it out with fighter escorts. Not usually in close formation like this, but then there'd been a couple of us that needed a little formation-flying practice, and we'd decided this was an excellent opportunity to catch up. The E-2 hadn't minded; the pilot had only warned us to stay out of his blind spot in that ungainly high-winged airframe he'd be flying.

"Viper 201, suggest we turn back." The E-2 pilot now, making it clear by his tone of voice that consenting to play pigeon in some Tomcat formation flying didn't include getting any closer to this SAM site.

Damn. Another paranoid aviator. What happened to the good old days? Gator would have pointed out that my good old days weren't all that long ago.

"Roger, Snoopy." It wasn't like I had a lot of choice.

The E-2 had us increase the separation between all three aircraft, giving him forty-five degrees and two thousand yards of lead on both of us. As my wingman slid back into position, I noticed him shaking his head, and he waggled his wings slightly in greeting. I waggled back.

"What the fuck—*missile launch, missile launch!*" My wingman's RIO was the first to pick up the radar trace of the missile leaving the rail and ascending into the atmosphere.

"Snoopy, get the hell out of here!" The E-2 knew I wasn't kidding. He curled into a tighter turn than I'd ever seen one of those birds pull before, and started beating feet for open water, leaving us to deal with the incoming threat.

"Take low position," I ordered our wingman. He slid down and below, peeling off into a steep dive to take him two thousand feet below me. I climbed up, keeping my aircraft interposed between the incoming missile and the bird we were supposed to be protecting.

"Two—no, *three*." Now Gator was holding them as well, singing out the range and bearings as the missiles spiked up from the tree cover.

"I'm going after the first one," my wingman said. I saw him bank hard right, heading for the course that he thought would put him on an intercept with Sparrows against the slower surface-to-air missile.

"Don't chase it—stay in formation and wait for it," I ordered. It was too late. Viper 202 was already well out of position, the pilot chasing that perfect firing slot that would put him in perfect firing position.

"Damn, damn, damn," Gator swore quietly over the ICS. "Asshole's going to—hold it."

The cry of "Fox two, Fox two" echoed over tactical as

202 toggled off two Sparrow missiles at the deadly incoming fire.

"No good." Gator's voice was slightly higher now as he relayed to me the details of the geometry between missile, fighter, and target. "He needs to go with a Sidewinder—now."

"202, Fox three time," I said over tactical.

"Roger, I'm on it, old man." 202's voice made it clear that I was a distraction rather than a help at this point.

I swore quietly, picturing Skeeter Harmon in the cockpit swearing back at me.

Skeeter Harmon—a hot stick, one of the best. Hell, Gator'd had the audacity to suggest that my problem with Skeeter was that I felt threatened. Threatened—not likely. Not from a junior nugget just starting his second cruise on board *Jefferson*. I had more time in the shitter than he had in the cockpit, and there wasn't a damn thing for me to feel insecure about.

Skeeter had gotten off to a rocky start in the squadron, but had quickly come around once we saw he could fly. That's all that really matters in the long run anyway—how hot a stick you are.

But Skeeter seemed to think that there were other issues at work in the squadron, and he was the first to start wailing whenever he didn't get exactly the flight he wanted. One night when we were out drinking in Singapore, Skeeter had even had the audacity to suggest that it was because he was black. I almost popped him at that point. Gator, that asshole, damn near agreed with him. Hell, if you can't count on your RIO in a bar, where can you count on him?

Anyway, that missile now getting too damn close for comfort didn't know whether Skeeter was black, white, or pink with purple polka dots. Missiles are like that. So are MiGs.

Skeeter rolled into position, slightly above the missile's altitude, and toggled off two Sidewinders. "Fox three, Fox three," he chimed over tactical.

"201, say your intentions." The voice was as familiar to me as Gator's, and almost as important.

Great. Now the carrier was getting in on the act. That was all I needed at this point, one other voice babbling out good ideas and suggestions while I was in a ready fire mode.

"I'll get back to you." I said it fast enough to let the Operations Specialist on the other end of the circuit know I was pissed. But hell, it wasn't really his fault. Some surface-puke Tactical Action Officer was undoubtedly riding his ass, howling for intentions and indications. Like there was anything he could really do about it.

"Got it!" Skeeter crowed seconds before his lead Sidewinder intercepted the first missile. "Man, am I hot or *what*!"

"Not as hot as the E-2 is going to be if you don't get the second one," I reminded him. "You take that one—I'll go for number three."

"Break right, descend to eight thousand feet," Gator ordered quietly from the backseat. "Recommend the Sidewinder for the first shot."

"You don't want to take a shot with the Sparrow?"

"No—let's just do it right the first time."

I nodded. The Sparrow had a longer range, but the Sidewinder was considerably more accurate at this kind of angles fight. Plus, the Sidewinder was faster. Not that the ground-launched missile could outrun a Sparrow, but the Sidewinder just felt like the right weapon to use. For once, Gator and I agreed.

I selected a Sidewinder and waited for the tone. The distinctive warbling of a Sidewinder that had acquired a sufficient-heat target filled the cockpit. I toggled it off. My Tomcat rocked slightly as the weight left the wing, and I corrected us back into a level flight immediately.

The missile wheeled off, picking up speed rapidly and nosing around a bit in the air as it found its heat source.

"Looks good, looks good—getting close now," Gator sang out, updating me on its progress on his radar. "Damn, Bird Dog, I think you've got it."

It looked like a diamond flashed in the sky somewhere, a brief flare of light that indicated a hit.

"Skeeter, talk to me," I demanded, leaving it to the backseaters to appreciate the damned fine shot. "Talk to me—have you got it?"

"I think so—it's a little too far north, so I'm—damn."

"Damn what?"

"Right engine over temp. I'm pressing on anyway."

"Any signs of fire?"

"Negative. Probably just a faulty gauge. Ready for Fox three. Now!"

"Shit." Gator's verdict from the backseat was good enough for me. Despite his unwillingness sometimes to go along with what I deemed an adequate tactical maneuver, Gator had an almost psychic sense of when a missile would hit and when it wouldn't.

"We're on it," I said, goosing the fighter slightly. I wanted speed, lots of it, to close the gap between me and the missile before I took a shot at it. The Tomcat screamed and the G forces pushed me back in my seat. It was a healthy, pounding thunder of powerful jet engines ripping speed out of thin air.

Closer and closer, until I got both a good growl off the

Sparrow and the high whine off the Sidewinder. Hell, go with what works. I toggled up another Sidewinder, glad it had only taken me one to nail the last missile.

The Tomcat felt markedly lighter now, more responsive and nimble under my fingertips. Not that antiair missiles weigh that much, but the drag they place on a high-performance airframe is always a factor.

"It looks good, it looks good," Gator said. "Not certain yet, but it might be."

"I'm coming in for follow-up," Skeeter announced. "I've got two Sidewinders left."

"Back me up," I agreed, waiting for that final confident howl of glee from Gator that would tell me we were on the mark. Hell, it was just a surface-to-air missile—I didn't need any help to nail one.

"Damn it, Bird Dog, it's dropping off!" Gator's voice held the note of confidence I'd been waiting to hear, but the words were wrong. All wrong.

"Shit, it fucked up?"

"Some sort of malfunction."

"Where's the fucking sun?" I swung my head around to see it. "No, not that. What the hell's got it distracted?"

"Maybe just a bad bird, Bird Dog."

I toggled off another missile, already feeling a sinking, twisting sensation in my gut that told me I was in a bad tail chase. Real bad. The geometry flashed through my mind, more instinct than an actual mathematical calculation, but often just as deadly accurate. Gator wasn't the only one who could predict a hit, and despite my wishes I was calling this a no-go.

"I'm there," Skeeter said. "Fox three, Fox three."

"You can't make it," Gator said, his voice panicked now.

"Bird Dog, get Snoopy down on the deck. She's gonna have to try to evade it."

An E-2 trying to evade a missile is like a snail trying to evade a flyswatter. I had five seconds to watch, five seconds longer than any I've ever had in my life. Even flying nap of the earth over the Arctic hadn't curled my balls back up into my torso and made me want to puke with pain like this.

Five seconds. The E-2 started to move, pitching down and pointing her nose to the deck. She picked up speed immediately, trading altitude for airspeed.

Four seconds. The E-2 went into full nosedive now, at an angle any experienced pilot would have been insane to try. Those airframes are sturdy but ancient, and the metal stress factors that play into extreme maneuvers like this are another thing to be worried about. I imagined what it was like in the cockpit of that bird, hearing the old structural members scream and complain, the ominous pops and cracks of an airframe exceeding her performance envelope.

Three seconds. The E-2 pilot was howling on tactical now, praying to every god he knew and damning the Vietnamese.

Two seconds. I heard it, those fatal last words that always echo over the airwaves, the ones that signify a pilot's final acknowledgment that he's really screwed the pooch this time. "Oh, shit."

One second. I had a visual on the missile now, so much smaller than the aircraft, streaming directly toward it with fire gouting out its ass.

The sky five miles away from me exploded into fire, violent, searing colors of orange and yellow. The black smoke followed, billowing around it like a shroud, then a secondary explosion, then nothing but black smoke and odd shards of metal cluttering the sky and Gator's radarscope.

"Chutes, any chutes?" Gator said urgently.

I tossed the Tomcat around in a tight curve, spiraling higher to avoid the black fireball now fouling the air. The sky was brilliant blue above, no trace of the fiery destruction down in my realm. Blue, innocent, and eternal. But that wasn't what I was interested in.

I spiraled down, staying well clear of the fireball that was now mostly smoke and a rain of shrapnel.

No chutes. No billowing arcs of silk white that would indicate any one of the four people on board had had time to punch out.

I dived lower, so close I could see the wave tops curling over and under, white-capped, covering deep sea fields of kelp. Just on the off chance that they made it out, had time to slip by me somehow undetected and make it to the safety of the ocean.

No luck. Not for me. Not for the E-2 crew.

"Let's get back to the boat," I said finally to Skeeter over tactical. "The helos are on their way—they can do a better search at this altitude than we ever could. If there's anything there, they'll find it."

Two clicks acknowledged my transmission, nothing more. Skeeter had spent his own time at sea level looking for any trace of the survivors. Hoping against hope, we both knew it was not going to happen.

Both of us were getting low on fuel. What we'd really like to do was head back in over land and nail the bastard who'd fired those missiles at an innocent, harmless E-2. If they wanted to fight, why hadn't they taken on one of *us*, somebody who had the maneuverability to at least stand a fighting chance? But no, they'd taken out the one bird in the sky that was more an ungainly seagull than a tactical aircraft.

And the one that could do them the most harm. Why were they objecting to the E-2's presence in their skies? In other words, what did Snoopy see that they didn't want him to?

"We're spooling up two F/A-18's now," the controller back on the carrier said, as though he'd managed to read my thoughts from a distance of fifty miles. "As soon as they're airborne, we'll recover you."

"Roger."

Skeeter and I fell into the starboard marshal, waiting our turn. As we spiraled around in our assigned spots, I keyed the mike and called the carrier one last time. "What are those Hornets loaded out with?"

"Ground weapons," was the short, satisfied reply. "And we're just waiting for clearance."

Fine. If I couldn't take the SAM site out myself, then at least we were doing something. Doing something this time, instead of doing what my father's generation had done, concentrating firepower on truck parks and POL sites. We needed to hit these bastards hard, where it could hurt them, where they knew exactly why we were doing it. As far as we were concerned, that SAM site would be toast.

I let Skeeter take a plug at the tanker first. As I hung back waiting my turn, it was easy to see that he was shaken up. Not that he would have admitted it, but it showed in his approach on the KA-6 tanker. Skeeter, normally the rock-steady precision flyer, was all over the sky. It took him three tries to plug the tanker, and even then he had one breakaway before he managed to suck down five thousand pounds. When he finally pulled away, I could tell from the tanker pilot's voice that he'd just about had enough of playing patty-cake with Tomcats.

"C'mon in, Bird Dog," Leslie "Loon" Luna said. He was normally the most unflappable of tanker pilots, but now his voice was short. I had a feeling we wouldn't be trading dirty jokes over the tanking frequency this time.

"On my way." I slid the aircraft forward slowly, eased into position, then, keeping my eyes on the lights around the basket, slid the probe home with a firm thunk.

"Good seal," Loon reported. "Ready to begin transfer."

I sucked down a quick five thousand pounds, glad I could at least manage to do this right.

Good eyesight and fast reflexes aren't enough to make a fighter pilot. You need something more—the ability to compartmentalize your mind, to shut out everything else in the world once you step into that cockpit. My wife, my dog, none of that matters when you have that many pounds of airframe wrapped around you, enormous firepower on your wings, and a guy in the backseat who's depending on you. It doesn't matter—it can't. Not if you're going to do your job right.

Like I knew what that was about. As I pulled away from the tanker, some tiny wall broke, and I saw again the bloody black fireball that was all that remained of the E-2. The Tomcat wobbled a bit as though she sensed my guts moving in different directions. Gator cleared his throat, then said, "You okay, buddy?"

"I'm fine." The words came out harder than I meant them to, but Jesus—what did Gator expect? Yeah, he'd seen the same things I had. But it hadn't been his fault. It was mine, completely and solely.

If only I had sent Skeeter off after that third missile. I'd been so certain that I could get it myself.

Too certain? I shoved the thought away, leaving it for another time. One when I wasn't trying to get a bird back on deck.

"Nice plug," Gator offered. I recognized that for what it

was, a little cheerleading from a backseater who thought the guy up front might be shaken up. Two years ago, when we'd first started flying together, it might have worked. It almost did this time too, especially coming from Gator, whose voice I knew as well as any man's on earth.

"Piece of cake, yeah," I said, trying to simulate the appropriate response so he'd go away and be happy. "Yeah, I sure can fly those tankers."

"All you have to do is get us back on deck now, Bird Dog," Gator said. I could hear the careful note in his voice, the one that treaded around the edges of an argument. No matter how strongly he felt about me—hell, I wasn't even sure he would ever want to fly with me again, not after today—he would never bring it up right before a trap. Not when he wanted every bit of my attention focused on the pitching, heaving deck below us, and the thin wires that ran perpendicular to my flight path.

Skeeter and I settled in to the starboard marshal pattern and waited for the call. We were operating on visual now, moving automatically into our next place in the pattern and waiting for our chance to roll out.

Finally, I was up. I went first, leaving Skeeter still in the pattern waiting for his turn.

I started my approach, and at two miles out I was rock-steady on glide path. The LSO voice—Landing Signals Officer—was just as soothing and encouraging as Gator's had been. Clearly, he knew what had happened, and he was prepared to talk a shaken aviator back down onto deck as gently as possible.

"Tomcat 201, call the ball."

Like I could miss it. In this weather, the Fresnel lens was a lock, clear and brilliant on the port side of the carrier's ass.

"Roger, ball," I acknowledged, and followed with a

report of my fuel state and number of people on board. Someday, just for the hell of it, I was gonna say three souls and see if anyone caught it.

I came in smooth, clean, adding a little power just as we came over the end of the ship.

It was one of the best traps I ever made, smooth, clean, and solid on the three-wire. Heck, if I'd had another hundred feet, I wouldn't have needed the damn wire at all.

So maybe that's an overstatement. Even the best carrier aircraft landing is a controlled crash, a violent intersection of aircraft and flight deck that throws you forward in the straps and rattles your teeth. It's not something you want to try with a full bladder. I felt the tailhook catch, and slammed the throttle forward to full military power. Standard procedure, in case the hook skips over the wire—called a kiddie trap, because the aircraft then looks like a kiddie's toy bouncing down the flight deck—or in case something else goes wrong.

If you do have a problem, you have enough forward speed and lift to get back off the deck. Then you go round, go back into the marshal, and take another pass at the deck.

I waited for the yellow shirt's sign that it was safe to power down, then throttled back to taxi speed. We backed slightly and I lifted the hook, clearing the wire, then followed the yellow shirt's hand directions into the spot. The nose wheel's steering gear felt a little rough—I made a mental note to gripe it when I signed the aircraft back in.

Once on the spot, I spooled the engines down and started my pre-shutdown checklist. Gator sang out his portions, and we finished quickly.

Behind me, I could hear the high scream, like a tornado inbound, of the next aircraft coming down over the deck.

Skeeter, probably—he'd been right behind me in pattern and should be next on deck.

I turned slightly and craned my neck to watch the ass end of the carrier. The youngster came in high and fast, almost seeming to ignore the LSO's increasingly frantic insistence that he power back. He caught the one-wire—but just barely. He was nose-high, and I saw the aircraft's nose slam down with an impact that must have been brutal.

"What the hell's going on with him," I said, half aloud and half to myself. "He's not the one who blew it today."

Gator leaned forward and tapped me gently on the shoulder. "Later, Bird Dog. Let's get this aircraft shut down first."

I shoved it away again, the last time I'd have to, and completed the pre-shutdown checklist. A few minutes later, the aircraft went cold and dark.

By the time we were on the tarmac, CAG was at the island door waiting for us. Big surprise, that.

CAG stands for Commander, Air Group. Except he's a captain, not a commander. And it's no longer called an Air Group either. It's an Air Wing. But somehow, the acronym CAW just never caught on. CAG is CAG.

There are three major players on board any aircraft carrier. There's the skipper of the ship, an aviator by trade but one who's on his way up from mere four-striper captain to admiral and has been through all the surface-track training he'll ever need. Then there's the guy that owns all the squadrons on board the carrier—the CAG. They both work for the admiral in command of the entire battle group.

CAG motioned us inside the island, and as soon as we were off the flight deck, he said, "The admiral wants to see you."

"I figured."

"Now."

"That I also figured."

We followed CAG down one deck to the Flag spaces, sweaty, stinky aviators in flight suits, still carrying their helmets and wearing their ejection harnesses, trotting the sacred cool corridors of Flag country.

CAG stopped us just outside the admiral's door and turned back to me. "He's been there, Bird Dog. If anybody understands, the admiral does."

The walls I'd erected in my mind broke down finally. It washed over me now, the sheer magnitude of the loss. Jesus, I knew those men—hell, I'd had chow with Dogpatch, the E-2 pilot, just yesterday. Gator grabbed my arm. "Don't go tits-up on me now."

I started to say something, tried to tell him I was okay, but it must have been very clear that I wasn't. My vision had faded around the edges, tunneling in like I was taking too many Gs, graying out, with color seeping out of the room. There was a black-and-white picture, bleached of all color—and of all life.

My knees buckled. Gator and CAG caught me on the way down. It didn't seem to matter—nothing did. My vision was now blurry as well as colorless, and the overwhelming sensation that the world around me was just mist and fog increased.

"Suck it up," Gator whispered harshly, glancing around at the people standing at the open hatches and doorways down the passageway. "Just a few more minutes, Bird Dog. Suck it up."

"Let's get him into the mess," CAG said finally. "Asshole's gonna pass out on us."

They dragged me into the Flag Mess, the dining facility just off the admiral's quarters. Somebody pushed me down on the couch, and I felt a hand on the back of my neck, shoving my head between my knees.

"Breathe." Gator's voice now, giving orders. In that state, if there was any voice I'd obey, it would be Gator's.

I took in a deep shuddering breath, felt my diaphragm flex and resist, then forced it in. With my head down, the fuzzy feeling and grayness started to seep away. I tried to sit up straight.

"Not just yet," Gator said softly. "Not yet, buddy."

Finally, the two of them decided I could be trusted not to be treated like a teenager. They let me sit up, and somebody shoved a glass of water in my hand. If they'd been any kind of shipmates at all, there would have been some bourbon in it.

"You feeling better?" Gator asked.

"Yes, Mommy."

Irritation splashed across Gator's face; then he gave a grunt. He turned to CAG. "Back to normal, I'd say."

CAG regarded me for a few minutes, and I saw an odd mixture of compassion and anger in his face. "No, he won't ever be," CAG said. "No man would be." He stood, motioning to Gator. "Let's see if we can get him on his feet."

I waved off their assistance and stood slowly. My vision wavered a bit, then settled down. My gut was letting me breathe, and my knees didn't feel like they were about to buckle anymore. Physically, I was all right.

"You up to talking now?" CAG asked. It wasn't really a question.

I nodded. "Yeah, let's get it over with."

CAG led the way to the admiral's private door to the mess, rapped gently, then stuck his head in. "They're here, Admiral."

Gator's hand was clamped around my arm again, just

above the elbow. Hell, if he kept touching me like that, we were gonna start going steady. I shook him off.

CAG motioned us in. As I stepped across the hatch and into the admiral's office, I tried to remember one thing. I was a good stick, one of the best. The admiral knew what I could do—hell, we'd been on three cruises together so far. He'd been in command of the Carrier Battle Group when I'd flown my ass off over the Arctic, and he'd been on board *Jefferson* from D.C. when everything went to shit in the Spratly Islands. And I knew him—he was a good guy.

The admiral knew I was a good stick. Even though I'd just killed four aviators.

THREE
Rear Admiral Edward Everett "Batman" Wayne

23 September
USS Jefferson
Admiral's cabin ·

God save me from good sticks. Whether they're male or female, they're never modest. They stalk the passageways of the carriers like grounded gods, arrogant and barely touching the deck. They can do no wrong, every trap is a three-wire, and they never, ever screw the pooch.

I know. I was one of them.

It can't last forever, of course. Sooner or later, they come down hard. Sometimes they're the only ones who know it, but you can see it in their faces. It starts with a quiet, reflective couple of days, an unusual look of thoughtfulness on the pilot's face. That fades—faster than you think. What you get at the end of it is a pilot who thinks, one who lets his mind rule his reflexes instead of the other way, one who knows he or she is mortal. In short, you get a better pilot. One who's likely to come back.

Of the five officers standing in front of me, only two had been through that process. One was Gator, Bird Dog's RIO. The other was CAG.

Bird Dog, Skeeter, and Lieutenant Laurel, Skeeter's backseater, were still too young to ever admit that they were mortal. God knows, Bird Dog was long overdue. I'd known it was coming.

But God, not like this. Never like this.

"Sit down." I gestured at the ring of chairs arrayed in front of my seat. "Tell me about it."

A knock on the door interrupted Bird Dog before he could even start. Lab Rat opened the door and stuck his head in. "May I sit in, Admiral?"

I nodded, a little bit annoyed that he'd caught me in a slipup. Or was it? Of course I'd wanted to hear the details first myself—deserved it, in fact. I was in command of this Carrier Battle Group, and everything that happened and every man and woman under my command were my direct and personal responsibility.

But Lab Rat, my senior Intelligence Officer, was right too. The first retelling of an incident is often the most accurate one, filled with the details that immediately stand out in each pilot's mind. Intelligence Officers such as Commander "Lab Rat" Busby thrived on that stuff, raw, hard data straight from the pilot's lips.

I pointed at the couch. Lab Rat slid into his accustomed space and perched on the worn cushions, his pale blue eyes alive and expectant behind thick spectacles.

"You were saying," I said to Bird Dog, although he hadn't been.

Bird Dog looked pale and shaken, as rocky as I'd ever seen him. He looked like he'd been about to keel over. A good thing—if he hadn't, he'd be popped tall at attention in front of my desk instead of sitting down. I had to know what had hit him and hit him hard.

"We were just flying escort on the Snoopy," he started, a

dazed, almost surreal quality in his voice. "Just a normal flight. Catch up on some formation, that's all."

Bird Dog led me back through the sequence of actions that had led to the downing of Snoopy 631, only occasionally stopping to backtrack or fill in some critical detail. About mid-debrief, his voice took on an eerie singsong sort of tone. I shot a glance at Gator, noticed his eyes were fixed on his pilot, a worried expression on his face.

Skeeter and his RIO were another story altogether. They didn't look happy, no, not that. More like relieved. And worried—deeply worried. Laurel, in particular, a young woman on her first cruise with the squadron, looked shaken.

"So I circled, looking for chutes," Bird Dog finished. "There were none in the air, so I checked at sea level. None there. No chutes, no bodies, no rafts. Nothing." I was almost relieved when his eerie voice stopped.

"Why did you choose to use the Sidewinders versus the Sparrows?" CAG asked, after shooting a glance at me. "What about the range?"

"I thought I could make it," Bird Dog said, his voice almost inaudible. "I thought I could—"

"Admiral, if I may," Gator broke in, attempting a save.

I shook him off. As admirable as RIO loyalty is, this one was all Bird Dog's.

"You thought you could make it," I repeated.

"My Sidewinders were the weapon of choice," Skeeter said, the first words out of the young aviator. Even as junior as he was, he should have known better than to break into an admiral's inquisition. His gaze met mine, confident and aggressive. "The Sidewinders were working, Admiral. Bird Dog had a bad load-out, that's all."

"That's all?" I came up out of my chair like a snake had bit me on the ass and leaned across the heavy desk to stare at him. I planted both hands palms down on it, and raised my voice. "That's all?"

A deadly, cold chill invaded the room. Skeeter and Laurel were slowly tumbling to what Bird Dog already knew—that overconfidence had killed four aviators in that E-2.

It wasn't my intent to be unkind, although kindness sometimes has little bearing on the decisions I'm forced to make. It was a combination of factors: sheer anger and sorrow over losing the four aviators, maybe the possibility that I could bring home the seriousness of this to the two junior ones in front of me. Maybe I could catch them before they made their mistakes, before they repeated Bird Dog's. But not unless they knew just how deadly, deadly serious it was.

"I mean—uh—" Skeeter fell silent, following a quick jab in his ribs by his backseater.

Bird Dog looked oddly crumpled, a still, motionless figure, in his seat. He was frozen in time, a time maybe only thirty minutes earlier when it had all happened. It was replaying in front of his eyes, in an endless loop, his imagination adding details that had never really happened. Things like the sound of the E-2 pilot's voice just before the missile hit, how clear and obvious it had been that he should have tried the Sparrow first, the fireball growing in size and intensity every time he thought about it.

I motioned to CAG, who reached out and shook him by the shoulder. "Snap out of it, Bird Dog."

Bird Dog looked startled, as though we'd awakened him from a sleepwalking episode. He glanced around the room, his eyes finally settling on the one most familiar figure in the room. "I blew it, Gator," he said softly, ignoring the rest of us. "That bird—they were counting on me. And I blew it."

"You got a bad missile," Gator said gently. It wasn't a denial, it was just another reason.

But bad missiles happen, even during peacetime missions. Or what should have been a peacetime mission. I looked over at Lab Rat, sitting on the couch. He was practically quivering in eagerness to ask a few questions. I started to shake my head, then thought better of it.

If ever a man has been accurately pegged by his squadron mates, it was Lab Rat Busby. He was a small man, pale blond hair cropped close to his head, with brilliant blue eyes that made him look almost albino. He was tougher than he looked—I'd seen him down in the gym bench-pressing a quite respectable stack of weights, and I suspect he'd always really wanted to be a Marine.

Or an aviator. But he must have known from the first that his vision would disqualify him, even for the backseat position. He'd gotten as close to it as he could, though, as an Air Intelligence Officer. He worked with what he couldn't have every day, and apparently took a great deal of pride in his aircrews being the best briefed on any ship—and the best debriefed.

I nodded at Lab Rat. He fairly sprang off the couch in his eagerness to ask his questions.

"This SAM site," he began, picking his words carefully. "You say it came up out of nowhere?"

It was Gator that answered, stepping forward as the man with more knowledge than the pilot. After all, it was his ESM gear that would have given the first warbling indications of the SAM site if they'd held it. "Snoopy got it first, and I picked it up a little later. No doubt, it was an SA-6 site. We were right at the edge of the envelope, proceeding inbound. We talked about it, and finally decided it was probably just a mission maintenance fire-up of the gear." A faintly challenging look came over his face. "Naturally that was our conclusion. Since there was no intelligence briefing on any real threats in the area."

Lab Rat nodded impatiently, as though he'd already considered how and when the intelligence briefing he'd provided to the aircrews might have been in error. If there had been a mistake made by his people, I had no doubt that heads would roll.

"But there was nothing else unusual about it?" he pressed, clearly after something, and just as clearly not wanting to put words in their mouths. "The parameters all fit?"

"From what I saw, they did," Gator answered slowly. The grief swept over him now, hard and deep. "But the guys who got the first good look were—"

Lab Rat looked slightly chagrined, and an oddly human and vulnerable expression took its place on his face. "I'm just asking about what you saw," he said. "I didn't mean to imply—"

Gator waved him off, now recovered. "The pulse repetition rate and frequency all matched. It looked to me like a normal SA-6 site."

"Did you see anything else unusual?" Lab Rat asked again. "Anything that might not have shown up in the link." He was referring to the tactical data net that bound the ships to the carrier, providing a comprehensive display of every single platform's radar and ESM contacts.

Gator shook his head. "Nothing."

Lab Rat sighed, evidently disappointed at the response.

"Were you looking for something in particular?" CAG asked. Now there was an uneasy expression on his face. I knew what was going through his mind.

It was the essential downside of intelligence, one that all aviators faced from time to time. Very excellent info can be quite highly classified, far beyond the level of information that would be given to a pilot flying missions over a foreign country. It's not that the intelligence is inaccurate—on the contrary, it is composed of the most precise on-scene reports and reports from national assets—read satellites for that— that the United States possesses. The information is detailed, dependable, and highly accurate.

And too classified to use. It was much like the problem with the British during World War II. Even though they'd broken the Enigma code and were reading German General Staff traffic, they were faced with the Devil's own choice. If they acted on the information, evacuating Coventry and other German bombing targets, the Germans would know that their communications were no longer secure. Since Britain wasn't ready to take the war to the Germans, they had to wait until they were to use the information. In other words, to use the information was to reveal its source and to compromise that asset forever.

Had the British evacuated Coventry, the Germans would have known that they were reading German radio traffic. The ciphers would have been changed, perhaps to something that could not have been broken in time for the D-Day assault. As massive as the casualties that the British took were, they would have been even worse had the British not held off on using that information.

Better gear, same problem today.

Then CAG looked at me, questioning. I kept my face impassive. Nothing on the ship was too classified for me to know, nothing. The same could not be said for CAG.

Finally, CAG recognized the problem and let it go. The entire exchange had taken place without words, and well outside the understanding of the aviators still preoccupied with the horror of what had happened.

Maybe not all of them, I thought, studying Gator. There was a guarded look on his face, as though he was pretty sure what was going on but was not about to let on.

A few more quick questions from CAG about flying conditions and decision points. Then I said, "That will be all, gentlemen. Turn over your aircraft and then report to Medical. You," I said, fixing my gaze on Bird Dog, "will go to bed." Bird Dog started to protest, and I cut him off. "You will tell the doctor I said you are to be out cold for twelve hours. After that, you will see him again. Further notice, I'm taking you off the flight schedule."

"Thank you, Admiral," CAG said as he stood up. He recognized the signs of a dismissal.

The other four aviators also stood up, with Bird Dog the last to do so. They followed CAG to the hatch, and at the last minute Bird Dog turned back to me. "I'm sorry, sir." His anguish was as evident in his eyes as it could be.

"So am I, son," I said. "So am I."

After they left, Lab Rat abandoned his precarious perch on the edge of the couch and stood in front of the desk. "Oh, sit down," I said, weary as I sometimes was of the reflexive courtesy of junior officers. "You know I want to talk to you, and you want to tell me something. Let's get it over with."

Lab Rat nodded, and took the chair that Bird Dog had just vacated. "You know what I was after."

I leaned back in my chair and laced my fingers across my stomach. It bulged out uncomfortably, and I concentrated on that sensation. It happens every cruise. I get caught up in the myriad matters that require my attention, from naughty personnel problems on board the ship to the constant pressure from higher up to generate positive publicity for the Navy. Being an admiral is a pain in the ass sometimes.

As a result of this, and my sincere dislike for running on

the flight deck, I tended to gain weight during a cruise. Now, four months into this one, I was already feeling the slight tug at my waistband that told me it was time to get serious about my diet again. That, and some running. Maybe I could just do one or the other, and not—

"It's the nukes," Lab Rat said calmly, interrupting my consideration of matters that were under control and interjecting one that was not. "That possible nuke site."

"I know. I was thinking the same thing. But your evidence is still pretty tentative, isn't it?"

Lab Rat nodded. "It's only a possibility at this point, not even a low probability," he admitted. "But the SAM site bothers me. And the shot at the E-2, of course."

"Damn, I hate this business sometimes," I said. I was thinking of the letters that would have to be written, the paperwork filled out. A sudden flash of insight hit me. The formalities that surround death at sea—maybe there was a point to them. It gave us something to focus on besides the loss of our shipmates, made us feel as if we were doing something as we filled out the innumerable forms, packed out personal gear after checking it for anything that might be embarrassing to the next of kin, and wrote those heart-wrenchingly difficult letters to the families.

"Admiral," Lab Rat said, "I have no explanation— none—for that SAM site being there and active. And for it firing on one of our aircraft. There is no reason, to my knowledge, that the Vietnamese would risk an open break with the U.S. like this. None. Unless that Intel spot report is true."

"Jesus!" I slammed my pen down on the desk, and saw it skitter across the surface and roll to the carpet. Lab Rat bent to pick it up. "How many generations have to spend their lives dying in this godforsaken land? How many?"

Lab Rat sat silent. It was one of the things I most appreciated about him, his ability to wait, absorb information and occasional outbreaks of temper without taking it personally. Every admiral needs someone to vent to. Command is a lonely thing. Lab Rat was, in many ways, my safety valve.

"Okay, run me through it again," I said, my rage fading as quickly as it hit me. "Tell me about this alleged nuclear facility."

Lab Rat nodded as though the last sixty seconds had not happened. "I sent out some queries yesterday, but haven't gotten an answer back. At this point, all I know is what I told you last time."

Not enough to go on by itself, but enough to make me extremely uneasy after the attack on the E-2. What Lab Rat had was a set of surveillance photos showing four huge eighteen-wheelers proceeding down a main highway and turning off onto a dirt road in northern Vietnam. The eighteen-wheelers had been preceded and followed by military assault vehicles, and a helicopter had dogged them the entire way. Nasty-looking, that—but it wasn't all.

Another satellite, one more specialized than mere photo or infrared imagery, had the ability to track sensitive nuclear emissions from cargo. It was the same technology used to insure that garbage trucks didn't dump medical nuclear waste in landfills, only infinitely more sophisticated. I've never followed the technical details—most of it is just magic to me. But the fellows whose job it was to be certain about these things had no doubts. There was nuclear material of some sort in those eighteen-wheelers, and not all that well shielded at that. They could tell me almost everything about the spectrum it radiated in, including a damned good guess about what might be in the other two vehicles. But there was one thing they couldn't tell me, and this is the always fatal flaw of raw intelligence—what the Vietnamese intended to do with it.

The SAM site that had taken a shot at the E-2 was only ten miles to the south of the compound where the trucks and their cargo had disappeared into the deep jungle. At that point, not only had national imagery lost sight of them visually, but the radiation had disappeared from their displays as well. From there, things got murky.

One group of theorists said that it could be commercial power-plant fuel that was now safely installed deep inside shielding. Another claimed the radiation could have been caused by large quantities of medical supplies, although they had no explanation for the supplies' presence deep in the jungle. Still another argued that their cutting-edge technology wasn't all that accurate and there could be a programming fault or a data-transmission error that resulted in a spurious image.

It was the last group that worried me most—and the ones I tended to agree with. Nuclear material of that grade means only one thing to me—weapons. The location fit, as well as the disappearance off the satellites as it was moved into deep shielded cover and the involvement of the military. And now, the SAM site. This report was either a big mistake or a big problem.

"What if it is?" I asked, knowing that Lab Rat would follow my meaning immediately. He was a professional paranoid like I was. "What do we do?"

It wasn't just a question for him, but a larger question for the entire United States. We'd never really formulated a national strategy for dealing with nuclear materials in rogue hands, not really. Oh, sure, there'd been the carrot and the stick, the promise of economic assistance and trade incentives to entice other nations to comply with the ban on these weapons. The reverse had also been tried, with trade embargoes and sanctions levied against rogue nations that refused to comply with any of the international treaties.

Sometimes it worked. Most times it didn't. Nuclear material lost in the breakup of the Soviet Union was scattered around the globe now, and technology was increasing so fast that the possibility of a high-yield manned portable device was virtually a reality.

"I'm not sure we're prepared to do anything," Lab Rat answered after a moment. "With the budget cuts in the last decade, we're strapped to even maintain a deterrent presence in the major hot spots of the world. We could just go in and bomb it, I suppose. And while, of course, it wouldn't explode in a nuclear reaction, the debris alone would contaminate that land for centuries. Eons, even. You saw how dirty it was."

I nodded. The spectral analysis had shown a number of long-half-life compounds, and the prospects of that much refined atomic material seeping into the groundwater and gradually infiltrating its way into the world's oceans was not a pleasant one. It could very easily be a case of winning the battle but losing the war.

"So we'd have to go in and take it and hold it," I said, thinking aloud. "A long, bloody ground war—one that we never really managed to win satisfactorily last time."

"There's something else," Lab Rat added. "You know how long it would take us to gear up for such an action. Sure, we might try Special Forces, try to get there quietly and eliminate the problems. Or it could be a surgical strike, just like the Israelis are always pulling on their neighbors, but then there's the groundwater problem. Whatever we're going to do, it has to be done fast."

"Why?" The shiver of alarm crossed up my spine. "Do you have indications that they're intending to actually use them sometime soon?"

Lab Rat shook his head. "No. Not use them. Sell them."

After Lab Rat dropped that little bomb on me and left, I hung around my office. There was no need for me to do so really. My pile of paperwork had been reduced to a manageable level, and I felt an urgent need to get out on the flight deck, to walk around and feel the fresh ocean air, see my aircraft—*my* aircraft—lined up hard and hostile in lines on the flight deck.

It doesn't take very long to reach anyone on a carrier. After all, they're not going anywhere. But even in this massive floating office building, it can take a while to find someone without using the 1MC. And if there were any news on the survivors from the E-2—I knew in my heart there wouldn't be, not after this long—then I wanted to be right where they could find me. Immediately.

There was something else too, an issue I was trying to avoid thinking about. It was completely out of my cognizance, and I had no power to effect the end result one way or the other. But a wingman never forgets his lead, and I couldn't rub out of my mind the fact that Tombstone was on the ground in Vietnam right now.

I looked up at the clock on the wall—the minute hand had moved slightly since the last time I'd done it.

Tombstone would be on the ground now, probably still stuck in meetings with the officialdom there. There was no way to reach him, no way sufficiently secure to talk this over with him, to warn him that he might be stepping into the beginnings of an American return to Vietnam. We'd never managed to establish a permanent peace there before, not with a massive military machinery behind it, and I doubted we could do it now.

If ever a man had demons, Tombstone did. When you first meet him, you think there's nothing behind that impassive face but good reflexes and a sharp tactical mind. It takes years of knowing him, mission upon mission in flight, before you know who he really is.

Still waters run deep, they say, and I've never seen it more true than with my buddy Tombstone. Two questions in particular haunted him—how much effect his uncle had had on his career, and the loss of his father over Vietnam so many years ago. I thought someday he'd learn to live with both of those—now it looked like he'd have a shot at answering the latter. He'd told me a little bit about the leads, and I'd felt my heart sink as I realized just how little he had to go on. These anonymous reports of evidence—hell, POW families around the U.S. had been tragically bilked for decades with those. The commission set up in D.C. to track down the rumors was always chasing some bogus report of an American still held captive in Vietnam, or one who'd settled in the countryside with a native wife, or of a mass grave turned up. They never amounted to anything more than a few shreds of metal remains or maybe some bones.

But Tombstone had to go check it out firsthand. In his shoes, I would have done the same thing. But I would have been prepared for what was to follow, and I think that Tombstone probably had no idea at all.

Yes, his uncle had let him go with his blessings, even provided some military assets to aid him in the search, as well as points of contact. Only a few people in the Pentagon knew what was happening. And they were sworn to secrecy.

If Tombstone's mission failed, the details would be lost in the eternal shuffling of paperwork within the Pentagon. But if he succeeded in turning up any trace of his father—ah, now there was the rub.

Tombstone had spent most of his career at sea, in command of squadrons or battle groups. He'd spent one obligatory tour in Washington early on, but hadn't been back for the extended tutoring in intricate politics that a flag officer generally receives. He couldn't see it coming—but I could.

If Tombstone turned up evidence that his father had been abandoned in Vietnam, the public outcry and political scurrying for cover was going to be beyond anything he imagined. People would be passing the blame, pointing fingers, and wailing loud and long about how they'd not been the ones to abandon our men in Vietnam.

And that was just if Tombstone turned up remains. But I knew what he was really after, and what he thought he would find—his father alive.

One of the hardest things about command is pushing aside things like that that eat at your gut and turning your attention back to business. With possible nuclear weapons in the hands of the Vietnamese, either for their own use or for sale to any one of a dozen rogue nations around the world, I had more to worry about than the fate of my best friend.

"Admiral, an update from the SAR helo." The Chief of Staff walked into my compartment carrying a brief summary of their last mission.

I looked at him, my hope evident on my face. "Any possibility?"

He shook his head sorrowfully. "It's been a long time, Admiral."

I'd known it, but even so, the report was a disappointment. Damn it, the U.S. had to take a stand—had to. Let this pass and every tin-pot dictator around the world with a Stinger missile would be taking potshots at us. It was only the fear of massive, overwhelming retaliation that kept them at the bay now, and it was a threat we were ill prepared to back up at best.

"Keep me posted," I said finally. Not that I needed to ask him to.

The Chief of Staff nodded, hesitating as he started to leave the room.

"I'd like to schedule a memorial service, sir," he said hesitantly. "Nothing formal yet—just to block out the time this coming Sunday."

"Do it." I stared down at the desk and shook my head.

On any cruise in the last twenty-five years, it could have been me or Tombstone. Only by the grace of whatever higher power looks out for aviators had we made it this far, although we'd both lost men under our command. And now, women.

"COS—make it a good one. They deserve it."

COS looked relieved that I hadn't bitten his head off. That provoked a momentary shiver of chagrin.

"I will, Admiral." He pulled the door shut on his way out, and left me alone with my thoughts.

FOUR
Admiral "Tombstone" Magruder

24 September
Vietnam

I heard the Tomcat even though I couldn't see it. The faint growl, as familiar to me as my own heartbeat, was barely audible above the constant whine of insects and the heavy harsh thudding of machete against jungle foliage. I would have known the sound anywhere, even if I'd been away from the cockpit for far longer than I had been.

I paused, waving a hand at our small troupe for silence. My command of the Vietnamese language was limited to a few polite phrases, some incredibly vulgar ones, and a few field commands I'd picked up since we left the hotel. Whether it was because of my butchered rendition of their native language or the expression on my face, the Vietnamese accompanying our small party fell silent.

Two Tomcats, I could tell now. High—ten thousand, maybe fifteen thousand feet. It was a standard tactical altitude, well out of the range of short-range surface-to-air missiles, but still low enough that they could sight significant ground landmarks and navigate by terrain alone if they had to.

But what were they doing so far inland? I listened to the sound of the aircraft fade away into the brilliant blue sky, then motioned to my guide that we could continue.

I'd spent the nights at the Downtown Hilton, relaxing in that peculiar combination of American-style facilities and native workers. You could get the *New York Times* and the *Wall Street Journal,* and the copies of *Sports Illustrated* were current. The cashier took my American money, charged me an outrageous exchange rate to produce a handful of Vietnamese bills, and smiled politely.

The first night I pleaded jet lag and got rid of Than and his entourage early on. Later, after I was sure they'd left the hotel, I ordered room service.

This morning, we'd set off early, even as the sun was just making its way over the mountains. The mountains themselves were just black shadows, backlit by the sun. Dark, mysterious, and unknowable, they cropped up around the country to separate long stretches of fertile wetlands.

Than brought along about ten of his countrymen that he said would serve as security and guides. He warned me about the conditions we were headed into, as though I hadn't already researched them. It would be primitive, wet jungle, hard climbing up the mountains and wet going around the rice paddies. He looked at me doubtfully, as though uncertain that I could withstand the rigors of the cross-country hike.

"Fifteen miles, maybe more," he warned.

"I work out." From the puzzled expression on his face, I saw that my response hadn't been all that clear. I pantomimed lifting weights, then added, "And run. Every day."

Than nodded, reassured more by my tone of voice and expression than by a complete understanding of what an American means by working out.

He'd chartered us three minivans to hold all the people and gear. We piled in, and I took a seat in the front of the lead vehicle, which Than was driving. We left the city quickly, careening along the crowded highways among native drivers who seemed determined to commit suicide in their automobiles.

Three hours later, the road degenerated to a roughly paved two-lane highway wending its way up the mountain-side. The drop to my right was terrifying—five hundred, maybe a thousand feet straight down. No guardrails. For the first time, it really came home to me that I was no longer in the United States.

We circled around one mountain range, coming down on the opposite side, then cut off onto a single-lane mud road still damp from the previous night's rainfall. Clouds were filling the sky, billowing and tumbling into immense cumulous shapes. I wouldn't have flown through them, not for any price.

Finally, the road stopped. Simply dead-ended into a wall of green foliage that was already creeping over the cleared space.

Than stopped the vehicle, got out, and began supervising the unloading. The ten men quickly picked up packs, and I asked him if there was one for me. He shook his head. "No, you and I do not carry." He pointed at the men. "That is what they are for."

I nodded, vaguely disturbed at the undemocratic resolution of the issue. Hell, I was an admiral, but I still humped my own bags. When my aide would let me.

There was no particular ceremony to entering the wilderness. It was almost anticlimatic, after the quick flight into the country and the bone-jarring ride to the edge of the wilderness. We simply donned packs—or at least the men did—and stepped off the track and into it.

Within a few steps, I could feel the jungle clinging to me. It was alive with the small sounds that forests make, birds, something skittering in the trees overhead, the steady drip of water somewhere in the distance. The sky was replaced by a canopy of green, looped overhead with vines entangled, almost as thick in places as the undergrowth was.

Black fertile soil, so rich you could smell the deep loam of it. Things sprouted, grew, and flourished over every inch of it, only occasionally dislodged by the tramping we made.

The men didn't talk, not for a while. I had the sense that they were reorienting themselves to being in the jungle, shedding away easier, more civilized habits for those that would insure their survival in here. They moved quietly, pausing occasionally to shatter the jungle noises with their machetes, their voices low and even. The sounds barely carried at all, not against the background cacophony of the wilderness.

Than edged closer. He handed me a rifle and an extra clip. I stared at him for a moment, started to wonder what regulations governed giving weapons to a U.S. citizen in his country, then caught myself at the sheer folly of it. "Every man must have a weapon." Than's voice was that same low, almost indistinguishable tone I'd heard the other men use. "Just in case."

"In case of what?"

He shook his head, and it seemed to me that he was not going to answer.

"In case of what?" I let my voice rise a little bit higher now, invoking the tone that had intimidated so many junior officers during my last twenty-five years. "In case of what?"

Than sighed, then gave up. "It is not only the wildlife we

have to be afraid of," he said. "Cautious of," he corrected himself immediately. "Snakes, the cats . . ." He made a gesture that encompassed the whole vast expanse of wilderness. "Those, of course. And you may have heard other stories from your intelligence people. The guerillas—they still claim some parts of the jungle as their own."

"The part we're going to?"

He nodded, his eyes for the first time filled with some dark emotion I could not peg. "It is a matter of history as much as anything," he began, now venturing slowly into the topic he'd avoided before. "The history between your country—and mine."

"They're not still fighting the Vietnam war?"

"Not exactly that. But the camp we are going to—the former camp—was of course deep within their territory. It would be, you know. Away from prying eyes, out of sight of your aircraft. When the war ended, we were not able to arrange for an orderly dissolving of all units. Some merely fell apart, with men picking up their few belongings and returning to their villages. It took years, but they were gradually reabsorbed into their homes. They had wives, families—all were still waiting for them, not knowing if they were dead or alive."

"You said some. What about the others?" An uneasy prickling was making its way across the back of my head, as though eyes were watching me from the jungle. I glanced back, saw nothing move, no trace of any other presence in the jungle save ours.

He started slowly, clearly reluctant to speak further. "There were other units—I have seen the reports. Ones that did not disband, men who had nothing left to go home to. The army was their only way of life, the only thing they had left. They remained as units, no longer provisioned or paid by our government, but still functioning." He shrugged, an oddly eloquent gesture. "How they have survived, I do not know. Stealing, certainly. There have been raids on our remaining camps for decades. Perhaps some of their former comrades are sympathetic to their cause and allow supplies to filter out from their commands into the depths of the jungle. There is really no way to know." He fell silent, and his eyes were down studying the ground.

"Are you certain of this?" I asked. There were precedents, of course. Reports of Japanese who'd still fought the last world war from remote outposts decades after peace had been declared. Small bands of Korean soldiers who'd never gotten the word that the war was over. Certainly, I could see how a unit could continue to function, could eke out a living in this warm and fertile land.

"They are still here." Than fell silent, clearly disinclined to elaborate.

"You shoot first?" I asked. In the military we have rules of engagement that govern our contact with enemy forces. But here, in his country, under his sponsorship, I would be extremely reluctant to take the first shot against a Vietnamese, even one who might intend me harm.

"We have scouts ahead," he said, motioning to the front of the column. I saw that we were short two men, who'd evidently gone ahead to mark out our path. "If the rebels appear, my men will try to determine whether they are hostile or friendly. Some are indifferent to our presence here, others are openly . . . territorial."

The terrain had changed slightly, had been rising under my feet steadily, and now abruptly increased in grade. I found myself trying to carry on a conversation with Than while struggling up a mountain, and gave up talking. There was no point in trying to get more information out of him—he'd tell me what he thought I needed to know.

Soon I noticed that the vegetation was changing, thinning out slightly from the morass of vines and undergrowth we'd run into below. The going was rough, though, and vines and thick bushes still barred our way. I was sweating, water pouring down my back and gluing my shirt to me. Insects swarmed around us, flocking to any bit of exposed skin. I pulled the tube of insect repellent out of my pants pocket and smeared some more around my neck and on my hands. God knows how long it would last with the sweat pouring off me like it was. Were there leeches? I shuddered, and made it a point to check that my jungle pants were bloused over the heavy boots.

The heavy growth of trees stopped abruptly, and we broke out into a clearing. The ground continued on up, and we followed it to the very top.

From the top of the ridge, I could see the ocean in the distance. On the horizon, a dusty, misted-over familiar shape greeted me. *Jefferson*—it had to be. There was no other aircraft carrier in the vicinity.

For a moment I felt a sensation of inchoate longing, the absolute conviction that I was in the wrong place. I belonged on the carrier, at sea, surrounded by a clean expanse of water. Not here, cloaked in mosquitoes and insects of every description, blinking to clear the dirty sweat from my eyes and trying to keep up with men born to this country.

Had it been like this for my father? The power of the thought almost stunned me, and all at once I had the uncanny sensation that I was trodding in his steps. Perhaps he'd stopped in this very spot and looked out at the ocean, seeing his ship out there so clearly visible and so far from reach. Maybe he'd had his radio, and it had been broken in the fall, or maybe he'd lost it when he punched out. How had he survived out here, alone and without his people?

No. Reality reasserted itself. My father would not have been here—not immediately after the ejection, at any rate. He'd punched out over the Doumer Bridge in downtown Hanoi, nowhere near here. His wingman had said he'd seen a chute, but despite the best efforts of the U.S., there was never any report of his surviving.

No, if he'd come here, it had been as a prisoner of war, under the escort of armed men. They would have set a faster pace, urging him on perhaps with his hands bound together in front of him as he stumbled over these paths.

"They brought them in in helicopters," Than said as though reading my mind. "Prisoners of war were collected at a central site, then transported by helicopter."

"Not always," I said.

He appeared to consider that for a moment, and then nodded. "Not always."

"How much further is it to this camp?" I asked.

He shrugged. "It depends on the pace. Much of the way is like this, mountainous and jungle. Another ten miles, perhaps a little bit more."

"We're heading north," I noted, observing the position of the sun in the sky.

"Yes. It is to the north."

"Then let's get going."

Than called out softly in his own language, and the men who'd been seated on the ground taking a well-deserved break moved quickly to their feet and gathered up their packs. We continued on for another hour before all hell broke loose. As we progressed through the jungle, I started developing a morbid dread of leeches. I'd heard too many stories about men in country in Vietnam, of the giant bloodsuckers that would affix themselves to any visible part of the skin and burrow in, bloating their vast bodies on human blood. It was an unreasonable fear—we were far above the small stream that had created the gully we'd first crossed, and probably well out of the reach of leeches.

Probably.

I started to ask Than about that, and then thought better of it. No, there were no leeches here. None.

After four hours of hiking, pushing my runner's legs past their normal endurance point with the steep terrain, the crawling sensation of sweat trickling off my body fed into the obsession with leeches. Each small movement of sweat across my body made me suspect that it was not just my own perspiration, but one of those horrendous leeches burrowing in. Then the itching started in my groin. It almost panicked me, the thought of a flaccid worm crawling across my crotch, looking for just the right point at which to feed. I'd heard that leeches first injected their victims with a small amount of numbing agent so as not to alert them when the leech finally selected its spot. Was that what I was feeling now? Was there a patch of numbness spreading across my thigh, stretching out tentacles toward my left nut?

It couldn't be. My rational mind was firm about that. Still, to appease the demons lurking in my mind, I bent over to check that my boot-pant barrier was still impenetrable. In the process, I brushed lightly at my groin, and was relieved to feel nothing out of the ordinary there.

I had just started to straighten up when the first light chatter sounded through the jungle. I glanced around, looking for the source of the noise. A hand clamped down on the back of my collar, the fingers hard against my neck, and jerked backward. I stumbled backward, lost my balance, and fell to the ground next to Than.

"Guerrillas." He mouthed the word. He pointed in the direction of the slope.

I squinted, and could make out nothing besides the same dense green foliage. I eased my rifle off my shoulder sling and settled it into my hands. It was bulky, uncomfortable, but the stock was worn in several places where other hands must have held it.

Than lay a quieting hand over mine to still the action of chambering a round.

From up ahead somewhere a thin, bloodcurdling cry started low and quickly crescendoed past any octave I'd ever heard a human utter before. It was a wild, keening sound, something inhuman and unholy. It lasted for about five seconds, then cut off abruptly.

Than nodded. "Now we wait."

"For what?" I asked, barely breathing the words.

Than gave me a look of slight disgust. "To see if that was them—or us."

The minutes stretched into hours, the jungle silent except for the noise of the wind through the trees. The animals had taken cover, and not even a bird disturbed the silence.

Finally, one of our point men emerged from the foliage. A severed head, eyes still moist but glazed with the unmistakable look of death, hung from his hand. The point man was grinning. He motioned to his fellows with his rifle with all the braggadocio of a fighter pilot, as if to say, "It's safe ahead, I've taken care of business."

The men climbed back to their feet, slowly now, casting looks around at the jungle around them. It wouldn't do any good—we'd not heard them before, and I doubted we would hear them next time.

We'd just started to reassemble into a column when the next shots were fired. This time I needed no prompting—I dove to the ground and rolled under some brush.

The shots were concentrated on an area about ten feet ahead of me, slightly above waist-high. I could hear no sounds save my own harsh breathing.

Beside me, someone moaned. I looked over and saw Than pale and grimacing in the next clump of brush. Could I risk it? Than was holding up one hand, motioning to me to stay where I was. He clamped his hand around his upper arm, then held utterly still.

I moved slowly, trying not to rustle the brush around me, moving at a pace measured in inches rather than knots. It took me five minutes to traverse those ten feet, but finally I was at his side.

I unpeeled his fingers from around his shoulder and inspected the wound. Blood soaked camouflaged uniform, running in trickles over the fabric until absorbed by a dry portion. I pulled the fabric back gently.

The entry wound was clean, a hole through his arm rather than ripping the entire arm off. I fingered it cautiously, hoping that the wound was still numb enough from nerve trauma for Than to tolerate it. There appeared to be no fragment of the bullet left inside, so I took his hand and placed it back over the wound and clamped down. I placed my hand over his and pressed firmly.

Wetness seeped between my fingers, dark red rivulets that coursed down my fingers and crept around my fingertips. I could see it under my nails, darkening them as though I were a mechanic.

Than pulled his uninjured arm free, and I felt the wound throbbing warm and moist under my fingers. He reached in a jacket pocket, extracted a small medical kit. With one hand, he withdrew a roll of bandages and tape.

There was still no sound from the jungle, and the gunfire had fallen silent. Still moving carefully, trying to make no motion discernible to the people that were shooting at us, I slowly peeled back the tattered camouflage sleeve and pushed the torn T-shirt up onto his arm.

From the little I know of wounds, this was a clean one. I dumped some alcohol on it, then wound the gauze tightly around it in multiple layers. When finally I saw no more red seeping through, I bound it over with tape. Than watched impassively, not so much as a groan escaping from between his lips.

Up ahead, one of our men returned fire. I saw the bright sparks from the muzzle of his rifle, heard the antiseptic rattle of his automatic weapon. An AK-47, I suspected—it had looked like that when I'd had a chance to see it earlier.

Lying motionless in the jungle was unendurable. Fear turned to rage, then to the urgent, overwhelming need to act, to do something to take my own destiny into my own hands. It is a trait bred into fighter pilots, reinforced through days and days of aerial combat maneuvering, and finally imprinted on your mind by your first at-sea combat experience. Unlike ground troops, for whom the survival of one man depends on all his buddies doing their jobs, aviators rely primarily on people within their own cockpit. For me, that meant the voice of my backseater in my ear, giving me vectors, calling off warnings as missiles were launched against us.

The closest thing I had to a backseater here was Than, and he was in no condition to help. I patted him once reassuringly, urged him slightly deeper into the underbrush, then crept forward toward the man who'd fired. Years ago, I'd test-fired an M-16 during OCS. Later, every few years or so, I'd have a chance to go out on a range and reacquaint myself with its capabilities. Not enough to call me a good shot with it, but then at that rate of fire you don't have to be good. You just have to be close.

The man saw me coming, and motioned me into position behind a tree. Evidently he'd ascertained the bearing of the threat. I crept behind the tree, then cautiously raised up, letting its bulk shield me from the snipers. The man to my right fired off another burst, and finally our assailants in the trees began returning fire again.

Their muzzle flashes gave them away immediately. With my M-16 in full-automatic mode, I hosed down the vicinity of the muzzle flashes, staying low to the ground to catch him in cover.

There was a scream; then a muffled wailing began up on the hill. The enemy gunfire ceased.

The man I'd identified as our platoon leader stood slowly and waited, exposing himself to fire. When none followed, he motioned to the rest of the men. They formed on him, and quickly took up fighting positions.

I returned to Than, only to find him struggling to his feet with one good arm. The bandage around his left arm was already soaked with blood.

With Than injured, our pace slowed considerably. Although the bleeding had finally stopped, he was fighting off shock by sheer willpower. I watched him carefully as we progressed through the jungle, noting the pallor beneath his burnished skin, the telltale tremble in his fingers.

The other men were aware of it as well, and one stood by his side at all times, ever ready to lend a hand during the steep upward climbs. At first, Than protested, shaking off the help. As the day progressed and there was no denying his increasing weakness, he accepted the assistance with bad grace.

The only thing he absolutely refused to do was stop. During one short rest break, taken at my insistence, he provided only a brief unsatisfactory explanation. "We are in danger until we arrive. Once we are there, I think we'll be safe."

I strained to hear the slightest unusual noise in the jungle, unconvinced that our attackers had been persuaded so easily. Where there was one, or two, there could be a whole platoon, lurking just out of sight in the dense jungle. I could feel their eyes on me, and even though there was no trace of them otherwise, not an unfamiliar noise or an odd flash of color in the jungle, I knew they were there.

For whatever reason, there were no further attacks. Late in the afternoon, when Than's strength was clearly almost gone, we broke out into a low valley between two sets of hills.

It was as though I had stepped back in time. Hard-packed ground surrounded cinder-block buildings, the materials for which must have been transported by unimaginable effort. Helicopter perhaps, I thought, glancing at the stand of trees. There was almost enough room to allow in a cargo aircraft, although the descent and landing would have been harrowing. Still, if the branches had been trimmed back, the trees thinned a bit thirty years earlier, it could have been done.

The buildings themselves were virtually intact. Someone had been caring for them—they could not have survived so well in the jungle otherwise. And there was the cleared dirt area around them, only a few green shoots popping up in the middle. It would have to have been cleared quite frequently.

The jungle around me was omnivorous, voracious, devouring any sense of order that man attempted to impose on it.

"It is here," Than gasped. Two of his men were lowering him to a sitting position on a barren tree stump at one edge of the compound. Than's color was markedly paler, and his breath was coming in deep, shallow gasps. His men moved in gentle eddies around him, murmuring uneasily. One ventured forward and began caring for the wound, tentatively at first as though he would be rebuked, then with greater confidence.

"You can't mean this has survived all these years?" I stared at the compound again, baffled at the orderliness of it.

We had entered the clearing at the southeast corner. Positioned at an angle to us was one large, central building, the glass that had been in the windows—if there had ever been glass—the only clear casualty of time. This building was flanked on three sides by longer ones, clearly configured as barracks. The low, utilitarian appearance was unmistakable to anyone who'd spent any time in the military.

A central tower two stories high stood at the back part of the compound, behind the barracks-shaped building that ran directly behind the main building. It was two stories tall, capped with a sunshade made out of poles. From it, a security detachment would be able to see everything that moved in the camp—and outside it.

There was only one fixture to the puzzle missing, one that had not struck me at first. I turned to Than, considered his condition, then asked anyway. "Defense—where is it?"

Than shrugged, then winced at the pain the involuntary motion invoked. "The wire—for people in this area it was the most valuable part. The rest of it, even disassembled, requires too much effort to move. Very heavy, of course. You can see that."

His voice was losing coherency, and he was tending to ramble. I motioned to the leader of the troops. He approached me, an expression of wariness on his face.

"He needs medical care," I said quietly. "You understand?"

"Yes," he said in a heavily accented voice. "Doctor, no?"

I nodded. "Do you have a radio?"

The man paused for a moment, then shook his head. I was certain he was lying.

"Because," I pressed, "it may be that we have to take him to a hospital." The man appeared to understand me. He replied in a brief, Vietnamese phrase, then appeared frustrated when I could not understand. He tried again, more loudly this time, and I heard Than laugh. I turned to him.

"He is telling you that he knows how to care for gunshot wounds," Than said. He closed his eyes, then let two soldiers coax him into a standing, half-carried position. They started walking him carefully toward the central building. "They know about such things," he continued, almost as though talking to himself. "They've had medical experience."

"More than I have." I let his men take him off to the main structure, oddly reassured by Than's comments. With my limited command of their language—although I suspected a good deal more of them spoke English than admitted to it—I would be relatively helpless without Than's interpreting abilities. Moreover, I had no real guarantees that the men would insure that I returned to civilization, such as it was, without Than's leadership.

After a short discussion amongst themselves, two men went over to examine the guard tower. Another conducted a careful inspection of the perimeter, poking at odd spots in the jungle with his rifle. Several others went to examine the barracks.

I followed the latter group, still unable to grasp what Than clearly intended. According to Than, this was the prison camp that had housed my father. For however long he'd lived, he had been imprisoned here in these window-less barracks, perhaps allowed out briefly every day to see the sun and exercise.

Or perhaps he'd been on a forced-labor crew, working every day under the raging sun, fighting the insects and heat as I had done. Not so very far from a major population center, but it might have been light-years away for all the good it would have done him. Even had he been able to escape, where would he have gone? What aid could he have expected to receive from these people? No, he would have had to have made his way south, far south—over three hundred miles, I estimated, and through terrain that was hostile and dangerous even to a man in good health.

And that wasn't counting the snipers we'd run into in the forest.

I stepped into the first barracks building, and paused to let my eyes adjust to the darkness. A square shaft of sunlight penetrated into it, but it was insufficient to effectively illuminate the place. I could see the first sets of bunk beds clearly, but the other ones faded off into the gloom. In the rear, one of the soldiers moved, checking out the room.

"A flashlight?" I said aloud, not knowing whether or not he would understand it. There was no answer.

I stepped further into the structure, keeping my back to the bright sunshine at the door. It took a few minutes, but my eyes finally adapted. I was able to make out the remainder of the bunks, see the surface of the cinder blocks that comprised the walls of the barracks.

I walked to the wall, still keeping my back to the door, and examined the surface. There were names, notes carved into it, letters and words etched into the cinder block by some painstakingly tedious manner. I read names, ranks, dates of service, a few details about when the men had been captured. Nothing that wasn't open knowledge, and information that a POW was permitted to give. I felt suspended in the air, as though reality had receded into some other plane of existence. A surge of eagerness, compounded with fear—would I find my father's name here? Had he been in this very building, sleeping perhaps in the bunk that stood right next to me? I moved a little bit more swiftly now, fully adapted to the dark and unable to contain myself. If it was here, I had to know it. Had to know it now. Every second of delay, even after over thirty years of believing him dead, was unbearable.

I made a complete circuit of the walls, scanning through the names quickly, pausing to read an unusually poignant note, then moving on to the next. Finally, after I had made a complete circuit of the building, I knew he had not been here.

Not in this building.

But there were two others, and I suspected each would carry its own graven record of the men who had passed through. There were far more names than bunks, indicating either that they'd shared racks, or more probably that some had died—or been taken elsewhere.

I squinted my eyes and stepped out into the sunshine, dazzling and painful after the prolonged darkness. I moved to the next building, the one directly behind the main structure. Again the wait while my eyes adapted.

Halfway down the third wall, I found it. His name, rank, scratched into the concrete. The date he'd been shot down, although no details of his mission. That would have been classified, even then.

Was I there? I scanned down the wall, searching for my name or that of my mother.

Nothing. Just details about his captivity, a prayer that he'd evidently composed himself, and one final, cryptic note. "Horace Greeley."

I stared at that one phrase until my eyes began to burn, sifting through my memory for anything of family significance, some key to unravel the phrase. It was not a random thought, I knew. No, it had taken too much effort to carve those words into the concrete, and my father would not have wasted his precious energy on inanities. It meant something—I just wasn't smart enough to figure it out.

Horace Greeley—my mind flashed, then dumped details in front of me. A newspaperman, one in the middle of the nineteenth century. He'd been noted for saying—

"Go west, young man."

I said it out loud, heard the words drift through the still air in this Vietnamese hell.

Go west? Is that what he had meant?

It had to be. It was the most famous saying of Greeley's, and my father would not have relied on something too obscure to be of assistance.

The words of the Ukrainian representative to the last peace conference on board the USS *Jefferson*, the one that had followed on the heels of the last Mediterranean crisis and had crafted an uneasy peace out of the conflict there, came back to me. The Ukrainian had said he knew my father. He'd refused to say anything further when I pressed, but there had been a look on his face, some odd, secretive sense of knowing, that had driven me almost to violence. It was that comment that had sparked this mission, that had burned itself into my mind and hung there, a constant, omnipresent ache.

I turned to my left, as though trying to look west. What was west of here? I shut my eyes and called up a visual image of a map of the world. Laos, Thailand, Burma. Then India, followed by the morass of the Middle East. Had he meant those countries?

Another possibility—maybe he'd meant it in a more general sense. Not west as in due west, running along this line of latitude, but more loosely. In that case, just slightly to the north—Russia. Or Ukraine. There had been rumors for years that some American POWs had been taken to the Soviet Union, maybe via Thailand or Cambodia. Who was to know which part of the then-strong Soviet Union was actually involved?

Russia probably, I concluded. Russians had always been the brains and leadership behind the Soviet Union, although Ukraine had contributed more than its fair share of superb military men, particularly to the navy.

So my father had gone west. Had gone, and had known he was going. At least far enough in advance to give him time to scratch this message.

There was an odd scuffling at the door, and I turned toward it. One of the soldiers stood there. He was backlit by the sunshine, just a dark, faceless shape. And wrongly shaped somehow. He stepped into the room, and all at once I could see that he was carrying a body. "Than?" I went immediately to his side and examined the body.

No, it was not Than. Outside in the compound, I could hear Than's voice raised in curses at the other men.

"Sniper?" I asked, looking at the dead man.

The soldier nodded. He motioned with the almost universal forefinger pointed and thumb extended to indicate shooting. Then he pointed at the man on the ground.

I knelt behind the man and felt for a pulse. None—not that I'd expected to find one with the bloody hole in his midsection.

There was another reason this man was not Than, one that caused me far deeper concern. I'd skimmed over it at first, but now it came back and hit me full force.

The size was my first clue. This man was at least six inches taller than any of the soldiers who had accompanied us out here, although his color was the same. But in him, it was the result of years—perhaps decades?—spent under the harsh Vietnamese sun. There was no doubt in my mind as I peeled back one eyelid to examine the dead, staring orbs.

He was Caucasian.

FIVE
Lieutenant Commander "Bird Dog" Robinson

26 September
USS Jefferson

I was working on the popcorn popper when the messenger stopped by to drop off the daily flight schedule. Normally, the next day's schedule is out early in the afternoon, at least during peacetime operations. However, with the world going to shit pretty damn quick, Strike Ops was taking a little bit longer to massage the matrix of aircraft, weapons, and people into a strike package.

Skeeter, that dumb shit, was Squadron Duty Officer. Actually, the popcorn machine didn't need all that much work on it—the junior officer in the squadron is responsible for its care and well-being—but I'd caught wind of a little something in the air and was using the popcorn popper as my excuse for hanging out in the ready room looking busy.

The skipper was in the ready room too, and it was a pure sheer delight to watch her chew a piece of Skeeter's ass into small, bloody strips. Commander Flynn—the Mrs. Admiral Magruder—is not usually one to rag on you just out of sheer meanness. With that red hair and those green eyes, you'd expect an explosive temper, but she wasn't like that at all. She was one of the first chicks to fly this big bad aircraft, and she'd paid her dues on more combat missions than I had under my belt. Somewhere along the line, she picked up this ice-nasty freezer voice that's a helluva lot worse than the screaming meemies would ever be. In the last month, I'd been on the receiving end of it twice, and didn't like it either time.

But not after the E-2 got shot down. I guess she figured I felt bad enough on my own.

Anyway, the right respectful young Lieutenant Skeeter Harmon was getting a royal, public ass-chewing. That was kind of odd for her too, because she'd usually call you into her stateroom when she was really pissed. But Skeeter had fucked up big time and publicly, so the pound of flesh got extracted the same way.

"See, it's just a buildup of old butter around the what-chamacallit," I said to the ensign who was watching me play with the popcorn machine. "It happens when you don't take good care of it." I shot him a hard glare, and was mildly satisfied with the way he flinched. Of course, the fact that the skipper was having at Skeeter in the background made it all that more effective.

"I cleaned it yesterday," my particular victim muttered surlily.

"Not well enough."

"But sir, it won't—"

I straightened up and put my hands on my hips and stared at him. "You telling me how to clean a popcorn machine, mister? Because if you are, I'd like to share one small fact with you. I've got more time cleaning this popcorn machine—the particular damn machine, which never during my eight months as SLJO, Shitty Little Jobs Officer, ever, ever fucked up in this particular manner. So when I talk to you about popcorn-machine maintenance, you may damn well assume that I know what I'm talking about. Got it?"

"Yes, sir." The surliness was gone, replaced by the bored, long-suffering tone that junior officers master far too early. Hell, I never sounded like that.

I paused for a moment, and let him think I was staring at him while I listened to the skipper run on up the scale. She was on a roll now, and it behooved me to pay attention to my betters. I could learn as much about chewing ass from Tomboy as this ensign could learn from me about cleaning popcorn machines.

"And the next time you are so inclined to refuse to sign a bird out for flight because it is dirty," she continued, reaching minus two hundred Kelvin easy, "please take it upon yourself to come see me. Or the Maintenance Officer. Or the Executive Officer. Any one of us will be able to adequately explain to you alternate methods of resolving the difficulty. Other than threatening to throw the plane captain overboard."

"I wouldn't have done it," I heard Skeeter mutter. I shook my head. At that point, the fastest way out of this for my errant wingman was to shut up and take it. Skipper had him dead to rights, and he ought to have known that.

Not that it wasn't actually kind of funny. The plane captain really had thought Skeeter was going to throw him overboard. Hence the complaint, hence the ass-chewing. I could have told him. But he didn't bother to ask, no more than this young asshole had bothered to ask me about popcorn machines.

"You do not—"

A shower of sparks arced out from the popcorn machine, splattered harmlessly against the deck with an ominous crackling sound. The ensign to my right yelped. The singeing, acrid smell of a short circuit quickly filled the ready room.

The skipper was at my side in an instant. I gestured futilely at the popcorn machine, now sitting quiet and peaceful, and said, "Guess I'd better have the electricians check it out again, huh, Skipper?" I tried for a concerned, diligent look.

It didn't work.

"I'm not a MiG, mister," she snapped. She turned back to glare at Skeeter. She seemed like she was about to say something else, then simply settled for a final snarl before stalking out of the ready room.

I heard a deep shuddering sigh behind me, and turned around to see my wingman slumping down in the Squadron Duty Officer chair. "Man, don't she have some bite," he said wonderingly.

"Sir, what's wrong with the popcorn machine?" the ensign asked, evidently with his priorities in order. "And what was that about her being a MiG?"

"Nothing. You clean those damn wires better, we wouldn't get the short circuits," I told him. The ensign nodded uncertainly, and a new, grave appreciation for the scope of his duties was evident on his face. He did a quick exit stage left, saying something about hunting down an electrician's mate to look at the power cord.

After he left, I turned back to Skeeter. "You could've even asked me—I would have told you you were about to be a dumb-ass."

"Like that would have made any difference. You're always telling me that."

Damn if we didn't have a lot of surly junior officers in this squadron. I was getting right put out about it, particularly seeing as I just saved his skinny young ass from permanent damage.

"And what was that crack about a MiG?" Skeeter continued. "Young dildo head may buy your explanation, but I don't. What did she mean?"

I sighed, and shook my head. "What the captain meant," I said, enunciating carefully for the edification of my wingman, "is that her preference would be that the only thing I shook off your ass was MiGs—not her."

I looked at the bafflement on Skeeter's face, followed by grudging, dawning respect. I basked in it for a moment. About time he got his priorities in order.

"You engineered that?" he asked. He pointed at the popcorn machine.

"Come here—I know you don't think there's anything I can teach you about flying, but there are certain things you don't know about a popcorn machine. Like how to make it spark on demand."

I was just delving into some of the intricacies of popcorn machine performance with Skeeter when the flight plan arrived. I snatched the first copy out of the messenger's hands and scanned over it eagerly.

There was something wrong with it. The neat, long line of aircraft, missions, weapons loads, and aircrew was missing one thing—my name.

"They screwed up." I held the offending document out to Skeeter and pointed at the line of missions assigned to our squadron. "Big time. Boy, are they going to be embarrassed when they see this."

Skeeter took the flight schedule and studied it carefully for a moment. When he looked back up at me, his face was glum. "I don't think it's a mistake, Bird Dog. We're just not on the flight schedule."

"Well, of course *you* might not be. You're junior, after all."

Skeeter shook his head. "They took you off, buddy. Remember?"

I snatched it back from him, anger ringing in my ears now. I knew why it was—there was plenty of ways to ground an aviator without actually grounding him. I didn't think the admiral had really meant I couldn't fly. But somebody figured it was my fault that the E-2 was in the drink and those men were killed, and they were cutting me out of the pack. No chance to explain, no questions other than the routine—I'm just off the flight schedule.

"They're not gonna get away with this," I said.

"I think they just did."

"Yeah, well I'm not gonna sit still for it."

"What are you gonna do?"

"I'm gonna go see Admiral Wayne—that's what I'm gonna do." I grabbed at the flight schedule, but Skeeter danced away and held it out of my reach. "C'mon, give it to me."

He dodged down a row of chairs and interposed a tall, high-backed chair between us. "I don't think so. Didn't you hear what the skipper was just on about? Good judgment, chain of command—all that shit."

I made a grab for the schedule, and faked an end run around the chair. But Skeeter wasn't buying it. "That's only for when you're doing stupid shit, like you were," I said. "Besides, the admiral says he has an open-door policy. And this is big, Skeeter—a helluva lot bigger than a dirty aircraft."

I had him in the corner now, with just the morning briefing crews in between me and him. I double-faked, and this time he tumbled. I snagged him around the waist, lifted him half off the ground, and pried the flight schedule out of his skinny little fingers.

"Bird Dog, you can't."

"I sure as hell can," I said, pushing away the nagging suspicion that he might be right. "You don't know what they're doing to me, Skeeter—this is just the first step. Pretty soon, I'll be out of qual periodicity, and then I won't be flying shit during this. We're gonna be flying over Vietnam dropping ordinance on targets and I'm not gonna play? They're fucking out of their minds."

"Where's Gator?" Skeeter said, changing tacks. "At least ask him before you go charging off and doing something stupid."

I snorted. "I don't have to ask any fucking RIO what I can and can't do while I'm on the ground. Or on the ship— whatever. It's not him they're grounding—it's me."

"Don't do it, asshole." Skeeter's voice followed me as I slammed out of the ready room and headed down the 03 corridor toward the admiral's cabin.

I knew where the skipper had learned it. It wasn't from PXO or PCO school, or anything like that. After five minutes of standing in front of Admiral Wayne, I knew where she'd got it. That cold, hard tone that could freeze you down to your testicles. She'd learned it from him.

My explanation sputtered out about halfway through, and I gradually realized just how damned stupid it was for me to be standing in front of the guy with the stars griping about the flight schedule. There were only about a million people I should have talked to before.

And if I thought I was in trouble now, just wait till the captain found out.

"What CAG says, goes." The admiral's voice damned near froze my testicles off. "You're out of order, mister."

It was suddenly becoming quite evident to me what a very, very bad idea this had been. If I just walked out right now, pretended that I was drunk, or fell down in a frothing fit on the deck, I might have a chance. Other than that—

"Admiral, you've got to let me go."

"I don't."

"But sir, you have to. It's personal with me, Admiral— don't you understand that? Those bastards shot down my E-2. There's nobody on this bird farm that's got more right to go after 'em than I do."

And just where the hell was all this coming from? I'd been absolutely certain I was about to turn and walk out of the admiral's cabin and report to my own skipper to get my ass chewed for screwing up. Instead, my mouth seemed to be running off ahead of me, off on some strange mission of its own that it hadn't bothered to talk to my brain about.

The admiral was standing now, coming around from behind his desk to go nose-to-nose with me. He wouldn't hit me, would he? And what would I do if he did?

No, he wouldn't. Would he?

"I understand how you feel, son," the admiral said. His voice wasn't a whole lot warmer, but it sure was softer. "I'd feel the same way, in your shoes. It's got to be personal— otherwise you're not worth anything as a fighter pilot. You think I don't know that?"

"Admiral, I—" I stopped mid-sentence, absolutely horri- fied and disgusted at the quaver that was in my voice. Damn—now I had no chance at all. The admiral wasn't gonna ever let me fly again, not when I couldn't even keep my own mouth under control.

I should have taken the advice I gave Skeeter—just shut up and let it wash over you.

"I've lost pigeons before too," the admiral said. Something went funny in his eyes and he looked like he didn't even see me anymore. "More than my share. It happens in combat, Bird Dog. We expect it to happen—why the hell do you think we send fighters out with them anyway?"

"I was supposed to bring them back," I said, my voice not much louder than his now. "When we get back to the States, I'll have to go see their families. Talk to them. Look at their wives, their kids, and tell 'em I was the one who didn't bring their guy back. Me."

"Not you." The admiral's hand was on my shoulder now, the fingers digging into the muscle. He started shaking me. I felt something wet slide down my face. "Not you, damn it. It was them—the Vietnamese. They're the ones who shot that E-2 down, not you. Don't you understand that?"

"I was there. I was supposed to stop them." Fucking-A shit—I tried to turn away from the admiral, get my hands up to my face and wipe away the goddamn wimp-ass tears. "I only had one thing to do on that mission, Admiral—to keep me and my Tomcat between them and the E-2. I got in over my head, trying to keep an eye on Skeeter and—hell, it wasn't his fault. I shut him up early on. Maybe he oughta be lead instead of me."

We stood frozen like that for a minute, the admiral's hands hard on my shoulders, so close he could have reached up and choked the shit out of me if he'd wanted to. Which he probably did. And I wouldn't have blamed him a bit.

"So it's like that, is it?" His hands fell off my shoulders, and I almost staggered at the unexpected freedom. "It's like that."

He turned away from me and walked back down to sit

behind his desk. His hand went to his flight jacket pocket automatically, and I recognized the gesture—an ex-smoker searching for a package of butts by reflex. Hey, he might be the admiral, but the no-smoking policy on a ship was damned clear. Not that I'd turn him in.

I took a deep breath that rattled around inside me before it settled into my lungs. The admiral tossed me a box of tissues, and I took one without commenting. About time— why couldn't that have happened ten minutes earlier?

"Back in the saddle then." The admiral's voice had a note of finality to it.

I looked up startled.

"I've seen this before—you don't know what's happening, but you're about to lose it over this. The only way I know to cure it is to put you back out there, let you fly right on the pointy end of the spear and kick some Vietnamese ass. It won't bring the E-2 crew back, but maybe it'll help you live with it." He looked up at me now, his eyes cold and distant. "And that's what you have to learn, you know. To live with it. Otherwise, you'll clutch up every time you try to get back on the carrier at night, make a difficult tanking flog in bad weather, anything that requires you to be right, absolutely and one-hundred-percent right, or you kill people."

He was going to let me go. I don't know why it took so long to sink in, but finally it did. The relief that coursed through me was almost overwhelming, running up my spine and floating around every muscle in my face. I started to grin, then realized what he really meant.

It was time to set things right, time to get vengeance. I either did it right this time, or I was washed up forever as a fighter pilot.

Deep in my heart, I knew he was right. I had to get back

out there—and now—or forget about ever flying another combat mission.

"Thank you, Admiral." Not elegant, but it was all I could manage.

He nodded, as if he was distracted by something else. "Go see your skipper. She's going to have a few words for you, I imagine."

If I didn't know better, I could have sworn he was looking amused. Me, I already had the cold sweats, thinking about what Commander Flynn was gonna do to me when she found out about this little stunt.

"Tomboy's a good skipper—she'll understand why I'm doing this." Damn admiral was reading my mind, I was convinced. His next words proved it.

"But you're right, she's going to make you pay for this." He sighed, then was back in the room all the way, back from whatever distant place he'd been at when he'd arrived at this decision. "Now get the fuck out of here, Bird Dog. Why is it that you're always in the middle of everything?"

I backed out of the room, moving so fast I damn near ran into the Chief of Staff glowering at the door. I murmured a quick apology, felt his equally icy glare try to nail me to the wall, and then just hauled ass out of there before the admiral had a chance to change his mind.

Like I said, I knew where the skipper learned it from. Talking to her was going to be a piece of cake after this.

As soon as we stepped out the door from the island onto the flight deck, the noise hit us like a tsunami. All those aircraft turning, jockeying back and forth into position whether under their own power or under tow by yellow gear. Not to mention the noise of the ship moving through the ocean at a good thirty knots, generating wind across the decks. "Where is she?" Gator hollered.

Like I should know. I'd just signed the aircraft out, not gotten a parking-lot diagram.

I turned 360, surveying the aircraft in various stages of launch preparation. The weapons were already on the wings, the silver and dark gray—not the blue practice bombs we flew with too often.

The helos were already turning, getting ready to launch for Flight Quarters SAR. Four thousand yards behind us, the tiny little profile of a frigate dogged our wake, standing by as plane guard in case something went wrong. Surface Navy translation—in case they had to pull an aviator out of the drink.

Finally, I spotted our aircraft. She was forward, almost to the waist catapult, her brown-shirted plane captain making a close examination of the weapons slung under her wings. A full load out—two Phoenix, two Sparrows, and two Sidewinders. Personally, I like going with more Sidewinders. And forget the Phoenix—they're the long-range antiair missiles, and you usually use those up early to put the other guy on the defensive. Nice concept and planning, but too many of 'em end up with mechanical problems. Besides, I like knife fighting better. The Phoenix requires that you maintain a radar lock on the enemy contact all the way into the last moments, and that just puts too damn many limitations on a pilot. Like I said—I like a good knife fight. And that meant the radar-guided Sparrows or the heat-seeking Sidewinders.

But since we were lead aircraft on this mission, the strike guys had decided to sling us off with the long-range Phoenix so we wouldn't be shooting through the pack if the bad guys showed up. They weigh a helluva lot more than

Sidewinders and Sparrows too. And their large bulk inter-
feres with the aerodynamics of your aircraft. Guess that's
why they put 'em on the wings of the best pilot around.

"There." I pointed out our aircraft to Gator, and then
grabbed Skeeter and shoved him toward the one up near the
forward cat. The little shit was flying wing on me again,
again the brilliant decision of somebody in Strike. I guess I
didn't mind—but at least they could have made him carry
the Phoenix instead of me.

Gator and I went through the preflight checklist carefully,
with the plane captain dancing attendance on us as we
checked out his bird. Either they hate it when you do this, or
they love it. Either they're looking for a chance to show off
how well they've taken care of the aircraft, or they're afraid
you're gonna find something they screwed up.

Either way, it's my ass that's getting strapped into the
four-point ejection harness and taking their little darling up
to fight the bad boys. I always do a good preflight—and
Gator feels the same way.

Finally, when we were all the way done, I was satisfied. I
saw Skeeter and his backseater starting to mount up, having
finished a little faster than we did. For just a second, I hoped
the dumb shit hadn't overlooked something that would get
his ass shot out of the air.

We climbed up the aircraft and settled into our ejection
seats. The plane captain followed us up, double-checked the
fixtures, and helped us get settled in. At the last moment, he
removed the safeties, the cotter pins, that kept the ejection
seat from firing. I counted the strands in his hand carefully,
then nodded. "Good hunting, sir," he said. He climbed back
down the aircraft and I slid the canopy shut.

A moment later, he appeared off the right side of the
aircraft, holding up six red streamers for my inspection. I

counted them, then asked Gator to confirm it. They were the streamers that safed the weapons on my wings. I'd be one hell of a constipated Tomcat if he didn't clear those off before I tried to take a shot at a MiG.

Our plane captain turned us over to a yellow shirt, and I followed her directions up to the cat. We settled in, and they pinned the front gear—those funny little sounds and movements of the aircraft that you get used to. At the yellow shirt's direction, I cycled the flight service, waggling everything that could waggle at him to show him I had a full range of motion on all my control services.

Finally, we were ready. At his direction, I jammed the throttles forward to full military power. He took one step back and rendered a sharp salute. I returned it. The aircraft was mine now, not his. Mine and the catapult officer's.

Two seconds later, it was all mine. There was a small little jolt, the sudden movement of the aircraft, then the gut-wrenching juggernaut down the catapult to the end of the carrier. It came up fast, too fast—just like it always did.

And thank God. One of my own personal nightmares is a soft cat, a launch where something goes wrong with the steam-driven piston that tosses us off the pointy end of the boat. The result is you don't obtain sufficient airspeed to remain airborne, and you dribble off the end of the aircraft carrier like a wet dream. They don't find much of you often—if you're lucky, you punch out in those three seconds that it takes to reach the pointy end.

I heard Gator grunt behind me. He always does that—even after this long.

Then there was the sudden, mushy sinking feeling as we departed the ship. The Tomcat was still screaming at full military power, fighting for altitude and safety. We dipped down below the front of the carrier slightly, and I held my breath as I urged her up.

I love this aircraft. She only made me suffer for a microsecond, then took command of the airspace around her and started gaining altitude at a healthy pace.

I heard the net chatter as Skeeter launched, but was still too busy paying attention to my own altitude, rate of climb, and turn to watch him. I took a straight vector out to about five miles and waited for him to catch up.

Behind us, the carrier was banging an aircraft off the catapults every twenty seconds. Forward cat port, waist cat, forward cat starboard, in a continuous rotation designed to place the maximum amount of metal in the air in the minimum amount of time.

Skeeter was on me like stink on shit, then took his normal glued-to-your-wing position to my right. The rest of the flight was up now too, forming into their combat pairs.

"Viper Flight, Viper Leader," I said into the mike. "You guys ready?"

One by one, they sounded off. A good flight launch, no equipment casualties or other problems to interfere with a full formation.

"Okay, you all know what we're going to do. Let's go do it."

We settled into a loose formation, cruising at seventeen thousand feet, and headed for the coast of Vietnam.

The plan was pretty simple, the way it had been laid out. Some of those weaponeers on board the ship knew what the hell they were doing. Two EA-6B aircraft were going in with us, fully armed with HARM missiles. A couple of us were going to sneak in, buzz around slowly pretending we were E-2s, and wait for the SAM site to light up. As soon

as it did, the aardvarks were going to let off with the
HARMs to take out the SAM's antenna.

As soon as that happened, we were going to reduce one
obnoxious, very, very nasty SAM site to a nice, clean,
sterile, smoking black hole in the ground.

Ten minutes off the coast, it lit us up. Gator called out the
warning from the backseat, and I knew every other RIO in
the flight was seeing the same threat indications. The
EA-6Bs didn't wait to be told—the HARMs were off their
wings and headed for their targets so fast the guys must
have been riding the button the entire time.

"Viper Flight, Home Plate. We have launch indications—
probable MiGs." The OS sounded almost excited about it,
something unusual for the air-intercept controllers on *Jefferson*.

"Roger." I just acknowledged the report—when I needed
to know more, I'd ask.

"Great—just what we needed." Gator was carping again.

"You think I carry these Sidewinders out here for my
health?" I demanded. "Not hardly—we ain't going home
with any weapons on the wings, Gator."

"Fine with me."

As I got to thinking about it, I realized that Gator was
probably as pissed at the Vietnamese as I was. More so,
probably. He's four years senior to me, and had been stuck
flying with me ever since my first cruise. He claims he
spends most of his time trying to keep me out of trouble. But
he and I both know that he's just a passenger, a guy in the
back, a scope dope.

Well, not exactly. Gator's pulled my ass out of the fire in
the air more than once.

I felt a bit chagrined when I thought about it. He was
bound to be just as pissed as I was about losing the E-2, but

he'd never let on. You wouldn't see Gator charging into the admiral's office demanding to lead the flight back. You certainly would not. I made a mental note to skip some of the aerobatics on the way back, just because I knew how much he hated them.

They were on us almost immediately. I saw the first one pop up out of the trees at a ninety-degree angle to the ground, full afterburners spitting fire out his ass as he achieved a rate of climb that my Tomcat would never be able to match. The MiG-29s were faster, and more maneuverable, but the Tomcat had sheer power they couldn't even begin to match.

And more weapons.

"Get that shit off your wings," Skeeter suggested. "The bird will fly better without 'em."

"You think I don't know that?" I demanded.

"Just reminding you," my wingman said casually.

Someday, someday, I'm gonna kill that little shit. It pisses me off the most when he's right. The moment to catch those MiGs was when they were fully committed to gaining altitude and thus less maneuverable.

"Fox one, Fox one." I pickled off the first Phoenix and held my Tomcat head-on to the ascending MiG.

My bird jolted to the left as I dropped the Phoenix off the right wing, and I fought her back into level flight. The massive missile seemed to move slowly at first, then quickly picked up speed. One thing I can say for it—it's a powerful warhead, and if you do hit something, you're gonna kill it.

Skeeter had taken high station on me, eight thousand feet above and behind me. This loose-deuce fighting formation has worked for two generations of Navy pilots, and it's still the best approach in tactical aviation. It's particularly effective against a smaller, more agile aircraft like a MiG.

There are basically two types of air-combat fighting

styles. Both of them are driven by the performance characteristics of your aircraft and the nerve of the pilot. You take a big aircraft, something like the Tomcat, and you've got all the power in the world. Those engines will pump out a helluva lot of lift, and you can gain altitude over the long run faster than any MiG around.

The MiG, on the other hand, is an angles fighter. He likes to creep inside your turns, pivot around, and drop into position for the perfect tail shot. That's why the two-man Navy formation is so effective—even as nimble as a MiG is, he can't keep up with two of us.

"Shit shit shit shit shit," I heard the refrain from the backseat.

"What the hell is the shit?" I asked.

"Bird Dog, we're about to get—" Gator never got a chance to finish the sentence. The canopy of treetops below us exploded with what seemed like a thousand sleek aircraft, all arrowing up like they'd been shot out of the same quiver. They were all MiGs, all carrying a full combat load, and all plainly intending to jump into our part of the sky, gain some altitude, and then beat the shit out of us.

"Fuck this." I broke radar lock with the Phoenix, saw it waver off course and fall away harmlessly. I took a shot in the general direction of the aircraft ascending from the trees, just to get their attention, then made my own dash for some altitude.

There were fourteen of us—seven pairs—and only twenty-four of them. Not a fair fight—but then, whoever said they had to fight fair?

"Viper Flight, engage at will. Watch the blue-on-blues, guys—pick your target."

"This one," Gator said, targeting one of the blips with his radar designator from the backseat. I nodded my agreement.

"Fox two," I said after the steady growl of the missile told me it had a solid radar lock on the nearest MiG.

The Sparrow is a fire-and-forget weapon. Unlike the Phoenix, it graciously lets me go kill other bastards while it seeks out the one I picked out for it. Assuming the Phoenix didn't get anything, I had enough missiles for four kills. Maybe five, if I could catch two MiGs in the same fireball.

"We're about to get in serious trouble," Gator warned. "Bird Dog, those lead three are at altitude. They're maneuvering, coming back down in on us. We got to get the hell outta here."

"Skeeter, you got them?" I queried.

"Fox three, Fox three," I heard my wingman say. Seconds later, a bright fireball obliterated my vision.

"Jesus, that was close!" I snapped. "Skeeter, don't you—?"

"Fox two," Skeeter interrupted, indicating he'd just toggled off a Sparrow. "Come on, baby," I heard him add softly, coaxing the missile along to its intended target.

My Sparrow finally found its target, and I saw the treetop canopy blazing in bright fire. My MiG had tried to go low, tried to break the radar lock by confusing the Sparrow's cute little sensor with the clutter from the treetops. Sometimes it works. This time it didn't.

"Break left, break left," Gator ordered, his voice a pitch higher. "Incoming! It's gonna be close!"

I threw the Tomcat into a hard left-hand turn, stamping down on the pedals and slamming the throttles home into full afterburner. She turned so tight I felt like I was in a dodge-'em car instead of an eighty-million-dollar aircraft.

Behind me, I heard Gator grunting. The G forces that build up in a tight turn are incredible, and Gator was performing the M-1 maneuver. You tense up all the muscles, tense your stomach up, and grunt. It forces the blood back up out of your legs and keeps it pumping to your brain. That keeps you from blacking out on a high-G turn.

Harder on him than it was on me. Sitting up front, I know when it's coming. Sometimes you catch the RIOs unawares and knock 'em out before you really know that you're doing it.

"You okay?" I asked as the G forces started to ease.

"Got it—target here." Gator kept radio chatter to a minimum as he fed me another target.

I craned my neck around, trying to see it. He was in front of the sun, hidden from visual by the brilliant glare.

"I don't have him, I don't have him."

"He's up there. I gave you the target." Gator sounded certain. "Take him with the Sparrow."

"Fox two, Fox two." The lighter Sparrow leapt off the wing like a weapon possessed and steered straight up toward the sun. It was the only weapon of choice at that point. Sidewinders become easily distracted by the sun. They see it as a giant, warm and fuzzy target, the mother of all targets for a heat-seeking missile. They wander happily off course, chasing it out of the sky until they run out of fuel.

"Break right," Gator ordered.

We were flying as a team now, the perfect trio. Gator was no longer a separate person but a part of me, a disembodied voice that seemed to be coming from inside my own head as much as through the earphones, and an extra set of eyes that fed me data and radar targets so quickly and seamlessly that it felt I was doing it myself.

And the aircraft that enclosed us—no more metal and struts and fuselage, but simply power, raw power carrying us back and forth across the sky. We were one entity, one being, with one single purpose in life—to kill other aircraft.

There were so many of them, so very many. We had the

missiles to take them, but the sheer target density and the necessity to avoid a blue-on-blue fratricide constrained our engagements. The chatter on tactical was at a minimum, as it should be. When you've got a MiG on your ass and you need somebody to take him out, you don't want any gossip cluttering the circuit.

"Billy, go him! I can't get turned around—yeah."

"Break hard right, Fred. On my mark—now."

"Fox three, Fox three."

"Jesus, did you see—where the—"

I heard six quick engagements, followed by six triumphant cries of "splash, splash."

And one of ours.

"Oh Jesus, they got it. Chutes, chutes—no chutes. They didn't make it."

The exploding fireball off to my right was one of my own squadron mates, a man that I'd served with since my first cruise. I'd known him well, spent many long hours with him in the ready room or in a sleazy bar on liberty solving the problems of the world over a couple of pitchers of beer.

"Bird Dog, head for the deck." Gator was almost screaming now.

I put my Tomcat into a steep vertical dive without even asking why. When your RIO sounds like that, you don't want to know first.

The Tomcat rolled violently to starboard, buffeted by the force of the missile passing close overhead. I almost wet my pants. It was so close I could make out the small aerodynamic fins of its body, see the deadly, sleek warhead mounted on the missile. It arrowed straight away, headed for another target. Along its flight path, Tomcats were jinking and diving, others jockeying for position on it.

"Splash two!"

"Yeah, I got it—Jesus, there's another one. Chopper, get him off my ass. C'mon, man—c'mon, c'mon—thanks."

"Home Plate, where's that backup?" I demanded. I'd put the call in for the all alert aircraft as soon as I'd seen the MiGs, and they still hadn't shown up.

"Hang in there, Viper Flight," the voice on the other end of the circuit said grimly. "Gonna take a few minutes—you've got to hold the line."

"What the hell is the problem!" I said, keeping my visual scan up trying to keep my ass from getting fried. "Just what the fuck is the problem?"

"FOD on the flight deck. Red Deck for now."

"Then pick it the fuck up," I screamed at the AIC. "Jesus, don't you realize what's—"

"Ramp strike, Viper Flight," the AIC said, cutting me off. His voice was cold with anger. "Don't you think we know what the hell we're doing?"

Ramp strike—too low on approach and too gutsy to take a wave-off. There would be pieces of pilot and aircraft smashed on the stern of the ship with flaming debris scattered down the entire flight deck. Who had it been?

I had no time to reflect on the possible identity of the ramp strike. Another flight of MiGs was rising up from the trees, adding another six airframes to the battle. Almost as many as we'd already shot down.

"Viper Flight, fall back and regroup," I ordered finally. The furball was getting too dispersed, a bad time-distance problem for providing support to each other. You don't want to be in too tight—you need a little elbow room—but you also want to have somebody delouse your six when it's necessary. Somebody besides your wingman.

Most of the Tomcats broke off their engagement and scampered out to our predetermined point. The MiGs followed them, and the Tomcats jinked wildly to avoid allowing them a perfect tail shot.

We pulled it back together and re-engaged. Gator fed me a third target, and I debated a moment whether to take it with a Sparrow or a Sidewinder. Finally, I selected the Sparrow, since the Sidewinder was truly my last weapon of choice. This MiG was a beauty, painted with something special that made it glint in the sunlight like raw gold. An odd, very distinctive undertone to its paint, one that did nothing for its low-observability characteristics.

But then again, maybe he wanted to be noticed. If so, then I'd just oblige him.

I tickled off the Sparrow, made the Fox call, then spiraled up to gain altitude. Altitude is safety. You can trade it for speed, which gives you increased maneuverability. Then things got nasty. Real nasty.

"SAM site," Gator said. "To the north. Bearing three two zero."

"Where the fuck are all these SAM sites coming from?" I asked. "Jesus, those intelligence guys don't know shit."

"Your turn, lead." Skeeter's voice was tight and controlled on the tactical circuit. "He's on me, Bird Dog, he's on me."

I snapped my head around to try to see what was happening out the back. Gator chimed in with an explanation. "Below us, about two thousand feet. Three o'clock. You got it?"

I did. Sun glinted off the wings of the two aircraft as they dodged and parried at low altitude. They were low, too low—I swore quietly. How had Skeeter let himself get suckered into a low-altitude fight with the lighter, more maneuverable MiG?

"Viper Flight, this is Home Plate. Friendlies inbound—

flight of four Hornets." The controller's voice off the carrier was clipped. "Watch out for 'em, fellows—they're the cavalry."

The cavalry. Yeah, like the Hornets were going to save our ass this time. They always thought they were on the front line, when in truth they were getting into this fight long after my Tomcats got it stirred up. Still, they carried air-to-air missiles, and I was getting damned low on them at this point.

"Need some help there, Skeeter?" The cheerful Texas twang grated across my nerves as it always did. "I'm inbound on your six—wait for it. I'll give you a break."

Of all the Marines to show up on station, it had to be Thor. Major Frederick Hammersmith, if you want his real name. The prototype for all Marine pilots—I'd seen him drop down on the brutally hot tarmac to crank out fifty push-ups before getting into his aircraft just to piss the Air Boss off. Given half a chance, he'd probably carry a knife clenched between his teeth while in flight.

Still, there was no denying his help would be welcome about now. Not that I'd ever admit it to him. But the lighter Hornet, while it didn't have the staying power of my own dear Tomcat, had some advantages in a fight with a MiG. Since it was smaller, with a higher thrust-to-wing-area ratio, the Hornet was a scampery little bastard, able to cut inside arcs and turns in a way that the Tomcat couldn't. Besides that, it has LERX—Leading Edge Root Extensions. These give it an extended range of angle of attack above and beyond sixty degrees, which is about what we're limited to. Also, it has a high-tech retrofitted fence running along the LERX that generates the right airflow patterns to reduce metal fatigue on its tail assembly.

"Come on in, Thor," Skeeter said. I could hear the relief

in his voice. Like what—he thought I wouldn't be there? I was already headed for the deck, trying to pick him out from the gaggle of other Tomcat pilots who'd let themselves get suckered. Too many—far too many.

"Wait for it, buddy," Thor said. I could see his Hornet now, the small, agile form of his two-seater night-attack variant arrowing in from the direction of the carrier. "Almost there—get ready—now! Break right, Skeeter. Hard right."

My confusion over which set of aircraft was Skeeter and his MiG was immediately cleared up. I saw an F-14 break hard right, the maneuver almost immediately duplicated by the MiG on his six in perfect firing position.

Almost.

Skeeter made the bright move of taking on some altitude at the same time he was turning, thus increasing his separation from the doomed MiG. The F-14 was almost on top of him now, seemingly being reeled in by some invisible fishing line trailing off the MiG's ass.

A slight twitch, a puff of smoke, then the heat-seeking Sidewinder blinking in the sunshine like a beacon.

The missile sought out the MiG's tailpipe like it was mother's milk. It streaked inbound, dead on target and never wavering, then the two images merged into one. The silver shape of the MiG was replaced immediately by a blossoming, ugly black and red fireball.

"That one's mine." Thor's voice was calm and confident. "Any other problems I can solve for you turkey jockeys?"

"Thanks, Thor," Skeeter said. I almost puked.

More Hornets were arriving on station, calling out their tallyhos and missile shots almost as soon as they were on station. I started getting calls from my own flight on a separate circuit, early indications that they were getting low on fuel or that they were Winchestered—out of weapons. The Winchesters I sent back immediately—there was absolutely nothing they could do out here except for a lucky shot with their twenty-millimeter Vulcan Gatling-type guns fitted on the left sides. The guns are bitching when you can take the shot, but even most knife fighters don't like to get that close. Their 675 rounds, even shooting small bursts, isn't a lot of firepower.

"Viper Flight, Dragon Flight, Home Plate. Two flights of Tomcats, one flight of Hornets inbound. Viper Flight, break off as needed."

At least we were getting some more Tomcats into the fight. And the controller was right to remind me—those of us who weren't low on fuel soon would be, and it was better to clear the deck for the fresh forces.

"Let's get going," Gator urged from the backseat. "Bird Dog, our fuel is—"

"I know what our fuel is," I cut in. Damn it, someday I'm going to tape a cardboard shield between the front seat and backseat on this aircraft so he can't stick his nose into my business. "You think I'll run out of gas?"

"Of course not. At least, you never have before." Gator's voice sounded just the slightest bit dubious. "Still, don't you think we ought to—?"

Without answering, I put the Tomcat into a hard, tight climbing turn. "One more quick look, then we're out of here. I want to make sure all of our guys are out."

"Whatever you say, Bird Dog."

We spiraled on up, slowing slightly as we poured all of our power into the climb. When I felt we had a bird's-eye view, I rolled back into level flight, and then into inverted flight.

I love this part. Gator hates it. It's a good thing for him

that our fuel-transfer mechanism doesn't allow me to remain inverted for the entire flight. There's something about hanging from the ejection-seat harness. Maybe it's the blood getting forced into your head by gravity that does it.

The ocean was spread out below me, looking almost calm and peaceful from this vantage point. The aircraft still engaged below were dull gray shapes against darker water, or brilliant specks of light like fireflies as the sun reflected off wings. They winked in, back to dull gray, then back into fiery brilliance.

I saw the remnants of two fireballs hanging in the air, slowly dissipating as the wind tore at them. Only one that I knew of was ours—and better them than us.

The new aircraft were joining up on the battle already in progress, picking out beleaguered Tomcats to delouse of MiGs and neatly nailing the enemy aircraft one by one. Other Tomcats were rising up from the fray, seeking altitude and shaking the last of their pursuers as they broke off.

"Viper Flight, say state," I asked, then waited for their responses. Each pilot called out his fuel status, then waited for the tanking order.

"Red, go on in—you're lowest," I ordered. "Then Smiley, Joe, and Theresa. Skeeter, you stick with me. I think we're better off than most of them."

"Not by much," Gator said tartly. "In fact, Theresa's got more fuel than Skeeter does."

"Ladies first. Besides, neither of them is in the red zone."

I heard the exasperated sigh over the ICS. As much as I hated to admit it, there was something to what Gator was saying. Still, more of us were at bingo state. A little low, a little light-winged of weapons, but basically in good shape.

Those of us who'd made it out.

Theresa had just cleared the tanker when I led Skeeter,

now wing-welded to me again, in a gentle turn toward the tanker. She called out and checked in with the carrier, then peeled off toward the starboard marshal pattern to wait her turn at the deck. She'd made it—Theresa was a good stick, and the weather conditions were optimal.

"Skeeter, go ahead," I said. "Plug and suck, buddy, then get the hell out of the way."

"Want to take any bets on this one?" Skeeter queried.

I laughed. "No, you asshole. I know you plug first time. Just go on and get it over with. Hell, you're probably as fast in bed as you are on the tanker."

"Now, that's not what they tell me," Skeeter answered, his voice cool and amused.

We were both in the throes of that exhilaration that sets in right after combat, the period of time in which it finally sinks in that your ass was almost grass and that you'd escaped once again. Plus you'd put a few bad guys at the bottom of the ocean along the way. It's a heady euphoria that's got no equivalent in civilian life. Except maybe bungee jumping, and that was one thrill I'd never tried out.

True to his word, Skeeter nailed the tanker right off. It was a smooth, fluid plug, probe right into the basket, and the tanker started pumping him right away.

Six minutes later, he was topped off enough to go take a look at the boat. I waited until he was safely away, then slid in to try my luck.

Well, not luck really. Skill is more like it.

"Take it easy, Bird Dog. You're coming in a little fast on me." The KA-6 tanker's pilot was a bit testy.

I guess I couldn't blame her. We had been coming in a little bit fast for her.

"Now, darlin', you just hold steady," I said, trying to make light of the situation. "Let me try this again."

I eased back off the tanker and lined myself up again. The mistake that most people make when they're trying to tank is they get fixated on watching the basket bob around in the air in front of them. You don't want to do that—you want to be staring directly at the lights on the tanker and maintaining the correct relative position between your two aircraft. Otherwise you get disoriented from the little bobbles and jerks the basket does in the air. It was something I knew better than to do—and I'd just done it.

The second time went smooth as silk, my probe sliding right into the hard plastic basket like—well, I wasn't going there. Not on cruise, not with the women on board the ship looking better and better every day that went by.

"Good seal," the tanker pilot said. "Ready to transfer fuel."

"Ready to receive."

I could hear the slight gurgle as the fuel fed smoothly into the probe and was distributed to the two wing tanks. Five thousand pounds, that would hold me until we got back to the boat. Enough to make two passes at the deck, although I doubted that I'd need more than one. It had been a long time since I hadn't gotten back on board on my first pass, and I didn't aim to break my record now.

"That'll do me, darlin'," I said finally. I shut off the switches that allowed fuel to flow in through the probe, and allowed her to do the same. Then I gently backed off, slid further back until I was well clear, and rolled off to the right. "See you back on the deck," I called out as a farewell.

"Not anytime soon," she answered tartly. "Got a bunch more customers up here soon enough."

"Those Hornets get thirsty fast," I agreed.

Despite some relatively decent performance statistics, that was the one problem with the F/A-18—it was a hungry little bastard. The trade-off for having a lightweight aircraft was that it could carry less of everything. Fuel, weapons, hell, probably even piddle packs. You never want to get into a fight with a bunch of Hornets without having a lot of gas in the air nearby.

I was just four thousand yards away from the tanker when I heard the tanker pilot start screaming. "Bird Dog, get back here! He's on me, he's on me!"

I slammed into afterburner and rolled and turned, heading back to the tanker. I knew what was wrong—one of those goddamn Hornets had let a MiG sneak through and make a run on their Texaco. That should have been the first thing they'd done, make sure that their tanker was protected. If I'd been down there—

The MiG was almost toying with her, like a cat with a mouse. It was a bit above her, and well aft, in perfect firing position.

I sighted in, got the low growl of a Sidewinder, then said, "Gina, break left. Now!"

Tankers aren't the maneuverable airframes that fighters are, but she did the best that she could. As old as those birds are, she probably damn near tore the wings off trying to get away. The KA-6 rolled hard, overshot, and exposed her underbelly to the MiG, then completed the roll and fell down toward the ocean in a spiral. It's always nice to use gravity if you need to gain some airspeed in a hurry.

I waited two seconds, enough time to get her out of range of the fireball, and just long enough for the MiG pilot to start getting truly pissed.

A missile leapt off his wings, the ignition of its booster blinding me slightly. I thumbed off the Sidewinder at the same time.

I had one second to see the canopy of the KA-6 peel off,

shatter into pieces, and two ejection seats rocket up at forty-five-degree angles from each other. They were barely clear of the aircraft when it exploded into flames.

The smoke and fire blanked out my view of the two chutes. Had they opened? I didn't know, and now I sure as hell couldn't see. The MiG I'd shot the Sidewinder at was a smoking black hole in the air.

"Get down—look for chutes!" Gator said.

"On my way." I took time to make a quick visual scan of the area around me, knowing that Gator was doing the same thing with his radar. "All clear?"

"I'll tell you if it's not."

I put the Tomcat into a steep dive, pulling up just about at the altitude where I estimated the chutes would be. We made a 360, each of us craning our necks trying to see them wherever they were. I felt a heavy, rotten, sinking feeling in my gut. There hadn't been time—not enough distance. Even though they'd cleared the aircraft, the fireball must have got them.

"Get down lower," Gator said. "Maybe we missed them."

I did as he suggested, far too low over the ocean for my own comfort, but desperate to see any trace of the tanker pilot and her RIO.

"Bird Dog?" Gator's voice asked. "Have you got 'em?"

"Not yet." I wished he'd just shut the fuck up and let me look for them.

"I'm joining on you," Skeeter said.

"No—get back to the boat," I ordered. The last thing I needed was Skeeter poking around down here while I was trying to find the two women who had gone down. "One of us is enough."

"But who's gonna cover you?" Skeeter asked. "Bird Dog, you can't—"

"Back to the boat, Skeeter," I said again. "Jesus, why don't you just follow orders for once without arguing?"

Two clicks on the circuit acknowledged my last transmission. I kept me eyes glued to the ocean, hoping for something, anything.

"He's right, you know," Gator said.

"Fuck him."

"No, fuck you." There was a note in Gator's voice I rarely heard, but knew better than to ignore it when I did. "Bird Dog, he's got enough fuel, we need another set of eyes out here, if not for the crew, then for any of those nasty little bastards that want to jump us."

"How about you keep your eyes on that radarscope and keep that from happening," I suggested.

"Damn it—too late for that. Bird Dog, MiGs at five o'clock, four miles off and closing fast. They're in targeting mode—Bird Dog!"

"I'm coming in," Skeeter said, still on the net. "Hold on, Bird Dog."

I was a little bit too busy to answer at that point, trying to get my turkey ass off the deck and back in the air where it belonged. How had I got suckered into this? I know better, I damn well know better.

"Targeting radar," Gator warned, his voice higher now. "Bird Dog, we're too slow—too low. We can't make it out of this one."

"I'm almost there," Skeeter said. "Please, Bird Dog, just—"

"We'll get some distance," I said, thinking furiously. "I've still got one Sparrow, the gun—we're gonna make it, Gator."

"The hell you say," Gator's voice had a note of quiet

desperation in it this time. "Bird Dog, get ready. You know we're gonna have to punch out."

"I'm not punching out. This is my aircraft, and no goddamned Vietnamese is going to take it away from me."

"Vampire, vampire," Skeeter screamed over the circuit, his voice losing every trace of cool it had ever had. "Jesus, Bird Dog—punch out. Punch out now!"

"I'm not—"

The wind ripped the words out of my throat and slammed my head back against the headrest. I had just a split second to realize what had happened before the canopy broke away from the airframe, tumbled backwards in the sky above us before falling back in the slipstream. A microsecond later, the pan of the ejection seat slammed me up. Over the noise of the wind and the explosion in my ejection seat, I heard Gator's seat go, saw out of the corner of my eye the bright flash of his ejection rocket firing. My vision was already going gray, and every bit of exposed skin felt numb and sandpapered. The gray crowded in on all sides, until my vision dwindled to a mere pinpoint of light in front of me. Then quietly, amazingly understated in the fury of noise and sound around me, that too winked out.

I woke up when I tried to breathe. Cold seawater is a poor substitute for air.

My gear had done its job as advertised. Sometime after I hit the water, the ejection seat had separated and the buoyant flotation pan had kept me above water. The life raft was already inflating nearby.

For a few moments, I focused on just trying to breathe. The seas were rougher than they'd looked from the sky, and every second wave slapped me in the face and tried to make me breathe it. I got my life jacket inflated, got enough air in my lungs to be able to think clearly, and then started swearing.

"Gator?" I hollered. Silly thing to do—I doubted he'd be able to hear me over the wave noise.

"Gator, are you here?"

I set out for the raft, breaststroking in my best fashion and trying to keep my head out of the water. All the while, I was looking for the other life jacket, the parachute, anything that would give me an indication of Gator's position. I'd seen his chute—the seats are timed so that his fires a split second before mine does, giving him enough time to get clear so his ejection rocket won't turn me into toast.

I grabbed the raft, hung on the side for a moment to catch my breath, then pulled myself into it. A flight suit, ejection harness, and boots were a hell of a lot heavier wet than dry.

I raised up on my knees, tried to stand, and almost lost my balance.

There—off in the distance. I could see a speck of something that looked orange, something that might be Gator. I grabbed the paddle out of the raft and headed for him.

"Goddamn RIOs," I said, as the events of the last few minutes flashed back in my mind.

I knew what he'd done. And he'd probably been right to do it. What was worse, I was going to have to admit it.

The missile had been on us, so quick and so fast that Skeeter hadn't had a chance to get to us. If I'd let him come back when he first tried to join on me, it wouldn't have been a problem. But it had been my delays—mine—that had kept him at arm's length and out of position.

There had been no time, no time at all. Gator had known it—and at some level, so had I.

Still, I never believe that anything in the air can get me.

It's one of those things about being a pilot. You start believing that it's possible for you to get hurt, that your bright and shiny new Tomcat wrapped around you isn't an invincible and all-powerful weapon, and you lose your nerve. The next thing you know, you're starting to stutter on your approach to the boat, you lose the edge, that thing that makes you the very best in the air.

Fear? You can't afford it. Not with the guy in the back depending on you.

But this time, it had been the guy in the back who'd saved my ass. RIOs have no ego compunctions about admitting when they're over their head. After all, they're not flying. Gator had seen what I wouldn't admit—that the missile was too close and that we were about to buy it.

Command ejection. When the ejection seats in a Tomcat are set to command-eject, activating either seat causes both to shoot out. Experienced pilots with a new RIO stay away from that, in case the guy in the back gets panicky and pulls the ejection handle. If they do, they're the only ones leaving the aircraft—and they're the ones who'll have to explain it to the Inquiry Board.

But with a guy like Gator, one who's been on more cruises than I have and has been flying with me for a couple of years now, you leave it in command-eject. For just such circumstances as this.

I was a little closer now, close enough to see that it was indeed a life jacket I was looking at. Gator had his back to me, and was floating uneasily on the top of the waves. He was still, except for the water-generated motion.

"Gator!" I hollered, and paddled over to him as quickly as I could. All this water—I was conscious of the overwhelming need to pee.

About three yards away from him, it suddenly hit me. The

life jacket—it looked wrong. And what I could see of the figure was too small for Gator.

I started swearing again, this time really meaning it. A damn Vietnamese—it had to be. Now I could see the skin color, and I was certain it was not one of our guys. Or girls. For a moment, I'd had a wild rush of hope that it could be the tanker crew, but no such luck.

I sculled the boat to a standstill a few yards away and considered my options. If I waited a little longer, maybe he would just drown. That would save me a whole lot of trouble.

Still—there's a kinship among aviators that transcends a lot of things. One of those being floating in the sea face-down.

As much as I wanted to, I couldn't let him die like that. I took a last look around the ocean, still searching for Gator, and saw another splash of orange off in the distance. What now? Head for Gator immediately and come back later for the gook?

Still, I was right there. I hauled ass over to him, grabbed him by the neck, and yanked him into the boat. I pulled my .45 out of my flight suit, chambered a round, and pointed at him. Maybe not the most logical thing to do, because if I shot him I'd undoubtedly put a hole in my raft as well. But maybe it would slow him down some.

He was unconscious, pale even under that golden skin, but breathing. Nothing stuck out at an odd angle, so I figured there was nothing broken. Not that it mattered—as long as he was breathing, I'd about reached the limit of my first-aid abilities.

I kept him where I could see him, right in the front of the raft, and headed for Gator. It seemed to take hours, much longer than it had to reach the stranger. But finally I was there.

Gator was conscious, sculling the water and clearly looking around for his own life raft. Obviously it had blown out of reach. One of his arms hung at an awkward angle by his side. I was a good deal gentler with him as I hoisted him into the raft.

"Got your radio?" Gator gasped. "I couldn't—my arm wasn't working. I couldn't grab it and paddle at the same time."

I felt in one long deep pocket and pulled out my emergency SAR radio. It was preset to the appropriate channel, and I keyed the flat switch on the side and spoke into it.

"This is Viper Leader, does anyone read?" I unkeyed the mike and waited for a response. Blessedly it came within seconds.

"Viper Leader, Angel 101 en route to your position. I have a visual on you."

Never have words been so welcome in my ears. I let out a wild shout, which Gator echoed weakly. Our companion in the raft still appeared to be unconscious.

I slumped back down on my butt in the ass end of the life raft—like you can tell one end from the other—and gazed fondly at my RIO. His face was battered and bloody, white with pain, and his arm looked like shit. Still, those SAR guys knew how to get us back up in their bird without doing permanent damage—I hoped. At least they claimed they did.

"First time for everything," Gator said finally.

"Last time too," I said. "And last time I leave us in command-eject."

Gator managed a weak frown. "Don't give me that

bullshit," he said, his voice faint. "If I hadn't punched us out, we wouldn't be having this conversation."

"Maybe you're right," I said finally. The urge to argue the point with him was overwhelming, but there was one factor that stood in my way.

He was right.

"So what do we do with him?" I said, gesturing at the Vietnamese pilot. "I vote we throw him overboard."

Gator shook his head slowly. "I know you're not serious."

"And what if I am?" I said, trying to salvage some degree of ego out this whole thing. "So it's okay to shoot 'em down but not to drown 'em?"

Gator sighed and shifted slightly. He reached out with one hand and touched the Vietnamese pilot. A low moan issued from the still form, and the Vietnamese stirred slightly.

"We take him back with us. On the helo."

"There it is." I pointed off toward the west. The tiny, ugly insect—Angel 101. "Hurry up, you guys," I said into the radio. "And we've got an extra passenger for you here— one of the bad guys we fished out of the water."

"Roger, copy three souls," the SAR crew chief answered. "We've got room for you."

Off to the east, I could see the air battle still raging. The fighters circled and danced in the sky, the Tomcats using their greater power against the MiGs' more maneuverable form. I saw another hit, but couldn't tell who it was. Please, God—not one of ours. I offered up the silent prayer, as contrite at that moment as I ever had been in my life.

Somehow, I'd always envisioned the war stopping when I left it. I knew it wasn't true, at least on an intellectual level. The flights who replaced me while I went to plug and suck on the tanker or back to *Jefferson* to rearm still continued the battle. Although it seems like you're at the center of the universe when you're in the cockpit, it really isn't so, as the battle off to my east was now making patently clear to me.

I saw one of the small figures break off in hot pursuit and head our direction. Gator was watching too. I heard him say, "Oh, no. No, not that."

My only excuse for what I said next was that I'd just come out of air combat, been ejected from an aircraft, half drowned, and wasn't thinking straight. It didn't make sense, not even as I said it, but I said it anyway.

"They're not gonna strafe us."

Gator shot me a look of sheer, hellish disgust. "Maybe not at first." He gestured with his good arm toward the helo. "They're after the Angel first."

It was simply no matchup. The MiG came no closer than two miles, circled for a moment, then fired two missiles at the CH-46. The helo dove for the water, trying desperately to shake the missiles among the clutter of waves, but the sea state was simply too light. I'd never seen a helo move that fast, or that nimbly. Their pilot did a helluva job.

It wasn't good enough. The first missile hit dead on, shattering the canopy, then plowing part of the way into the fuselage before exploding into a fireball. The second missile detonated upon hitting the suspended shrapnel in the air, creating a secondary explosion that was completely unnecessary. The crew had died in the first moments of impact.

"No!" I was trying to stand now, shaking on my feet in the fragile life boat and lifting one hand at the air and shaking it. "No, you bastards."

I felt a hand on my back, and something yanked me down hard. I lost my balance, fell half out of the raft. My head was submerged in the cold water, and it must have cleared my brain. I grabbed for the side of the raft to keep from falling out, and in the process lost my gun. Two hands hauled me back into the raft and tossed me across to the other side. I sputtered, choked, then puked over the edge.

The Vietnamese pilot was awake—and clearly had been for some time. I clenched my right hand reflexively, felt the absence of the pistol as keenly as I'd ever noted a loss before.

Our eyes met—his black, battered from his own ejection and colder than the water. No blinking, just staring. I broke the gaze first and looked down in his left hand. A pistol, not an American one.

"Oh, Bird Dog," I heard Gator say softly. "Jesus, Bird Dog."

The Vietnamese whirled on him, pointing the gun in his direction. He made a motion, clearly indicated that Gator should move to my end of the raft. He did so, dragging himself and his crumpled arm painfully down the length. As soon as he was within arm's reach, I grabbed him and pulled him up toward me. "Just hold still, buddy. They'll be back."

Gator groaned, now past the point of having a coherent discussion.

In the far end of the raft, the Vietnamese settled down, seated, but with the gun pointed implacably in our direction.

We just sat like that for a long time, staring at each other. I checked Gator over, did what I could to make him more comfortable. There was nothing I could use on the boat to splint his arm except the oar, and the gook had gotten hold of that.

The other fellow pulled out his own version of a SAR radio and spoke briefly into it. My heart sank as someone answered.

It took them about thirty minutes, but the patrol boat

finally found us. We saw them well before they saw us, and our not-so-good friend guided them straight in on us.

They took him aboard first. Then two of them climbed down in the raft to hand Gator up. They went pretty easy with him once they saw he was injured. I saw Gator start to scream at one point when his arm joggled the wrong way, and the guy we fished out of the ocean said something in a nasty tone of voice to them. I don't speak Vietnamese, but I could guess what it was by the expression on their faces.

Something else struck me odd about the entire exchange. Our good old buddy in the water, the one I'd been so tempted to drown, looked like he might be something a little bit more than your average fighter pilot. There were no insignia on his uniform, nothing to give away his rank—a standard precaution when flying combat patrols—but I could tell from the way the rest of the men on the boat reacted to him that he might be somebody special. Maybe real special. I should have drowned him when I had the chance.

But for what it was worth, it got Gator fairly decent treatment. The fact that I'd fished him out of the water to begin with seemed to count for something.

It took us two hours to get to shore, a rolling, gut-puking journey in what looked like a converted fishing vessel. It must have had no draft whatsoever—we bobbed around even in the mild seas like a cork with a trout on the other end.

Finally, we pulled into a naval base and pulled up to the pier. Once again, my buddy departed the boat first. That clued me in too—last on, first off is the rule for senior officers. He stood on the pier, a bedraggled, soaked, and exhausted figure, with something burning inside of him that kept him upright and snapping out orders. A stretcher was waiting for Gator, and two men who looked to be the Vietnamese equivalent of medics were at his side immediately. Not a routine evolution from the looks of it—I expected our friend's extended conversation on the ship-to-shore radio had something to do with it.

Nobody paid much attention to me, other than a tough-looking guy patting me down real thoroughly. He took away my knife and my radio. He left me with a chocolate bar and my plastic bottle of water.

Finally, old Fred—and that's how I was beginning to think of him, because I was tired of thinking of him as a gook or simply that guy—motioned to both of us. We marched off to an ambulance and a panel truck. They tried to pull me away from Gator's side and stuff me in the truck, and I protested vigorously.

"You are American?" The words in English surprised me, and I spun around to see a small, delicately made Vietnamese woman looking up at me. She smiled. "I am the translator," she said carefully, her words precise and accented. "You are American?"

I nodded. "Lieutenant Commander Curt Robinson, 783–22–9872. United States Navy."

She nodded, as though she'd expected nothing more. "And your friend?"

"Commander Gator Cummings, United States Navy. I don't know his Social Security number."

Again she nodded, an odd, cryptic expression on her face. "I have some questions to ask you."

"I don't answer questions."

"They are very easy."

I shook my head in the negative. "No questions. And I go with him." I pointed to Gator, who was being loaded into the ambulance.

It was her turn to shake her head, and a frown appeared on her face. "You had General Hue in your boat," she began, and pointed at Fred. He was standing off to the side and watching this all with a cynical expression on his face.

"A general?"

"Yes. He has ordered for us to take care of you in light of that fact. And your friend. But your friend must go to the hospital, and you will go to . . ." She struggled with the phrase for a moment, then came up with it. "A holding facility."

She blew it when she glanced over at the general to see if she'd gotten it right. I knew at that point that good old Fred spoke a good deal more English than he'd let on. I turned to him and spoke directly to him.

"You know what happened. So you just explain it to her. And I gotta go with my buddy." The rear doors to the ambulance were now closed, and Gator was out of sight. I was growing increasingly desperate. "C'mon, you'd feel the same way if it were your backseater, wouldn't you?"

General Hue regarded me for a long moment, as though trying to decide whether or not to admit that he spoke English. Finally, without a word, he nodded. He rattled off a short series of commands in Vietnamese, then turned back to me.

"Thank you." The words were harsh and guttural, and barely understandable. It was evidently one of the few phrases he was willing to admit that he knew in English.

I stared back and gaped. None of this was making sense, none of it. I was certain that the general understood a good deal more than he was letting on.

But then again, you're not really in a position to challenge a general's word when you're a prisoner of war. I settled for being handcuffed and placed in the back of the ambulance with Gator.

With a rough squeal of tires, the ambulance took off from the edge of the pier. They lit up the siren, but only for a few minutes, evidently to clear traffic out ahead. I looked back at the pier through the rear window of the ambulance, and saw the general standing there talking to our interpreter.

The hospital looked like any hospital—smelled funny, lots of white walls, a lot of people doing things that seem either painful, embarrassing, or downright pointless. Nevertheless, they seemed to treat Gator pretty well. I refused to leave the room, so they just ignored me as they wheeled in a portable X-ray machine, took some shots of his arm, then motioned to me to follow as they wheeled him down the hall.

An hour later, Gator had a real fine smile on his face, the result of whatever painkiller they'd pumped into him shortly after we arrived. He also had a nice white cast on his arm, and a neatly tied scarf in place for his sling.

"How you feeling?" I asked quietly. "Listen, you know where we are?"

Gator smiled dreamily. "Hong Kong?"

"No." It was as bad as I thought it might be. Gator was disoriented, and there was no telling what he might say until the drugs wore off. "Gator, listen to me. You punched us out, we were in the drink. The Vietnamese picked us up. Listen, good buddy, they're taking real good care of us so far. But I don't know how long that will last. You need to keep your mouth shut, don't say anything. Not about the ship, not about the aircraft, not about anything. You got that?"

"You're always telling me to shut up," Gator said vaguely. He looked up at me, and his pupils were dilated until they ate up the whole iris. "You never listen to me."

"I will from now on, Gator." I laid my hand on his good one, and held it tight. "You were right this last time, buddy. You were absolutely right and you saved my ass. But you gotta listen to me, Gator—pay attention now. Don't say anything. We're POWs, you understand?"

Gator nodded. "Don't say anything." His voice trailed off into a sleepy mumble. I sat right next to him in the room as activity teemed in the passageway. Through the open door, I could see more pilots being brought in, all of them Vietnamese. The sounds of a working hospital were almost overwhelming.

For a while, I thought they'd forgotten about us. But no such luck. Finally a big heavy guy, a security fellow of some sort, showed up.

"Come." The word was clear and understandable.

I stood up, then motioned to Gator. "He can't walk just yet."

That damn panel truck was back, parked right by the ambulance entrance. It must have followed us back from the pier. I couldn't be certain it was the same one, but it looked like it. It had that faded, oxidized green you get on Army vehicles, streaked with rust on the sides. It looked pretty rickety, but the engine sounded decent.

The guard motioned us to the back of the truck, and I helped Gator in first. Damn, it was so hard not to jar him—thank God the drugs hadn't worn off yet. He moved like a little schoolkid, sort of clumsy and awkward, with a trusting expression on his face.

I handed him up into the truck, and whispered to him, "Don't forget. Don't say anything." He nodded once dreamily, scooted back into one corner, and seemed to doze off. I turned back to our guard. "Where are we going?"

He motioned at the truck again with his rifle.

I took the hint. As soon as I sat down, he slammed the door shut and I heard the lock turn. He walked around, got into the passenger seat, and talked to the driver for a minute. We pulled away, out of the parking lot, and onto a paved road.

Thirty minutes later, we were deep in the countryside. The road had degenerated to a rutted track, mostly paved but often not. Gator was awake now—the first teeth-rattling jolt over an enormous pothole had brought him awake with an anguished moan. Now he just sat there, staring out into the air, holding his arm close to him and trying to keep it from jarring. It looked like the drugs were wearing off—his face was getting tight, and his pupils were contracting.

"How're you doing, Gator?" I raised my voice to be heard over the rattling of our vehicle.

He groaned and turned white as we jolted hard to the right. I knew, whatever he said, he wasn't doing well at all. Not at all.

"I'm okay," he said finally. The words were forced out between clenched teeth. "My arm—they fixed me?"

Okay, so maybe he wasn't all the way there yet. The last couple of hours must have been a blur for him. I debated rehashing them, then glanced toward the front. There was nothing separating us from the security man and the driver, and I had evidence that the security man knew at least one word of English. "Yeah, they set your arm."

Gator nodded, then looked back up at me. "What happened?"

I shook my head. "Not here, Gator. It's not safe." I pointed to the guys up front. His eyes followed my gesture, and it seemed to make sense to him. He nodded, then said, "Are you okay?"

Jesus, how could the guy even think of it? Here we were, trundling off to God knows where, his arm in a sling and my ass in one, and he asks if I'm okay? I don't know what I ever did to deserve flying with a guy like Gator, but whatever it was, it wasn't enough. He'd been taking care of me for years now, going along with some of the wild-ass schemes I cooked up—the one over the Arctic came to mind first, where we'd whizzed along blind nearly at ground level to chase down some bad guys living in the ice spears—and he'd damned near never said a word. Oh sure, he complained from time to time, but he went along with it. And so far, I hadn't done anything serious enough to get us killed.

At least not until now.

If I ever got out of here, I was gonna have to make it up to him somehow. Be more considerate, not roll inverted in a steep dive just for the sheer hell of it when I know it pisses him off. Listen to him occasionally, even laugh at those dumb-ass jokes he likes. Hell, I'd even make his rack every day if it would get us out of this situation.

"I'm fine," I said finally. "As fine as I can be."

Gator nodded. It looked like the medicine had kicked in just a little bit more. His eyes, unfocused and glazed, drifted shut, then jolted back open wide as we hit another bump.

"Where are they taking us? Did they say?"

"They're not the most talkative of fellows," I said.

I'd taken a long hard look at the sky when we walked out of the hospital and headed for the truck, wondering if the air battle was still going on. I hoped not—it had looked like it was turning in our favor when we departed the pattern, but I couldn't be sure. Still, given enough Tomcats and Hornets, the United States Navy can whip the ass of any fighter air force around. And that included the bad-ass MiGs that were flown by the Vietnamese. Hell, I'd shot down a couple myself in the last Spratly Islands conflict.

I hadn't seen anything, but I was glad I'd at least looked. There was no chance that we would see it now, not this deep in the jungle. Trees towered overhead, tangled with vines and undergrowth. The sky was just patches we'd occasionally catch a glimpse of. The real overhead was the jungle.

I was halfway expecting it when we got there, but it still depressed me. Wire fencing, with guard posts set in every corner. One main building, no signs of barracks or anything like that. But behind the building, a structure in the ground that slanted downwards, about eight feet across at the entrance and maybe six feet high. The entrance was fortified with huge wooden girders, a nicety of construction that degenerated further back into unfinished tree trunks.

The open cavern inside was pretty big, and seemed to be well supported by timbering and boards. It was maybe fifty feet by twenty, illuminated only by a single strand of electric lights that ran across the middle of the ceiling. Near the rear, there were eight sets of bunk beds. A primitive bucket evidently constituted the sanitary arrangements.

One of our guards flicked on the lights, pointed us down the ramp, and gave me a gentle shove. I started to swing at him, but Gator caught my arm with his good one. "Not now."

I looked around the wire enclosure outside. Twenty, maybe thirty uniformed ground troops were milling around smartly, their curiosity about us evidently at a fever pitch. Our two guards held them back, waving them away with their weapons.

We went in and settled down on two bunks, the lower two that were side by side near the forward part of the cavern. It seemed important to me to be as near as I possibly could get to that one blank patch of natural sunlight. Gator stretched out on his rack and fell asleep. I lay down on mine and tried to think.

What were the odds that anyone had seen us taken by the Vietnamese? The helo had seen us in the water, sure, and had probably gotten a report back to *Jefferson*. But after it had been shot down, what had happened next? Had any of the aircraft overhead actually seen the Vietnamese fishing boat come out and pick us up?

And what about Fred—General Hue, I mean? If he really was a general, what was he doing flying? You don't do that when you get stars, at least not in the United States Navy. You barely get to fly when you're a captain. And if he wasn't a general, what exactly was he?

My mind ran around in circles, trying to make some sense of it and wondering whether anybody even knew we were still alive. Finally, despite my best intentions of standing guard over Gator the entire time, I fell asleep.

SIX

Admiral "Batman" Wayne

27 September
USS Jefferson

I hauled my ancient ass up six decks to Pri-Fly to watch the preparations. We'd lost three Tomcats, one tanker, and one helo. That in addition to the E-2C that went down four days before.

It wasn't just the aircraft, although that was the way we phrased it to keep from facing the ultimate tragedy. Airframes could be replaced, but the men and women who'd flown in them could not. Not in my air wing, and not in the families—wives, husbands, children, and parents—that they'd left behind. I would be writing those letters all too soon, facing the hard reality of what we do as day-to-day business. Then there would be time to mourn, time to think about them as I knew them, as I saw them in the mess every day and in the passageways of my ship.

But for now, we went by the numbers. It reduced the war to what it had to be for us to fight it—for if we really thought about our people too long and too hard, or even about the other guy, we'd lose what you have to have to get shot off the pointy end of an aircraft carrier and go into battle.

"Every aircraft you have, CAG," I said for probably the third time. It wasn't necessary—he'd heard me the first time.

CAG nodded. "We have contingency plans, of course," he began. "Actually drafting up the flight plans and getting all the birds on deck in the right spots with weapons on wings will take a little time." He shot me a glance that said he knew that I knew exactly how much time. I ignored it.

"Two hours—every aircraft," I said. "Unless it's an out and out hangar queen, I want it in the air."

"We'll do it." CAG stood. "And if you could excuse me, I probably need to be down below keeping an eye on it." He pointed one finger in the direction of Vietnam. "Get a good look at the coastline, Admiral. In a couple of hours, there's gonna be too much smoke and fire to see anything."

CAG headed back down to his office on the 03 level, trailing a couple of Strike Warfare people in his wake like pilot fish. He was a good man, and if anybody could pull this off, he could. The tower was fully manned up because we had SAR assets airborne. I'd sent out four helos and three S-3s, hoping that by carefully quartering the area we might pick up some trace—any trace—of our downed aircraft.

Of our crews.

So far, the results had been zero. Three oil slicks, one chuck of a fuselage floating. No signs of any aircrew anywhere, and that was all that mattered. Evidence that they'd gone into the drink didn't matter—hell, that was something we already knew.

The SH-60s and CH-46s had one advantage over the S-3. They could hover, get a good close look at the water, and see if there were any men in it. The S-3, on the other hand, had a lot longer legs. With tanking, she could stay airborne for five hours easy, although the noise and vibration would reduce crew efficiency considerably before then.

Under the circumstances, I thought they'd probably tough it out. In fact, I was certain of it.

After I'd committed a second squadron of Hornets to the battle, the Vietnamese had finally broken off and fled for home. They had an airstrip deep in the jungle, one that had been carefully camouflaged before except for heat sources and that was not the subject of constant intelligence updates. CVIC—Carrier Intelligence Center—was already working the problem real-time. Lab Rat had called me three times so far to let me know that Strike was getting the full picture on it.

I think of all of us, if it were possible, Lab Rat felt the worst. It was his intelligence the crews depended on—and he hadn't known about the SAM sites. A simple equation from an Intelligence Officer's point of view. Bad intel equals lost aircraft. I wondered how bad it would eat at him.

The Air Boss turned to me and said, "Admiral, the first two helos are coming back in for fuel. No sign so far, other than those oil slicks."

Unspoken was the bigger question—how much longer did I want to keep it up? We knew where the aircraft had been, had already covered the area pretty thoroughly. But there was a chance, a small one, that somebody hadn't been looking in the right direction, or that a current had carried the crews further out of the area. I'd already dispatched two destroyers as well to ride at the twelve-mile limit, and put them patrolling the outer limits of the area.

"Another full cycle," I said to the Air Boss. "We've got to do it."

He nodded, clearly with something on his mind. "May I be blunt?"

"That's what I pay you for."

The Air Boss took a deep breath, then spoke quietly. "Admiral, we're going to need most of our SAR assets and support during and after the strike. My only concern here is making sure we have that."

It was a real concern, but one that I didn't think the aircrews would go along with. As long as there was a chance, no matter how slim, that there was a pilot or RIO out there in the water, they would insist on going back out. I had more crews than aircraft, and could rotate them through helos and S-3s at will, but eventually even aircraft start breaking down.

"Another full cycle, then we'll see." I could see that the Air Boss was glad it was my decision and not his.

I waited until everyone had come in to recover, fuel, and head back out. Then I went back to my cabin to wait.

There was a pilot waiting for me there, standing just outside my cabin. I stopped when I saw him, then shrugged. Why should I be surprised? After all, Skeeter Harmon had been flying wingman on Bird Dog long enough to pick up most of his bad habits in the air—why not on the ground too?

"What do you want?" I asked. I had a pretty good idea, but I wanted to hear it from him.

"Admiral, I need to go on that strike," Skeeter Harmon began.

Just what I thought.

"You'll go if they put you on the flight plan," I said, aware of a rough edge to my voice I hadn't really intended. "And why the hell are you pop-tall in front of my patch?"

Skeeter shook his head, not listening to anything I said.

"Strike won't let me go—they're putting me in the second wave. Admiral, I have to—"

"I had this conversation with your lead not so long ago," I said. "And look what happened to him. I know you're furious about this, Skeeter, everyone of us is. But damn it, I'm not intervening in the daily planning anymore." I tapped lightly on my collarbone at the stars there. "That's not my job. And for you to come in here and start insisting on—"

"Admiral, it was my fault," Skeeter said, his voice low and crumpled-sounding. "I made the same mistake Bird Dog did with the E-2—hell, I saw him make that one, I knew it was wrong, but I didn't say anything. He's kind of a tough guy to argue with sometimes, you know." He looked up at me, and I could see that those hard, shiny eyes were glazed.

"We all make mistakes in the air," I said. "You make them at the wrong time, and it kills you. End of lesson—now get out of here."

"Admiral, he's alive. I'm certain of it."

I had started to walk away, but that phrase stopped me dead in my tracks. Without turning back to him, I asked, "How can you be so sure? The helos haven't found a thing."

"I know he is, I just know it," Skeeter said, his voice insistent. "Admiral, there were chutes—I'm certain of it."

"Did you debrief chutes?"

Skeeter shook his head. "No, it was only when I got to thinking about it—it happened so fast, Admiral. God, you wouldn't believe—"

"Of course I would believe," I said, turning back around to face him. "And just who the hell do you think I am? Some ship driver? Jesus, mister, I've got more time in the chow line on an aircraft carrier than you've got in the cockpit.

And you barge in here and presume to lecture me on how my pilots need to be treated?

"You want sympathy for how you're being treated, young man, you go see the chaplain. Not the admiral. You got that?"

I saw him stiffen, drawing himself up into a rigid posture of attention. "Yes, sir, Admiral, I surely do." A soft Southern drawl had crept into his voice. "I apologize for disturbing you—I just thought that—"

"You didn't think," I said, cutting him off. "And if you don't think while you're on the deck, then how do I know you're going to think while you're in the air? Have you ever thought of that? Good judgment is good judgment—it's not something that overcomes you the second you drop your ass into one of those babies. Now get out of here."

I watched him turn and head down the passageway, wondering just what the hell his point had been. Did he want me to make sure that he was personally on the flight schedule? Hell, there are too many pilots on the carrier for me to even know all their names, much less watch how they're assigned on missions.

And why had I been so rough on him? The man's lead had just been shot down, and by most standards any wingman would feel it was his fault. No matter that I'd heard Bird Dog order him back into the stack, tell him to keep his distance while Bird Dog was searching for the tanker crew. That didn't matter to Skeeter Harmon—anymore than it would have mattered to me had it been Tombstone who'd been in the drink.

Then why was I an asshole about it? With a flash of insight, I knew. I'd known Bird Dog for several cruises now, watched him grow from a brash young aviator with more mouth and balls than ninety percent of them, seen him pull off some incredible stunts of airmanship. Every single loss we take hurts, hurts more than I ever thought possible, but it's even worse when it's someone you know that well. As well as I knew Bird Dog. As well as Skeeter knew him.

And that was the unpardonable sin that Skeeter had just committed in my presence. He'd reminded me that at least one of the men in the water—too junior to really call him this, but this was what he was—was my friend.

I went back into my office, got on the horn, and made my second call of the day intruding into Strike Operations.

If Skeeter needed vengeance to be whole, then that's what he'd get.

Or at least the chance for it.

CAG beat his deadline by five minutes. I don't know how he accomplished it—and I guess I don't really want to know. The shortcuts alone would have terrified me.

The deck was packed, as full as I'd ever seen it. Every aircraft that could fly was manned, with engines turning or crews doing preflight. The SAR helos were already turning on their spots, blasting the deck with incredible downdrafts from the rotors. They would go first, in order to be on station in case an emergency occurred during catapult operations.

After that, the E-2C Hawkeye would launch, accompanied by a pair of fighters. Once he was airborne, my radar coverage extended to well over the land mass. More importantly, he could provide direct control of all the fighters on station, vectoring them off to intercept inbound bogies or vampires as necessary. Maybe the AWACS radar coverage is better over land, but there's nothing that can beat an E-2 controlling an air battle.

After that would come our main strike assets. Tomcats

loaded with five-hundred- and one-thousand-pound bombs, along with a couple of Sidewinders tucked in for good luck on their wing tips. Then the Hornets, those thirsty little bastards, would want to get airborne, then immediately take on fuel. Their carrying capability was more limited. Each one carried two one-thousand-pound bombs, but Strike had designated most of them for air-to-air combat roles. Given their performance characteristics against the MiG-29, that was the best choice for what I hoped would be a quick strike, burn to the ground, and back out again.

I'd asked the Air Force for tanker assets, and they were scrambling to get a couple of KC-135s and KC-10s in the area, but I didn't think they'd make it in time. The Air Force has been always oddly reluctant to commit tanker assets to a battle on short notice, preferring instead at least a couple of days of planning, polite requests, and other butt-kissing to get them on station. While the massive KC-10 could outrefuel anything I had on board, it had a couple of disadvantages as well. First, it carried a minimal crew—no navigator, just pilots and a boom operator. Their entire flight program was loaded into the computer, supported by redundant backup SINS systems. The Air Force always swore to me that there was no chance—none—of all their independent backup systems going down at once.

Don't count on it.

Under grueling conditions, things go wrong. Additionally, call me old-fashioned, but I at least like to have one person on board every aircraft who has a clue as to where they are. Computers are great, and they've certainly revolutionized warfare, but there's no substitute for a guy with a compass, a piece of string, and a damn good set of charts. Unfortunately, practical real-world experience has proven this point over and over.

A KC-135 might be a smaller aircraft, with less refueling capability, but it would still be a massive advantage over our own organic tanker assets. But they were still a day away, staging out of Japan, and Japan was none too happy about it. Massive diplomatic battles were being fought over whether or not Japan would grant us landing rights, overflight rights, or anything else having to do with the suddenly sprouting war against their neighbors.

In theory, the tankers could support our squadron from Hawaii, or even some other Asian nation. In practice, however, the long flight time, crew fatigue, and the ever-changing tactical picture would often render it difficult for a KC-135 to be present in-theater. Besides that, if they did get in trouble, they had to have somewhere to bingo. It wasn't like I could take him on my deck, not even with the barricade nets strung across the flight deck.

There were more people on deck than aircraft. Yellow-shirted handlers directed the flow of traffic. The brown shirts were plane captains, each either standing next to their aircraft and preflighting with the aircrew or carefully watching the fuselage for signs of problems as engines spooled up. Most of the purple shirts—aviation fuel technicians—and red shirts—weapons—were already well clear, having worked at a breakneck pace during the last one hour and fifty-five minutes to arm and feed the hungry beasts already growling on the deck.

Six decks directly below me, in the Handler's Office, there was one lieutenant commander who was responsible for all the movement of aircraft across the deck. He had a scale mock-up of the ship, along with accompanying wooden overhead silhouettes of each aircraft. I had no idea how he'd managed to get so many aircraft packed so tightly on the deck. I'd never seen that full complement readying for launch, but somehow he had.

Finally, the last helo bobbled unsteadily into the air and veered away from the ship. Seconds later, the Air Boss called a green deck for fixed-wing aircraft. Just as he'd finished giving the order, the first set of fighters were shot off the forward and waist cats simultaneously.

From the tower, I could see the waist-cat aircraft launch, sagging a bit as it lifted off, but still always in view.

Once all the aircraft were off the deck, there was no point in remaining in Pri-Fly. It stayed fully manned, of course, as it did whenever we had aircraft up. The vagaries of combat are too unpredictable—hell, of carrier aviation in general. If an aircraft suffered a serious equipment failure or mechanical problem of some sort, they needed a green deck—now. There wasn't time for them to wait around while we manned up.

But you couldn't fight a war from Pri-Fly. The aircraft I just had launched were now black smudges on the horizon, then not even that. I needed real-time information, the big picture, and I wouldn't get it here. And not just over radio circuits.

Six decks back down, then forward to CVIC. The sailor at the security door buzzed me in as soon as he saw me. I stooped long enough at the large coffeepot just inside the hatch to grab a quick mug, then ambled on back to SCIF.

"You've got connectivity?" I asked Lab Rat as I slumped into the chair next to his.

He pointed up at the monitors, a slight smile on his face. "As good as we've ever had it, Admiral. The next best thing to being there."

Some of the technological advances in war-fighting are almost out of Star Trek. This was one of them.

For years, we've had the ability to mount a photo-reconnaissance pod underneath an aircraft and use it to obtain real-time BDA—Battle Damage Assessment. The big drawback was always that we couldn't put weapons on the TARPS bird, and we had to wait for it to come back to the carrier, download the film, and then have it developed. It was still light-years better than anything else we had. We've never been able to rely solely on pilot reports of their own performance on bombing runs.

Not that they lie. It's just that they tend to be a little overly optimistic about the damage they've inflicted during a bombing run.

TARPS gave us the capability to conduct real BDA, albeit after the fact. Still, it was invaluable in deciding whether or not we needed to go back and bomb a target again or whether we'd taken it out the first time.

J-TARPS took the whole thing one step further. The J stood for joint, which meant that the system was capable of being deployed on aircraft in all the services, not just the Navy. Another part of the modern trend, developing technology that's not uniquely service-bred, that can be exported and used by your sister services.

There was one other thing about J-TARPS—it was real-time. In addition to the photographic capabilities of the pod mounted on the beast's underbelly, there was one little section that contained a high-data-rate transmitter. Now, instead of waiting for the film, we saw what the pod saw—real-time as it happened. The pilot could switch between a regular video display, a low-light one, and infrared. While the pilot couldn't monitor the data in the cockpit, he could respond to requests from the carrier to change displays. I had no doubt that in the next generation of J-TARPS technology, that limitation would be overcome as well.

SCIF—Specially Compartmented Information—was the most highly classified space on the ship. Into it was fed the most esoteric and high-tech data we had, in addition to the normal slew of incredibly sensitive message traffic. Reports from informants, human sources on the ground, and stuff so highly classified that they'll barely tell *me* where it comes from. But it's like any intel—it can be wrong or incomplete at times. That's why we'll never take the man out of the loop. Somebody's got to decide what's nonsense and what's ground truth.

This room had been configured as a new experiment, one that would allow me to monitor and direct the battle from here. It sounded like a good idea, but there was a danger too, the tendency to micromanage. It had already gotten us in trouble when the same technology allowed the pundits in D.C. direct control of an arsenal ship's weapons, and I was determined not to make the same mistakes they'd made. The same mistakes that had been made in Vietnam the first time—micromanagement of targeting choices by politicians.

"Who's who?" I asked.

Lab Rat pointed to the monitor on the far left of the room. "That's the lead—from there, I have 'em up in order of egress."

"All Tomcats?"

Lab Rat nodded. "Strike wanted all the hard points on the Hornets devoted to weapons. I don't think it'll make a difference."

I grunted, not sure I liked that. Since when did Hornets have priority over Tomcats in an air battle.

Since MiGs turned out to be the target, one part of my

mind suggested. Don't go getting parochial about this—you know they're right.

"The satellite imagery is over on that wall," Lab Rat continued, pointing off to the right. A large-screen display dominated that wall, an overhead view of the area from a geosynchronous satellite. It was currently in photo mode, but it also could toggle into infrared if needed.

On the far-left screen, from the TARPS camera on the lead Strike aircraft, the coast of Vietnam was materializing out of the haze. Dark, jagged along the coast, a few dreary brown areas of civilization carved out of the lush terrain. It was like being there, like flying over it myself, except that my view was not obstructed by my own aircraft. A stunning picture, one only occasionally shot through with static.

The screens to the right of it, the two others, still displayed just ocean. Just at the edge of the horizon, I could see the coastline starting to come into view.

"Wow." It was all I could manage.

Lab Rat looked smug. "We're pretty pleased with it," he said offhandedly, as though he alone were responsible for the entire project. I let him enjoy his triumph, as a partial mitigation of the terrible embarrassment he felt over the SAM sites.

The lead was feet dry now, the radio call coming over one speaker as the camera showed the aircraft transitioning to over land. The other cameras were now showing the coastline, only minutes away from going feet dry themselves.

The primary target was the covert airfield that satellites had just revealed hidden deep in the jungle. It was the same one from which the last, aborted strike had deployed, and from what we could tell, most of the aircraft had returned to that airfield after withdrawing from the air battle. My intention was to strike a quick, retaliatory blow aimed primarily at the airfield and its aircraft that had attacked us. No civilian population centers, no other targets, other than a secondary airfield we'd just discovered north of that.

The strike was divided into two missions, one heading for the main field, the other briefed to pull north to the secondary airfield. Depending on the results I saw via J-TARPS, I would be able to vector the second flight in to restrike the primary airfield or allow them to continue on to their northern airfield mission.

The trees loomed closer now, and I could make out individual trees and foliage. The aircraft were down on the deck, coming in low and fast. Precision bombing at its best, with the results highly dependent on individual pilot skills. But the airfield was a good target, one that would be easy to pick out. And it was big enough that we should be able to neutralize most of its capabilities even if we didn't nail every square inch of it. Of course, it was the aircraft I was really concerned about. Airfields can be fixed quickly, with the combination of quick-set concrete and temporary steel airfield mats. But aircraft—and the people that flew them—weren't quite as expendable.

The airfield was coming into view now, a dull, silvery stripe against the green of the jungle. There were maybe ten aircraft parked along it, wings folded, ancillary equipment swarming around. One main building spouted flames and smoke, an indication that the EA-6B Prowler HARM missiles had found at least one antenna radiating. Good— maybe we'd caught them by surprise. One of the first things any enemy does when an inbound strike is detected is shut down all electromagnetic radiation to avoid the HARM missiles.

If they'd had any doubts about it before, they now knew

we were coming. The detail was amazing—I could pick out technicians running across the airfield, yellow gear called huffers that provided compressed air for quick engine starts next to some of the aircraft, and even one pilot slamming down a canopy. Faces were turned up to look toward me.

The picture shuddered violently. The radio circuit revealed why—the lead Tomcat had just lofted his five-hundred-pound dumb bombs at the airfield, and pulled into a hard turn to clear the area. The clearance maneuver was designed to not only get him away from the explosions that would soon occur, but also to clear the path for the incoming flights.

The J-TARPS camera was stabilized to remain locked on the designated point as long as possible, but the pilot quickly outstripped its capabilities. He pulled back, and the picture of the airfield was replaced with the immenseness of the jungle again.

I switched my gaze to the second camera. He was just coming up on the airfield, and concrete and smoke splattered up from the runway where the lead's bombs had hit. There were more people now running, scampering toward the illusory safety of the main building as the strike force pressed on in.

Smoke was obscuring the picture, and would complicate the targeting picture. As it wafted across the screen, blocking out part of my picture, I realized that something was bothering me. I turned to Lab Rat. "Where are the rest of the aircraft?"

He frowned, a worried look on his face. "We counted twelve on the deck. There were more than that in the air last time—definitely more."

"Revetments?" I suggested.

He sat still for a moment, his face expressionless. "May-be," he admitted finally. "But we saw no indication of it on the satellite pictures. Usually there are mounds, some sort of clearly definable entrance to them. But not here."

"Then where are they?"

He shook his head. "I don't know. But at least we'll get the ones that are out there now. Twelve aircraft have got to be a significant blow to their capabilities."

I didn't want to decimate the Vietnamese air-combat capabilities, not just hurt them a little, force them to slow down. I wanted complete and utter destruction, smoking black holes in the ground where aircraft, fuel dumps, and spare parts inventory had been. Scorched earth as vengeance for my people—nothing else would suffice.

But if the aircraft were in revetments, we had a problem. Concrete reinforced structures buried under the earth were a tough target. It took a lot of firepower to damage them, much less destroy them. Weaponeering can do it if you know that's the problem, using some special high-penetration bombs designed to take on hardened targets, but that wasn't what our weapons load carried. Big old plain fat dumb bombs, that was it.

Now the second aircraft was dropping its bombs, and I studied the picture being transmitted back carefully, search-ing for some indication of where the aircraft might be. Jungle, just jungle surrounded the entire airfield. It was unusually flat for that part of the country, probably the reason they'd built the base there. "Switch to infrared on number three," I said.

Lab Rat relayed my order to the Tactical Action Officer in the Combat Direction Center, who had his Operations Specialist pass it on to the pilot. The picture flickered, then dissolved into the black-and-white display of the infrared.

"See anything?" I asked Lab Rat. He motioned to the Intelligence Specialist standing slightly behind him, an expert in photographic imagery. The man stepped up beside the monitor.

"These heat sources appear to be from the bombs, Admiral," he said, pointing out two or three bright white flares on the screen. "Smoke may cool the picture off a little bit, but it can't disguise the main heat source. These appear to be pretty much in the area where the aircraft were parked."

"What else?" I asked.

He studied the picture for a moment, then continued. "Here's the main building—see, those heat sources come from the gear in there as much as the people. And a couple smaller spots—probably yellow gear. Maybe some secondary fires."

"So what would the revetments look like?" I asked.

"Tough to say, Admiral. There are ways to design the exhaust systems to conceal a heat signature—just like we do with our Stealth birds, cooling the exhaust down so it's not distinguishable from the ambient atmosphere. However," he continued, seeing my doubtful look, "I doubt that the Vietnamese are that sophisticated. If they're not obviously visible from the photo display, then they're camouflaged in some way, although we can make some logical assumptions about their location. First, they need to be near the airfield—or if not, there's gotta be a well-marked path from the revetments to the airfield."

"Could they be built into the side of the mountains?"

He shook his head. "I doubt it. I've read some science-fiction books about aircraft landing in concealed mountain caverns, but that's not a strong probability. No, if they're there, I'm betting that they're near this airfield." He pointed in an area ringing the airfield, now splotched with bright heat sources indicating fires.

"Maybe—what about there?" I said, pointing at a small spike of peaks off to one side.

"I was just looking at that." He squinted, stepped back a few feet to get a bigger overall picture, then nodded. "If the revetments are in the area at all, that would be my bet." He shot a sly, sideways glance at me. "If you ever get tired of being an admiral, I could use a good photo interpreter."

I laughed, more at the shocked, outraged expression on Lab Rat's face than anything else. I like an enlisted man that has enough balls to treat an admiral like a human being. "I'll consider it," I said. "After this raid is over."

The technician nodded, a pleased expression on his face. Then he slipped back into a professional mode. "Commander," he said, addressing Lab Rat, "your opinion, sir?"

Lab Rat nodded. "If there are revetments around, that's where they are, I would think. As you said, it fits all the criteria."

"Then let's get some ordnance on top of it. We may not be able to break through the top of the revetments and get at the aircraft inside, but we ought to be able to muddy up the entrance enough to make it difficult for them to dig out."

"The secondary strike, or divert some aircraft from the main one?" Lab Rat asked.

"The secondary strike—hell, both. If we can put those aircraft out of commission, then we've accomplished our mission."

Again, Lab Rat relayed my orders to the Tactical Action Officer. I heard the pilots acknowledge the change of mission over tactical, and sat back to watch the show.

The satellite picture was now almost totally obscured by smoke. The one small area we had been bombing was only about one twentieth of the large-screen display, and I was struck by how vast and vital the country was around it. This was such a small area, but if the mission went well, one with major tactical implications for the Vietnamese. It was, I hoped, truly a surgical strike.

The third J-TARPS camera was now over the scene, and the photo image showed billowing clouds of black smoke. Down at the bottom of the screen, one small ball of fire seemed to take on a mind of its own. It was moving, traveling slowly from left to right on the screen. I stared at it for a moment puzzled, not understanding what I was seeing.

Lab Rat choked off an exclamation. He turned away from the cameras for a moment, then looked up at his Photo Tech, his face pale. "Screaming Alpha?" he asked.

The photo intel expert nodded. "That would be my guess."

I tried to ignore them, but my eyes were drawn back to that spot again and again. It had stopped moving now, settling down to look like any other fire spot on the ground.

A Class Alpha fire was one composed of combustible materials such as paper and wood. A Class B fire was fuel oil of some sort, Class C electrical, and Class D burning metal such as an aircraft on fire.

In the profane jargon of Damage Control, a Screaming Alpha was brutal shorthand for a human being on fire.

One of the advantages of fighting from the air instead of on the ground is distance from targets. Sure, you know that your bombs are hitting people, but you try not to think about it. It's like taking out an enemy aircraft—the target is the aircraft, and the crew are merely incidental matters. You feel you've killed an it—not a him or them.

But this was something that ground troops faced all the

time, both the Army and the Marines. They looked into the eyes of human death far more frequently than we did, shielded as we were by our aircraft and altitude. I thought, after seeing the picture, that perhaps it was a good idea that the J-TARPS pods had no display inside the cockpit. I wanted pilots focused on missions and threats, not on the hard facts of the destruction they were wreaking on the ground.

"Second flight leader acknowledges the new mission," Lab Rat said. "They should be on station in two minutes—a little less now."

Now that I knew what I was looking at, I could see other small spots of fire moving erratically around the burning airfield. The more I stared, the easier it became to pick them out. The people were the ones that moved in short spurts of speed, then fell burning on the melting tarmac. My imagination started suggesting that I could see the figures inside the flames, and I shoved the thought away. Not now, no more than I would think about the men and women I'd lost in my fighters. Not now.

Suddenly, everything seemed to be moving on the ground. I turned to Lab Rat for an explanation.

"That heat generates strong local wind currents," he explained. "You heat the air, it rises, and cold air rushes in. That's how you get the mushroom effect from any bombing, and that's what you're seeing on the ground now."

The third camera showed the flight leader was almost over his target. Again the shudder as the bombs were dropped, making the aircraft suddenly lighter and more maneuverable. I knew that feeling, of dropping heavy weapons off your airframe. There's an immediate increase in your airworthiness, and your speed and maneuverability.

You feel lighter, like you've just lost fifty pounds after sitting in a sauna.

The camera jiggled, and steadied back down. The bombs dropped, almost invisible, lofted toward the revetments on a parabolic arc.

Explosions, heat, and light—the picture was a blur.

"Commander, there's something—" The Intelligence Specialist broke off and stepped over to stand directly in front of the monitor. As the aircraft veered away, the area where the enemy aircraft had been lined up on the airfield came into view. "It's not hot enough," he said. "Not for a Class D fire. It should be burning brighter than anything else on the screen, absolutely unstoppable. It should be—no, it can't be."

"What?" Lab Rat and I demanded simultaneously. "What is it?"

"I saw something similar once," he said slowly. "It was a test-range film. They were touting the accuracy of a new guidance system, and a couple of Tomcats were making precision bombing runs on a mock enemy airfield. That picture looked just like this one."

"So what's wrong with that?" I asked, shifting my gaze back and forth between the burning area over the revetments and the technician. "That's what we wanted, right?"

He shook his head, a deep look of concern on his face. "No, I don't think so. Because in the training tape I saw, the Tomcats were dropping ordnance on wooden mock-ups of enemy aircraft. The point wasn't to test the destructiveness of the weapons, you see, but to demonstrate the effectiveness of the targeting. You don't need to burn up real aircraft for that."

I stared at him aghast. "You said it's not hot enough— you think we're burning up wooden targets?"

"Shit." The disgust in Lab Rat's voice convinced me that he was in agreement with his technician. "Shit shit shit."

I turned back to the display and stared at it again. "The heat sources are the same intensity as the burning jungle and buildings."

"That's what I mean, Admiral." The technician's voice was grim. "If there're aircraft around that airfield, they weren't lined up along the side. We've been suckered."

"Can you play this tape back?" I asked Lab Rat.

He nodded. "Now, or after the mission?"

I considered it for a moment, then said, "After the mission. I want to watch this one play out first. Then I want every set of eyes you've got on the tape from the flight leader. Get a good look at those aircraft, see if we've been suckered. Do an analysis of the revetments again as well. One way or the other, Lab Rat, I need to know where those aircraft are."

"There's one thing that wasn't cardboard," the technician said. "Those people on the ground. That I'm sure of."

I repressed a shudder. I didn't want to know during which part of his training he'd studied classified imagery of human beings running while they burned to death.

"The fire's spreading, Admiral," Lab Rat said. He directed my attention back to the satellite overhead imagery. "The wind's picking it up and carrying it along—see, there are spot jungle fires cropping up all over."

"Any nearby villages?" I asked.

"I don't know—I don't think so. The people are so thinly scattered in some parts of the jungle, it's hard to tell. Maybe."

I needed to know, to see whether or not the fires that were spreading would inflict significant collateral damage. I told myself it was in order to make a complete report to my superiors, but in reality it was more than that. Command can be a terrible thing sometimes, but it demands that one understand the consequences of every order and decision. I'd made the decision to conduct this raid, even without Air Force support. It was up to me to face the consequences.

"Vector the flight leader—the first camera—down toward those jungle areas," I said.

"Might be a problem with SAMs," Lab Rat warned.

"Then get the EA-6 back up there to cover him."

Lab Rat nodded. He spoke to the TAO for the third time, directing the lead Tomcat to fly a low, high-magnification sweep of the direction in which the fire was burning. I switched my attention back to the first camera and waited.

Sure enough, the picture changed almost immediately. "Back to photo," I said. Lab Rat nodded and complied.

We were back in the jungle again, skimming over treetops so close it seemed I could touch them. Lab Rat had set the J-TARPS pod to maximum magnification, and I knew the pilot was well clear of the treetops.

"Mark on top," I said, as a small cluster of structures zipped by me on the monitor. "I want another look at that. Maximum magnification."

Lab Rat slaved the J-TARPS to that geographic spot and asked the pilot to orbit overhead. He did so, and the picture was remarkably stable.

It was a small cluster of huts, along with one main building built out of wood. Smoke from the fires was drifting into it, and I could see people running and probably screaming, their mouths moving and wild expressions on their faces. Where they were going, I had no idea. The fire was moving up on them rapidly, and I could see no place nearby that they'd be safe.

"Who is that?" Lab Rat said suddenly. He jumped up and

pointed at one figure on the screen. "She's not Vietnamese."

"Get in closer," I said. "Now—Jesus, now."

The picture flickered, then zoomed in hard on the figure that had caught Lab Rat's attention. It was a woman, a tall white woman, clearly distinguishable from the families of Vietnamese flooding past her. Unlike her counterparts, she was facing toward the fire, pointing and talking to a large man in her company.

There was something about her posture, about the way she moved, that reminded me—oh, dear God.

"It's Pamela Drake," I breathed, scarcely daring to believe it myself. "God damn, Pamela Drake, the ACN reporter. And that man must be part of her video crew."

"What's she doing in a small Vietnamese village?" Lab Rat said, his voice beyond surprise and into sheer shock. "She's gotta get out—Admiral, the fire's moving that way and she's not making any effort to get to safety."

"She wouldn't," I said grimly. "Pamela Drake is as bad as any fighter pilot. She's invulnerable, don't you know? Just like all of the rest of them."

And indeed, that had been the case in most conflicts that Ms. Drake had covered. She'd been a continual pain in the ass to both Tombstone and me, but her sheer, raw courage and tenacity had always evoked a grudging admiration from both of us, even when she interfered with military operations.

"Finally—she's leaving," Lab Rat said. Pamela had turned away from the fire and was following the path of the Vietnamese. A few had remained behind, dragging at her arms and urging her to leave the area. "But where are they headed?"

"See if the pilot can follow them," I said.

Lab Rat spoke in the radio, relaying my request. The pilot's voice was doubtful.

"They're disappearing into the trees, Home Plate. I may fly low, but I can't get that low. I can't see them under the canopy, and there's no indication of a road."

"Is there anything around? Anything that can provide them shelter?" I demanded. "Water? Some stretch that's bare of vegetation?"

"Nothing I can see. Hey, Home Plate, glad to oblige you guys"—the pilot clearly had no idea of who he was talking to—"but I gotta get the hell outta here. My visibility's getting obscured and this rising hot air is playing havoc with my low levels. So, if it's just the same with you guys, I'm outta here."

"Tell him to go ahead," I said to Lab Rat.

The picture stayed locked on the burning village as long as the J-TARPS pod was capable of doing so, but eventually it wavered and then slaved back to the forward view from the aircraft. I had Lab Rat freeze the last frame of the village on the screen.

The flames had crept to the edge of the clearing, and were now nibbling at the small building inside it. There were no people anymore—they'd all fled. One pig wandered around the compound, confused and lost.

Where had they gone? The villagers had looked as if they'd known where they were going, but what refuge did they have from the flames there? What was it I didn't know about these mountains, these hills?

Another worry intruded. Where was Tombstone? I knew he was on the ground in Vietnam, but the circumstances and conditions of his mission meant that he was completely out of touch with us. Was he anywhere near the burning airfield, the fire spreading out in giant plumes around it?

I could only hope and pray not. Collateral damage to this small village that I'd watched was bad enough, but the possibility that I'd just torched my old lead was almost more than I could bear. The devastation that nuclear weapons would wreak on this beleaguered country was just beyond imagining.

One thing I knew for certain. If Pamela Drake was around, Tombstone couldn't be far.

SEVEN
Admiral
"Tombstone" Magruder

28 September
Northern Vietnam

After two days in camp, I'd uncovered far more than I'd ever thought possible about the lives of the men who'd lived and died there. At first, the cryptic markings meant little, other than the comment from my own father to "go west." Even that was open to interpretation—how far west? Russia, as I'd originally thought? Or another camp to the west somewhere in this part of the world, perhaps Laos or Cambodia?

The other messages I found scratched into wood and etched in concrete were less meaningful. Some were clearly parts of prayers, left to encourage either the writer or others that followed. Others bespoke immense pain, anguish beyond anything I could imagine. There were simple ones: "I am dying." The longer I stared at that particular one, the more I began to see images of the man who must have written it.

I'm not some New Ager that believes in ghosts and channeling spirits from the other world, but I've had some experience with the inexplicable. The scratchy feeling I always get along my spine right before I hear an enemy fire-control radar. The impulse to wake up and tour my squadron in the middle of the night, back when I was in command, only to find something that had gone wrong and needed my attention—or just a sailor who needed to talk. Call it ESP, call it command instinct, or just call it survival skills. Whatever it was, I knew about it. This was something different, and I chalked most of it up to my imagination. The longer I stared at those words, the more a face began visualizing in my mind. Gaunt, terribly drawn. Stubble clipped short along the jaw. A massive bruise along the right cheekbone, spreading over to encompass a black eye shot with purple and yellow around the eye.

I imagined him to be a man slightly shorter than myself, the same sort of build when well fed, but emaciated now from lack of food. He would be a brave man, although I doubt he would have believed that himself. The face I imagined bore scars from repeated beatings, the body bruised and welted in an ominous, indiscernible pattern. One arm looked as though it had been broken and reset badly, with a limited range of motion.

This man—I had no name, merely this vision I created in my mind—was a survivor. I imagined him bearing up under pain beyond anything I'd ever experienced, yielding only when it drove him completely out of his mind into sheer survival desperation. Then the words would come halting, slow, revealing as little as possible as he tried to lie. They would have known that, when he started lying, and the beatings would have gotten worse.

Still, he would have never broken completely. He would have been one of those men of incredible depth who are able to face their own limits, go past them, and rebound into some form of resistance. He would have brought strength to the others imprisoned there by his sheer determination and example. Had he been very senior? I considered the matter, then decided not. No, there have been others who'd taken command in the close-knit POW community, others who'd borne the ultimate responsibility for the performance of the men held captive there. But this man, the one who'd scratched those simple words on the wall, would have been one of their mainstays, the example that they held out to the others.

Had he died here?

Probably. I'd read the reports of the POW camps that were examined thoroughly, and I'd never found one that matched this location. But his message seemed more one last calm attempt to convey information than the anguished howl of a man who knew he would not survive.

But why had he not signed his name? Why not add that one word, just a last name, that would have identified him to the rest of the world?

Perhaps he wrote those words not just for himself, but for those men around him who were made of lesser stuff. They were all dying, they had to be. Abandoned here by their own country, their existence not even suspected until I'd come here on this tour, they had died one by one.

Other images came to me as I studied the rest of the secret messages scribbled on the walls. "Tell Sally I love her." It was signed "Rieger," probably a last name. Or maybe a nickname, something that he left as a message only to his relatives.

I saw a few more messages that I came to believe were left by my father as well. One had my own name, Matt, scratched into it. "Be strong, Matt." Whether it was a prayer or an admonition intended for my eyes someday, I could not decide. Yet it was more evidence that my father had been here, that he'd thought of me, and that somehow perhaps the image of me as he'd last seen me, as a very small, barely talking child, had helped buoy him through the torture and deprivations.

After two days, I was finished. I had compiled an extensive photographic record of the messages I'd seen, as well as a detailed pictorial overview of the camp and its location. I'd made sketches, suggested possible meanings to some of the more cryptic notes based on their location, and generally done what I could to document the camp and its existence.

Than was healing rapidly, regaining strength every day. His constitution was such that while the injury still limited his range of motion, it seemed barely to affect him. I marveled at his recovery, not sure I would have done as well, particularly not in the stifling heat and humidity that plagued the camp.

On the third day, I roused out of an uneasy, sweating sleep to an ominous smell—smoke. I could see nothing, but the scent was unmistakable.

Around me, Than was organizing the rest of his crew, packing up gear and preparing us to move. I'd told him the previous day that I thought my work here was finished, and asked about camps further to the west.

The question appeared to surprise him, because he had examined the walls almost as carefully as I had, albeit with different reasons. "There is one location," he said finally. "We can go there if you wish." He shook his head, as though disapproving of the notion of another trek through the jungle. I had a feeling that there were reasons that he did not want to go that had nothing to do with his own physical condition.

Later, I would learn that Vietnamese aircraft had made an

unprovoked attack on fighters from the USS *Jefferson*. But I had no inkling that that was the case at the time, and Than had steadfastly refused to admit that one of his men carried a radio capable of reaching their base station.

Now, the question of moving west was less of an issue. Than came running up to me, clearly agitated. "We must move."

"Where is the fire?" I asked.

He pointed to the east. "Very big—some distance, but we must hurry." He regarded me levelly, as though trying to make sure I understood what he was saying. "It is very dangerous here, Mr. Tombstone. Very dangerous."

"From the fire?" I asked.

He shook his head, appeared to want to explain more, then settled for; "The fire. Yes. Come on—we must leave immediately."

I packed up my own gear, then passed it off to the man who insisted on carrying it. By now I'd become accustomed to, though not comfortable with, the idea that Than would allow me to carry none of my own equipment. What had at first seemed like an elaborate courtesy for a field operation, intended solely to placate the ego of a flag officer, now took on a more ominous meaning.

Without my gear, I had no way of surviving in the jungle away from Than and his crew. Additionally, carrying my pack would allow them plenty of opportunity to search it every night, to make sure that I was not carrying a radio myself or some other locating beacon. While no questions had been asked about one, I was certain that such a device would raise innumerable problems on this delicate mission of trust.

Within twenty minutes, we were ready to leave. Than took point, setting a smart pace through the jungle. I wondered for a moment about the snipers, but he assured me that they had been cleared from the woods during the two days that we had camped there.

The smell of smoke was stronger now, and growing more so with every breath. If it were to the east, then it was gaining on us. Could we outrun it? What had at first seemed a foregone conclusion was feeling entirely less obvious now.

We were at a brisk walk, almost a trot, following the path of a creek bed through a narrow canyon. We moved steadily for two hours, not stopping for anything. Water breaks were taken on the run, and I saw one of the guards stuff a field ration in his mouth as the pace quickened.

It was the noise that brought me to a crashing halt. One so out of place and foreign in this decade. And one I knew well.

A jet engine, something powerful and military, I suspected from the high-pitched whine. It was coming in from the east, low over the trees, directly toward us. At first it was indistinguishable from the background buzz of insects, but I soon recognized it for what it was.

Than heard it too. He glanced back at me, saw that I had stopped, and yelled, "Move—quickly now!"

We were running now, moving along the cleared area between the stream and the trees at breakneck speed. The first tendrils of smoke were now visible, and it was getting harder to breathe.

The aircraft continued inbound on us, and now I thought I could put a name to it. It wasn't American, that much I was certain, and in this area of the country that left only one choice—a MiG-29.

The noise built to an almost deafening intensity, crescendoing until I thought it would permanently deafen me. Then the canopy overhead rattled, treetops whipping like pennants. A dark, black shape screamed overhead, filling the world around me with the sound and the smell of hot jet exhaust.

It must have been like this during the Vietnam war. Jungle troops on patrol, hearing the high-pitched scream of the enemy aircraft inbound, fleeing for their lives before the devastation and destruction that rained down from the skies. It was an entirely frightening experience, being on the other end of an air attack.

The noise of the fighter faded far more quickly than it had started, passing overhead and then continuing straight on ahead of us. Then the ground under my feet rose up to smash me in the face, shuddering and shivering like a massive earthquake. The noise again, a thick, dull roar this time. Another explosion rattled the jungle, and I realized what had happened.

Not a bombing run—a crash. The fact that the aircraft had been skimming the treetops, the odd stutter in its engine, those had been the signs of a fatal injury. It had gone past us before auguring into the ground, but just barely.

Had the pilot gotten out? I had no way of knowing, but since it appeared to have impacted the ground directly ahead of us, there was a possibility that we might see him.

We were headed uphill now, breaking free of the smoke, for which we paid with aching calf and thigh muscles, as we negotiated the steep incline. Away from the creek bed, the trees were thicker now, the undergrowth almost impassable at times. Our progress slowed, but we appeared to be moving away from the path of the fire—and from the aircraft that would undoubtedly be burning ahead of us.

We neared the top of one ridge, and Than called for a halt. After four hours of moving at almost breakneck pace through the jungle, my legs could barely hold me up. Than himself seemed indefatigable.

"We wait here," he commanded, and gestured toward the barren, rocky outcropping along the mountain.

"Why?" I asked. There was no doubt that in matters effecting our survival in the jungle, Than was the expert. If we survived, it would be because his decisions were the right ones, not because anything had been left to me to decide.

He regarded me for a moment, then appeared to reach some decision. "There is shelter here. Come, I will show you."

We crossed the rocky clearing, rounded three large boulders, clinging to them as we negotiated a narrow path, then arrived next to a sheer cliff face.

I stopped and stared up at it, amazed. There was a series of steps leading up the mountain face, maybe fifteen in all, to a narrow ledge. Just behind that ledge there was a dark, black opening. A cave—one that was invisible from almost any angle except this one.

"If the fire comes closer, we will take cover there." Than gestured at the cave. "There are ways to survive fires. These I know."

A small, wintry smile, one that reminded me that he would have been a very young man during the days of the Vietnam war. Very young, but most probably a fighter. During the latter years, the Vietnamese drafted everyone including women, grandmothers, and children into the continuing fight against the strangers on their land. It was this action on their part that had led to some of the major atrocities of the last war. U.S. troops in the field began to distrust small children, knowing that the Vietnamese were not above strapping booby traps on the children's backs and sending them off to beg food from the all-too-generous American troops. More than one woman had been sent to decoy other men, playing on their great weakness and loneliness, and then slitting a man's throat at an intimate moment.

From this elevation, I could see the progress of the fire in the jungle below us. It was moving rapidly, and had already encompassed the area where I thought the camp was. I gave silent thanks that I'd made a complete visual record of it, knowing that the memories contained in it were now lost forever. Mine would be the last—and only—record of those messages echoing down through the decades.

I am dying.

The fire was following a general westerly course, leaping back and forth on either side of the creek bed we'd followed. It was approaching the position we would have been in had we not cut up the side of the mountain, and I could see now that there had been no chance of our outrunning it.

Additionally, it was creeping up the sides of the hill, more slowly than its forward progress, but still clearly moving. It was a long, narrow wedge that broadened gradually, eating up the countryside around it.

Than appeared to be unworried. He watched the fire with me, then said, "To the cave. We have preparations to make."

It isn't the heat of the flames that always kills men in fires. The dangers, even for those that are out of reach of the more obvious threats, are more subtle. Fire requires oxygen to burn, and a good forest fire will suck the oxygen away from areas near it. You can survive the heat and flames and still suffocate, and I was afraid that would be what would happen to us.

The men were moving now, filing into the cave with their packs.

I could hear the fire now, chomping the valley as it moved toward us like a giant beast devouring the terrain. It was punctuated by high-pitched squeals, as the heat flashed moisture inside large tree trunks into steam, splitting them open like roasted pigs. The wind was picking up now too, rushing in toward the fire, billowing up smoke in huge gouts into the sky.

We were all inside the cave now, and men were pulling large, folded packages out of their packs. Clear sheets of plastic, heavy lengths of canvas. I watched as they rigged them over the door, dousing the canvas first in water from their canteens, then covering it with plastic. The canvas faced outward, the plastic inside. They worked carefully but quickly by the light of flashlights, fastening the canvas and plastic securely to the edges of the entrance into the cave, driving metal spikes into the wood and then positioning clamps on those.

"It keeps the air inside," Than explained briefly. The force of the wind outside was already sucking the canvas up against the edges of the cave entrance, and it billowed away from us, creating what appeared to be an excellent air trap.

"Are there any other air vents in this cave?" I asked.

He glanced briefly at the ceiling, then shook his head, "I am not certain, but I think not. You see the smoke—it pools near the top, not rushing out." Now I knew why he had lit the candle shortly after the men had started erecting the barricade.

"Where did you learn this?" I asked.

He shot me a dark look, then said, "Experience. We know to come prepared."

"I wonder how the fire started," I said.

Another unreadable glance from Than, and then he turned away. Something in his response puzzled me. While he was often providing less than complete explanations for what we were doing, he normally had at least some response. Then it hit me.

The MiG. The fire. There was one thing I knew far too well that could ignite incendiary fires across a wide swath of country. While not the only cause, certainly, a ground-strike attack with heavy weapons could do just that.

We had seen it too often even during practice runs. Even practice SAR missions, where troops on the ground drop smoke flares and then wait for helos, could fan into brush fires, particularly under the heavy downdraft of a rescue helicopter. Another lesson we'd learned during Vietnam.

The MiG—the damaged MiG. And how had it been damaged? Through some mishap in a routine training mission?

From Than's response, I thought not. It had been in air combat, and that left just a few possible candidates. The Chinese to the north—or the *Jefferson* to the east. And if Than had a radio, he would have known what had happened. Known, and been prepared to move out and flee from the fire.

The fire was on us now, the noise all-consuming. It sounded like a tornado, or the sound of some odd jet engine spooling up. The canvas and plastic barricade was sucking hard against its clamps now, and the men were lining the entrance, adding their strength to hold it in place against the difference in pressure between the inside of the cave and the outside. The canvas itself was smoking, and I could see a thin layer of smoke trapped between the canvas and the plastic.

How long could it hold? Even wetted down with water from our canteens, the canvas would soon dry into a thin, combustible layer. The fire was on us now, dancing and howling just past the thin temporary air lock we'd jury-rigged out of what he had. Flames danced and skittered along the canvas, sheets of fire steaming off the last remnants of water. The canvas was beginning to smoke. Or burn. The noise was unholy, and the small cavern was filled with groans and creaks of rock heating and expanding. A new danger now—that the flames would crack the rock, opening air vents to the outside and quickly sucking out our oxygen.

The men were crouched around the lower edges of the canvas, which was stretched tight to immobilize its top, holding it with all their might against the rock walls. The clamps alone could not hold. The heat was unbearable, radiating in and raising the temperature inside to excruciating levels. I had thought the jungle hot, but it was nothing compared to the scorching, killing heat.

One of the men standing along the right side of the entrance let out a low, howling moan. He swayed, and I could see the canvas corner he was holding sag. There was a thin, whistling scream of air escaping. I jumped forward. Just as he collapsed, I seized the edge he'd been holding and slammed it hard against the rock. The whistling stopped. He went down with a dull, sickening thud into the rock floor. Than grabbed him by the collar with his one good hand and dragged him back away from the barrier.

I could feel it full force now, the heat, the unbearable heat. Fire swirled just inches from my fingers, kept at bay only by the canvas and plastic. I could feel the heat redden my fingers, scorching them now, and still I held on. It was not a matter of courage—there was simply no choice.

Just as suddenly as it was upon us, the main fire stormed past. It was consuming fuel at a prodigious rate, and the scant vegetation around the cavern gave out quickly. I could hear it as it passed, the Doppler lowering of the frequency of the noise, just like the change in sound an aircraft makes as it passes overhead, or a train whistling off into the distance. The heat abated noticeably, but was still well above my pain threshold.

The air was hot, almost too hot to breathe. I took shallow breaths, sucking it in between clenched teeth and trying to let what little moisture remained in my mouth cool it before it seared my lungs. We were all breathing like that, short quick pants, held uptight and in place only by fear and adrenaline.

But there was hope now, as there had not been before. The temperature continued to drop, and I felt the tug of the canvas in my hands decrease slightly. The wind continued, though, as the fire sucked in fresh air behind it. Still, we held on.

It might have been minutes, it might have been hours. I'd lost all sensation of the passage of time, my world defined simply by the urgent need to hold onto the fabric in my hands, the dead, throbbing pain in my hands. We waited, silent.

Than spoke. "It is safe now." Still, I held on, and it wasn't until one of the other men pried my hands from the rock wall that the reality sunk in.

We were alive.

My fingers refused to move at first, locked into position by fear and heat. The men were oddly gentle now, easing me back from the wall and gently prying my hands off the canvas. I sank back against the wall, slid down into a sitting position, and studied my hands. They were red, blistered, and crusted now, black in a couple of spots. There was no real pain—the nerve endings had been seared by the heat—but that would come soon enough. I looked across the small cavern at the other men, who were similarly injured.

"How is he?" I said to Than, gesturing at the man on the ground.

He shook his head, stared down at him, and prodded him gently with one foot. "The heat. I do not know—the heat kills more quickly than anything except perhaps the fire."

"Or suffocation," I reminded him.

"Yes, that too." Than knelt down beside the man, touching his forehead briefly. He looked up at me. "He needs water, something cool—we have none here."

Indeed we did not. We'd all emptied our canteens onto the canvas, expending every last drop dousing it. It hadn't seemed important at the time, not with the fire almost upon us. Besides, we knew that the lower regions of the mountain range were honeycombed with creeks and rivulets.

"I'll go get some," I offered. Another man, evidently understanding my suggestion, stood up and walked over to stand next to me.

Than shook his head again. "It is still too hot outside. The fire, it is past, but the ground is nothing but burnt wood and coals. It is still on fire."

I stepped out of the cavern and onto the rock ledge to look at what was left. The heat radiated up through my jungle boots, immediate and painful. Than was right—I couldn't even stand on the rock ledge, much less hike down to the stream through the charred embers that had once been such lush vegetation.

The land around me was a harsh, barren devastation. The trees were stripped of leaves and limbs, and the sky was now visible. In place of the brilliant greens and yellows, there was only black, and a little gray where ash had formed. The only color that remained was in the sky, brilliant and serene. Smoke wafted up from the charred landscape, thick and cloying.

I turned back to Than. "In a few hours perhaps."

"He does not have that much time." Than's voice was blunt and matter-of-fact. "If he survives, he survives." With this final assessment, he turned back to the man and made him as comfortable as he could. He extracted a first-aid kit from one pocket, the same one we had used to treat Than earlier, and a preloaded hypodermic. He found a clear patch of skin on the man's shoulder and plunged it home, depressing the cylinder to eject the full dose into the man. "Morphine," he said in response to my questioning glance.

I nodded. Absent water, morphine was the next best thing. If we could not save him, at least we could keep him comfortable during his final hours.

That night, we posted no guard, secure in the frail protection of our sheltered cave. I woke once at about two that morning, and wondered what had disturbed me. No nightmares that I could recall, and I was still so tired from surviving that day that it seemed impossible I had woken at all.

As sleep drifted back in, I pondered the possibilities. The fire had been moving west, the same direction as the second camp. The lifeline to my father that had seemed so strong in the earlier camp now seemed the thinnest of leads. Was that what the message had meant? And how far west? The possibility that I'd misunderstood his meaning, or even that Horace Greeley was the name of another man in the camp, ate at me.

I drifted back down into sleep without any answers. At the very edge of consciousness, I heard a sound that brought me bolt upright from my hard pallet on the rock floor.

Aircraft—a helicopter to be specific. And not one of ours, not from the sound of it.

I rolled out of my pallet and went to Than, to wake him and tell him of the helicopter. Even though he had no guard mounted, he would want to know.

I should have been expecting it, but the night held one more surprise for me. The spot where I'd seen Than curl up under a coarse cotton blanket was empty.

I walked to the edge of the cave, stared out into the night, and wondered.

EIGHT

Admiral "Batman" Wayne

28 September
USS Jefferson

I could tell by the look on his face that Lab Rat had bad news. When it's good, he's practically bouncing as he stands at my door and waits for permission to come in. When it's bad, his already small form seems twenty pounds lighter. He shrinks into the door frame, slinks into the room, and his voice is barely above a mumble.

This was one of those times.

"It's still operational," Lab Rat said flatly. "The latest imagery shows aircraft moving in and out of the hangar. And they're already repairing the airfield. We knew that wouldn't take long, but it's going even faster than we predicted."

"What about the SAM sites?" I asked. I was convinced I could eventually knock a hole in the top of those nasty little revetments, but I had to be able to get my aircraft in to do it.

"They're mobile. Not fixed sites."

More bad news. We'd maintained meticulous plots on the

electromagnetic transmissions from the antiair sites, and I was hoping to take them all out the next time.

"Can you tell where they're headed?" I asked.

Lab Rat shook his head. "They're moving under cover of the jungle canopy, Admiral. I get a few glimpses of them, some heat sources, but that's about it. We've looked at the terrain, the tactical disposition, and I've simply got no good predictions."

I leaned back in my chair and considered the matter. Intelligence was fine, but sometimes I needed ground troops. "Have you talked to the Marines? They might have some other ideas on where they'd put the SAMs if they were the bad guys."

Lab Rat nodded. "A few estimates, but they're not any more confident about it than we are."

I should have known he would have tried it. When it comes to intelligence estimates, Lab Rat is the least likely officer I know to invoke parochial interests. You've got something to say, something to make sense to him, then he'll listen. With ground weapons positions, of course he would have sought out the senior Marine on board and asked his opinion.

"So what do you suggest?" I asked finally. "We can send in another strike, but . . ."

Lab Rat sighed, then looked up at me. "It's time for Special Forces, sir. We could use them one of two ways. Send them in, send them after the SAM sites, or target the revetments." He grimaced, indicating that neither of those were particularly attractive alternatives. "Or we can just try what we've done before."

"And lose more aircraft probably," I said.

"Probably."

I stood up and started pacing the length of my office. It

helps me to be moving while I'm trying to think. It would help even better if I were in the cockpit of an aircraft, but that's a luxury not often allowed to me as a flag officer. I barely make it out on the flight deck once a week just to get a whiff of fresh JP-5.

"What do the SEALs say?" I asked. We have a platoon on board, with a lieutenant commander in charge of them. Brandon Sykes was one of the smarter SEAL officers I'd met in my time, and he'd proved his tactical savvy to my satisfaction before. If he had an idea, I wanted to hear it.

"Lieutenant Commander Sykes wants to go for the mobile SAMs, but he thinks the revetments are the better targets," Lab Rat replied immediately. "He says you can always use the HARMS against the SAMs, but that the revetment is the real problem."

"He's right, of course," I answered. "Did you ask him when he could be ready to go?"

Lab Rat smiled. "He knew you'd ask that—he told me so. And he said to tell you that they were ready to move out at your very earliest convenience."

"So what does that mean?"

Lab Rat thought for a moment, then said, "I think he'd like about twelve hours, Admiral, but I'm sure he could pull it off right now. If Brandon Sykes says he's ready, he's ready."

I nodded. "Twelve hours would put us into the night-time—he wants to go in with the RHIBs—the Rigid Hulled Inflatable Boats?"

"Or maybe helos—he hasn't decided yet," Lab Rat said.

We'd rendezvoused with the underway replenishment ammunition ship earlier, and I'd onloaded a ration of heavy-duty bombs designed to penetrate concrete bunkers. They'd worked well in Desert Storm and Desert Shield, and

I thought that probably they'd do the job against the Vietnamese revetments as well. Still, I didn't have all that many of them—it would make them a better target if I could have the SEALs soften them up a little beforehand.

"Tell Brandon to get ready," I decided. "I want to see him as soon as he's ready to talk."

They make bigger SEALs, they make stronger ones, but they don't make them any tougher than Brandon Sykes. He'd been pulling aviators' asses out of the fire his last twelve years in the Navy, along with conducting the other types of covert-insertion missions for which his community was justly famous. You look at him, you see a guy who looks like he's in pretty good shape. Not the bulging arms and forearms you get with Marines, but just a guy who works out a lot.

You'd be making a mistake. What's more, he's smart as he is tough. That makes Brandon Sykes a very deadly combination.

"Admiral, I'd like to go in by helo to the two-mile point, then drop and inflate RHIBs and proceed by boat. From what Commander Busby says about their surveillance assets in the area, I figure that gives us the best chance of getting in undetected." Brandon was soft-spoken and polite.

I started to ask some technical questions about the insertion, but looking at Lab Rat and Brandon, at the united front they were presenting, I knew there was not much point in it. We hire the best talent we can, then turn them loose. "You cleared this with CAG?" I asked.

Brandon nodded. "He's good to go with it, sir."

"When do you want to leave?" I asked.

Brandon looked thoughtful for a moment, then said, "With your permission, I'd like to get underway about zero one hundred. That'll put us on the beach by two, and in the area of the revetments by three. A little while to sneak and peek, do some damage, then we haul ass out of there. We'll be using timed explosives—a little bit risky, but I want to make sure we're clear of the area before they know they're fucked."

I nodded. "Let's make it happen, gentlemen. You go boom in the early hours, then I'll follow with an early morning air strike. How's that?"

Both men nodded. "Of course, we thought that might be what you wanted to do," Lab Rat added. "Strike's already signed off on it as well."

I grunted. "Not much point in having an admiral around, is there? Seems to me like between you two and Strike, you've got it all figured out."

Brandon stood, a slow and easy smile on his face. "Oh, there's plenty of reason to have an admiral around, sir. We can come up with the plans okay—but you're the only one who can say yes."

I threw the two of them out of my office so they could get some work done, then turned back to the unending pile of paper that continually seeped into my in basket.

J-TARPS wasn't the only innovation in virtual reality that had entered the fleet. Even though I'd seen them discussed in newspapers, and on television, I'd never actually worked with the new visual-link helmet that the SEAL community now owned. As Lab Rat switched on the monitors, I sat quiet and stunned.

Sykes had shown me the headset. It looked more like a hairnet built out of steel than anything else. Mounted along his left temple was a very tiny pinpoint camera. The usual whisper communications giving satellite voice comms with units in the field had been improved to allow for an open-mike capability. Now, Brandon could leave it turned on and transmit everything he heard straight to me. He also had a control switch to prevent me from transmitting, so that he could be certain that no questions from higher authority would echo while he was in the field and give him away. I didn't intend to put him in danger that way.

We'd agreed that Brandon would not activate his headset until after the helicopter drop and when they were safely en route to the beach. Lab Rat had been keeping track of the time, and woke me from a quick nap when they were under way.

At first, all I could see on the monitor was black. Vague shapes and forms, shifting shadows, but that was it.

Then Sykes turned his head. I could see the other SEALs in the boat, a little bit fuzzy, but their faces clearly discernible. They were communicating in hand signals, even this far out from the shore. A good habit to be in when you're making a quick foray into enemy territory.

The small boat engine was a muffled puttering sound in the background, hardly even audible over the link. The silenced engine also cooled the exhaust, another small innovation courtesy of Stealth technology, so the boat itself produced no discernible heat signature. The men inside it were another matter—even clad in wet suits, I knew they would soon be radiating visible signatures.

"Any sign they've been detected?" I asked Lab Rat.

He shook his head. "I just checked the TAO, and there's no indication of any unusual activity ashore. Not there, or on our other assets," he said, glancing back at the array of sophisticated electromagnetic listening equipment that terminated here. "Not a peep."

"Let's hope it stays that way." Watching the boat move in

to the shore quickly became boring, unless you kept in mind what they were actually doing. It was like watching OJ drive down the freeway at thirty miles an hour in a white Bronco—meaningless, unless you knew the context.

Brandon was looking forward now, and I could see the shore looming into view. It was a dark smudge against the blacker sky. It was slightly overcast tonight, with a new moon. That had been the deciding factor in the decision to go in at night, I suspected.

The boat ground onto the shore with a soft, sibilant sound. I caught glimpses of their activities as Brandon supervised the disembarking, and hiding the RHIBs in nearby cover. He left one man on guard, and the rest of them set out for the airfield.

"Is something wrong with the sound?" I asked Lab Rat.

He checked his instruments, then shook his head. "No. Why?"

"No reason." I wasn't about to explain that the SEALs were moving so silently through the dense jungle that I thought we had an equipment failure. I didn't want that getting back to Sykes, even as a backhanded compliment.

It took them an hour and a half to make it to the perimeter of the airfield and base. Once there, Brandon sat motionless for at least twenty minutes. I tapped my fingers impatiently, waiting for something to happen, then realized that it probably was. As the leader of the team, Brandon was hanging back and coordinating.

Then he moved, so silently and slowly that at first I missed it. It was a slow, careful slither through the underbrush, and from what I could see, not a branch around him moved. Without the pictures, I never would have believed just how invisible a SEAL can be in deep cover.

Then I saw what had attracted his attention. A two-man

patrol, their voices now reaching the microphone at his lips. He'd heard them well before I had, and had moved into position. But for what?

I got my answer shortly. Brandon raised one hand and positioned it in front of the camera. There was a long, pale strip in his hand. It loomed at me now, filling the screen, wiggled, then held still.

"What the—?" I turned to Lab Rat. "We've lost the picture?"

"It was a stupid comment. Lab Rat didn't say anything, just stared at me.

Then I understood. Maybe Brandon had briefed him, but probably Lab Rat had just figured it out himself. There was something going on on the ground that Brandon didn't want me to see. Whether because he was protecting me or his men, it was important to him that my silent, watchful presence at the scene be eliminated.

Then the sound went dead. For about five seconds I was completely cut off from the SEAL team. Then I saw Brandon's hand appear, ripping away the covering over his camera, and I heard the small night noises of the jungle. I caught another glimpse of the thing that had obscured my vision earlier.

"A Band-Aid?" I asked. "Do they carry them all the time for just that purpose?"

Still, Lab Rat was silent.

And the guards were nowhere in sight.

Just exactly what had he done? Shot them? He must have, because there had not been time for him to approach them on foot and eliminate them. And I was certain that that was exactly what had occurred.

"He can't—" I began.

For the first time in our relationship, Lab Rat cut me off.

"You sent him in to do a job, Admiral. He let you come along for part of the ride, but only as long as it didn't interfere with his capabilities. Do you really want to see what just happened? Do you want to know and be forced into some action? Or will you settle for having things just the way they would have been before this newest toy?"

"Damn it, I'm responsible!" I stood and started pacing again, angry at more than just Brandon Sykes.

"Of course you are," Lab Rat said. "But do you really want to know what just happened?"

I considered the matter for a moment, cooling off as I did so. The truth—no, I didn't want to know. No more than I wanted a bird's-eye view of the men and women who died following our bombing run, the tiny sparkles of flame that spurted briefly across the J-TARPS screen, then collapsed.

"They're in," I said, and took my seat again.

Indeed they were. What I at first took for shadows on the ground were two SEALs, now edging closer to the back end of the revetments. This thing was massive, extending back into the jungle and shaded by the trees. Each could have easily held thirty or forty aircraft, though why they would have concentrated all their assets in one area was a mystery to me.

They crept around the side of the revetments still in Brandon's view, barely discernible moving shapes against the night. They moved out of his field of vision, and I heard Brandon's breathing pick up speed. Had the microphone been any more sensitive, I was certain I would have heard his heart pounding away as well.

It was over fast, so fast. Five minutes later, they were creeping back out as carefully as they'd gone in. They joined on Brandon, then the three of them moved out, picking up the other two along the way. They moved more quickly through the underbrush now, it seemed to me.

I had just started to breathe again, when all hell broke loose. A loud, wailing siren went off and the jungle behind the SEALs lit up like daylight. Someone had evidently discovered the two missing guards on patrol, and the response was fast and deadly.

I couldn't see them yet, because Brandon was concentrating on his own path, but I could hear the screams and commands being shouted out behind him. All five men had abandoned their complete stealth mode for a quiet but much speedier exit from the area.

What had taken them an hour to cover quietly, they did in less than ten minutes hauling ass. Before any effective patrols had been sent out after them, they were back at the boats and hauling them out, and were already en route to the ship when the first patrols appeared on the beach. All I could see was the rubberized side of an RHIB—Brandon was evidently crouched down low in the boat, making as small a target as possible for the spatter of gunfire now splatting in the water around the RHIB. There was a heavy, consistent thud-thud-thud—the bow of the RHIB slamming down against the waves as it hauled ass back out into deeper water.

"The helo is airborne, sir," Lab Rat reminded me. "All he has to do is make it to the five-mile point—then the helo will rope them up and have them back on deck before the Vietnamese know what happened."

We'd established fives miles as the safe point to keep the helo well out of the range of Stinger missiles as well as any other shoulder-portable weapons the Vietnamese might carry. The helo was going in low to avoid search radars, running a mere ten or fifteen feet over the tops of the waves to the intercept point.

"Shit." I heard one of the electronic warfare technicians say. "Not now, damn it!"

Lab Rat turned and surveyed the numbers flickering by on the Signal Intercept equipment. Whatever he saw drained the blood out of his face.

"SAM sites, sir," he said, his voice low and level. "They're lighting up all over the coast."

"Have they got the helo?"

"No indication if it, yet. They're still in search mode, but they're definitely alerted. He's going to have to fly low level all the way back."

Lab Rat knew what that meant just as well as I did. At night, without much ambient light, low-level-over-water operations were particularly dangerous.

But not as dangerous as being in a RHIB with people shooting at you.

"How much longer?" I asked.

"Another two miles," Lab Rat answered. "The helo's got a visual on them—says they're doing well, evading all the fire. No indication there's been any casualties."

Those two minutes were some of the longest I've sat through, made particularly painful by the fact there was nothing I could do to help these men. Time has a way of stretching out when you're under fire, when seconds become minutes and minutes eternities. Your nervous system is so flooded with adrenaline that you're thinking faster, moving more quickly than you ever have before in your life. Survival depends on making the right decision, and making it seconds before you have to.

But at least you have some control over your own destiny. If you're just a little bit faster, a little bit smarter, or a little tougher, you know you'll make it out. And if you've got the right stuff to be a fighter pilot, you're all those things and more.

But it's entirely different watching someone else go through the same thing, unable to help or hurt them.

Brandon was talking now, his words faint over the roar of the engine and the slap of the sea against the rubber-bottomed boat. "Admiral, if you can hear me, I think we may need to move up that schedule a little bit. The devices are in place and set to go off right before the strike is on top, but I think you need to move a little quicker. They're alerted now, sir. They're gonna be searching the revetment, and they might find our little presents. Suggest you command-detonate now, get the strike airborne as fast as you can, and play the cards as they lay. We're almost home—the helos just blinked their lights at us, and I'm turning toward her."

I turned to Lab Rat. "You bet the cards?"

He nodded. "Do it now."

One corner of the CVIC's space was occupied by a signal generator linked to a high-frequency transmitter. It had a dedicated antenna on deck right now, hard-wired for just this purpose.

I watched Lab Rat as he set the signal generator to the appropriate sequence, then thumbed the switch on. We heard nothing. At least not inside CVIC.

From Brandon Sykes's microphone, I heard a small, muffled thud. Then a scream of exultation by the SEAL. Sheer joy, followed by a hurried commentary. "Good work, guys! Hell of a light show out here. Man, did it ever go boom." The sheer, reverent wonder in his voice at the size of the explosion was gleeful.

Lab Rat handed me a microphone. He pointed at a red

light on top of the SEAL receiving gear. It blinked green. "Want to congratulate them yourself?" Lab Rat asked.

I cleared my throat, then picked up the mike. "Good work, men. Now get your asses back here."

With the helo airborne, we were already at flight quarters, but now the hard rolling thunder of a Tomcat engine spooling up rattled the 03 level. Strike was one step ahead of me, as usual.

The first launch took place five minutes later, just as Brandon Sykes's headset camera swung around in a gut-wrenching panorama, briefly inverted, and then steadied on the helicopter above him. He'd just hooked the rope they were dangling to hoist him and the other SEALs up into the helo. The camera steadied on the inside of the helicopter, then turned to the open hatch on the side of it. Brandon was staring down at the water, and I saw a dull flash of light, followed by a geyser of water. He'd just blown the RHIBs.

"Admiral, we're launching the first wave." Strike's voice over the bitch box was spooled up. "J-TARPS mounted on one Hornet and two Tomcats, Admiral."

I motioned to Lab Rat. "Go ahead and switch the picture—I think we're done with the SEALs."

How quickly we'd become accustomed to new technology, capabilities that would have seemed sheer magic just ten years before. The J-TARPS display had awed me just the day before, and now I was casually directing my Intelligence Officer to display an air battle and strike for me real time.

Lab Rat quickly complied. "They've got MiGs in the air," he warned as he glanced at another piece of gear. "Launch indications now."

"It figures." The catapult was thumping steadily now, shooting off another one of my aircraft every twenty-two

seconds. Twelve aircraft airborne so far, one of which had to
be a tanker. We'd agreed that the SEAL helicopter would
serve temporary duty as SAR bird during launch while we
shot everything we had off the deck. After the bomb-laden
fighters were airborne, we'd launch another SAR helo and
bring the SEALs back on deck.

The first J-TARPS was mounted under Hornet 301.
"Who's flying?" I asked.

"Thor Hammersmith. You remember him," Lab Rat
answered.

Indeed I did. Thor was a Marine's Marine, an infantry-
man on temporary assigned duty in the cockpit, as they
called in. Every Marine underwent basic indoctrination in
ground combat and infantry tactics, a fact that made Marine
Close Air Support—CAS—a deadly potent capability.
Marines wouldn't leave Marines, they were fond of reminding us.

The other two cameras were mounted on Tomcats configured for bombing runs—bombcats, we called them.
Once Thor got within killing range of the MiGs, however, I
barely even glanced at the other two monitors.

I was raised on Tomcats, the biggest, meanest fighter in
the fleet. Sure, I knew the Hornets were more maneuverable, had even seen them in action myself. But watching it
from another aircraft or from the flight deck, or even on a
radarscope, is nothing compared to the picture you get when
you're slung onto the undercarriage of one.

The Hornet darted and whirled, playing an intricate game
of cat and mouse with its MiG opponent. It was a different
fight from the kind I was used to, given that they were both
angles fighters. They were equally matched in thrust to wing
area, giving them similar performance characteristics. The
battle was not the harrowing series of power climbs and

scrabbles for altitude that I was used to, but rather a close-in, parry-and-dart knife fight. Thor was closer to a MiG than I'd ever been in my life—and closer than I ever want to be. But the movement of his aircraft was swift and sure. There was no hesitation or sudden changes of angle on the MiG that would lead me to believe he'd miscalculated or changed his mind. The Marine was a deadly fighter in his aircraft, a lethal capability that took on a whole new meaning as I watched the battle progress.

Thor's Hornet was loaded with Sidewinders and Sparrows, along with a full charge of rounds in his nose cannon. He used the Sparrow first against the incoming MiG, forcing it into a defensive position. The MiG pilot was good, but not that good. Thor had harried him into a mistake with the Sparrow, then slipped neatly into a perfect firing position behind him. Fox three, and then the MiG was a smoking fiery hole in the dark night.

Now what? Thor was down to one Sparrow and two Sidewinders.

Listening to the air battle over tactical as well as watching it through the three-camera displays was more comfortable now, the second time through. I heard the cry for help, saw Thor's Hornet bank hard to the right, the stars wheeling crazily across the camera screen through the broken cloud cover. The MiG appeared center-line, and I waited for Thor to launch one of his remaining missiles.

What the—Thor wasn't launching. I had a sinking, foreboding feeling that I knew just exactly what he was planning.

His Sparrow-Sidewinder tactic was clearly a favorite. He was planning on saving all the remaining missiles for a second shot of his own, but still needed to shake this MiG off his buddy's butt. I groaned out loud. "No, Thor, don't do it—don't do it."

But he did. With the MiG preoccupied with jockeying into firing position on another Hornet, Thor swooped in from above like an avenging angel. There was no sound, but I saw the staccato stream of tracer fire arc out ahead of me and stitch a line across the MiG's fuselage. The Hornet it was following broke hard left, on Thor's command, and Thor pulled up and hard to the right. The J-TARPS camera caught the first microseconds of the fireball that had once been a MiG.

I slammed my hand down on the table. "Damn it, that glory-hogging—" I stopped abruptly, and reconsidered my analysis.

Sure, I was an admiral and in command of this entire battle group. I'd even flown Hornets, had qualified on them, as it was necessary to do before assuming command of this battle group. It was part of the long, tortuous process of taking this job, one that included far too long at the nuclear-propulsion training command in Idaho, command of an aircraft carrier, then requalifying on every aircraft that landed on the deck of a carrier. Hell, I even had my time in helos.

But despite my experience and the genuine qualifications I had for wrestling a Hornet down onto the deck, I wasn't a Hornet pilot. Nor was I a Marine. Thor knew far better than I the capabilities and tactics that worked with his aircraft one-on-one against a MiG. If I wanted to go along for the ride, I damned well better shut up and just watch.

I wondered how many admirals after me would experience this same temptation that technology now provided us, this yearning to try to coach the pilots through each air-to-air engagement. I'd almost made a fatal mistake, giving red orders to Thor while he was in the air. I hoped the guy—or woman, eventually—that followed me would do better than I had.

Thor broke off with a dizzying series of barrel rolls that swapped open sky every other second. Then the camera steadied down, surveying the clear sky dotted with aircraft. It swung back and forth slowly as Thor assessed the current state of the battle and selected his next target. Then it steadied down again, rock hard, on a single MiG diving into the engagement from on high.

The shape grew larger quickly now as Thor kicked in the afterburner. Soon the MiG filled the camera screen, the sleek, deadly aircraft jetting gouts of its own afterburner fire out the tailpipes. The camera bobbled unsteadily as Thor hit the jet wash. He was too far away for guns and too close for Sidewinders. I could tell what he was thinking now—trying to decide whether he should pull back and let loose the Sparrow, or simply press on in with the guns. In the end, he made the same decision I would have, pitched up in a hard, gray-out-inducing climb, then pivoted back down into position.

Not that the MiG was waiting for him. He'd cut, rolled, and gone into a long climbing loop intended to place him in position on Thor. The two craft passed each other belly-to-belly on opposite ends of the altitude-airspeed curve. Thor rolled out of the turn, converting his downward movement into a sharp, breaking curve to the right. The MiG rolled out of his climb and dove to meet him.

I groaned out loud watching it, seeing the inevitable fighter geometry take shape. The MiG was behind Thor now, closing rapidly and maneuvering so that the bright heat of Thor's tailpipes would serve as a perfect missile synch.

Thor sensed the same thing, because he broke hard in a

roll, cutting inside the MiG's arc of turn and jockeying back into position himself.

That was the essential difference between a Hornet-on-MiG engagement and a Tomcat-on-MiG engagement. In the first, the battle tended to take place in a vertical plane since the aircraft were evenly matching power and agility. With the Tomcat, you use your greater power to gain a height advantage, keeping the MiG from cutting inside your turns as Thor had just done.

The MiG pitched nose-down and headed for the deck. It was a last-ditch maneuver, one designed to shake the hard lock of a Sidewinder on its tailpipes.

Thor was too quick for it. I saw first one Sidewinder, then the other leap off his wings and streak unerringly for the MiG.

The camera caught just the upper edge of the explosion, black and oily as it billowed burning fuel, shards of metal, and a few traces of the pilot into the serene sky.

So Thor was Winchestered now—no, wait. He still had one Sparrow left. Would he go for it, without the potent Sidewinders as a close-in backup? He probably had some rounds left in his cannon too. I recalled the delicate way the rounds had traced their path across the hull of the MiG, and knew he hadn't shot his load on that.

Of course he'd find another one. No pilot comes back with weapons—that's an unspoken rule.

The camera was back in that general to-and-fro hunting motion, a good retriever sniffing the air looking for prey. It took a little longer this time, but Thor picked out another one, one widely separated from the rest of the gaggle. A nasty, black cloud and the frantic cries over tactical told me why. The MiG had just nailed a Hornet and was rejoining the fray itself.

They were nose-to-nose now, each accelerating to well over Mach one. The closure rate was well over twelve hundred nautical miles per minute, increasing every second as the two aircraft accelerated. A game of chicken, one fought at seventeen thousand feet instead of on some dusty country road, but no less deadly.

Thor had the Sparrow selected, and I imagined he was hearing the high, wavering growl of the missile as it tried to obtain a lock. He was just inside the weapon's envelope, it appeared, judging from the appearance of the MiG. My mind automatically converted what I was seeing on the camera into distance.

A bright flash of light, then another missile off the wing, Thor's last.

"Break off," I said out loud. "C'mon, Thor—you shot your load, get your ass back to the ship."

Lab Rat looked at me curiously, but said nothing. We both knew what the score was. A Hornet without weapons was simply a target waiting to happen.

But the camera stayed rock steady on the approaching MiG, tracking the missile as it bore in on him.

The MiG blinked. At what seemed the last possible second, it cut hard to the right, intending to break the radar lock and allowing the missile no time or distance to reacquire. It was a good move, one that should have worked. It almost did.

The Sparrow clipped the MiG on the canted tail structure, knocking off one portion of it. It was happening so quickly. All I saw was the thin, triangular shape tumbling away from the aircraft, then the fragments of missile pelting the air behind the MiG.

For a moment, I thought the MiG might make it. They were incredibly airworthy little beasts, and it was just possible that the pilot might be able to pull off a controlled descent, at least one long enough to give him a chance to eject.

But Thor had other plans. He was on him now, stitching the canopy and fuselage with the rapid-fire Vulcan cannon. I saw the MiG canopy shatter, bright shards of it reflecting in the hard sunlight.

The ejection seat fired. It must have been the pilot's last conscious act before the bullets penetrated the canopy and hit him. It slammed out of the aircraft at a forty-five-degree angle to the fuselage, hung in the air for a moment, and then the parachute deployed. By some miracle, the bullets hadn't shredded the ejection seat. It worked, just as its Russian designers had intended. But the pilot hung lifeless and inert below it. He and his aircraft both headed for the sea, one in a deadly flat spiral and the other drifting down gently.

"Now, Thor." I reached for the microphone. This time I would act, order the brash Marine back to the carrier rather than let him take on another MiG with his guns alone.

Evidently Thor had the same idea. The camera swung away from the battle, found the horizon, then hunted for a moment before settling on the massive shape of *Jefferson*.

"Admiral, look." I turned to see Lab Rat pointing at the large-screen tactical display. "It's Hunter 701—he's got a visual."

The NTDS—Navy Tactical Data Display—symbol made it clear just what Lab Rat was talking about. A submarine, classified as hostile by the S-3 Viking orbiting above it. I could see the symbol for the aircraft almost superimposed on top of the hostile submarine mark.

"Well, it's about time," I said heavily. "They've got them, don't they? Why wouldn't they use them?"

"I'm putting up the ASW C&R—the Anti-Submarine

Coordination and Reporting Circuit." Lab Rat fiddled with the speakers and the dial-up box next to it. It crackled, then came to life in the middle of a sentence.

"—certain it's a Romeo," I heard a voice say. A familiar voice—I strained to put a name to it.

Lab Rat saw my questioning look and said, "Commander Steve 'Rabies' Grills, another *Jefferson* homesteader."

I nodded, calling up a face to match the voice. Rabies had been a regular mainstay of our ASW evolutions for the past several cruises. He was a lusty Texan, I recalled, one who drove his flight crews to sheer desperation by singing country-western songs on the ICS during their long hours on station. Another strong player, in his way just as good as Bird Dog or Thor.

"He's still holding it?" I asked.

Lab Rat nodded. "And from the looks of it, he's got so many sonobuoys in the water around it that we'll be able to track it just by the noise alone," he added. He tapped a few keys and the sonobuoy lines popped into being, a regularly spaced line of listening devices that would keep track of the submarine if it decided to pull the plug and go sinker.

"What's he doing on the surface anyway?" I asked.

"Maybe he's got those antiair weapons on board," Lab Rat suggested.

A nasty prospect, but one that we had to consider. The new generations of submarines all had them, a small surface-to-air missile that could be extruded through an extension to the conning tower and fired at aircraft overhead. It was particularly effective against the smaller and less maneuverable helicopters, but I'd known one or two to take a shot at fixed-wing aircraft as well. If anything, it would keep the S-3 crew on guard. Rabies had personal experience with the weapons system, and I knew he wasn't eager for another encounter.

"I guess Rabies doesn't think so," Lab Rat said. "His altitude is three hundred feet."

"If he sees anything—" I began, and then broke off. Of course he'd be watching, and of course he'd get the hell out of the area if he saw anything suspicious unfolding from the conning tower. Like a missile launcher.

Lab Rat spoke up. "I haven't heard anything about them being back-fitted on the older submarines, and I'm not sure they have the power supply for it. Or the guidance systems." He looked thoughtful. Then he continued. "But I suppose it's possible. As miniaturized as some of these circuits are these days, the space wouldn't be a problem. It would just be a matter of tacking the missile assembly onto—"

"How far from the carrier?" I asked, interrupting his train of intelligence speculation and theorizing. All very interesting, but what mattered to me was whether or not the submarine was in a position to do damage to one of my ships.

"Well out of range, Admiral," Lab Rat assured me. "Almost twenty miles."

"Not to say he couldn't close that distance eventually," I said.

"Well, now that we know she's there, we can take some precautions."

The appearance of a submarine in our area worried me. Worried, hell—it scared the shit out of me.

There's something particularly terrifying about submarines, at least to an aircraft carrier. For sailors everywhere, ships are more than just weapons platforms or floating airports. A ship is the one little space in the world that's home, at least for months at a time. It's where your stereo lives, your spare set of civilian clothes so you can go on liberty, and those few precious possessions that you can cram into the small lockers and staterooms assigned to you. In short, it's home.

Ever since their earliest days, submarines have been weapons of terror. Until the last couple of decades, we'd had no way of knowing where they were, no way of tracking them with any degree of certainty, other than by saturating the air around the ships and hoping the submarines came up to snorkel. But with the advent of the nuclear-powered submarine, snorkeling had become unnecessary. Besides that, the age of Hyman Rickover and the nuclear submarine had upped the tactical stakes in two ways. First, the nuclear submarines were fast as hell underwater, while their diesel brethren were limited to either slow speed or being submerged for a short time. Second, the weapons were far more deadly. Without even getting into the devastation that one ballistic-missile submarine can wreak, the nuclear-tipped torpedoes alone could crack the keel of any ship. Even a big ship like a carrier.

Submarines just seemed so damn sneaky. They were undetectable, slipping silently beneath the water. It seemed so fundamentally a terrorist act to deploy them. At least, that's how the British had classified it in several world wars. I was inclined to agree with them. And now that they could shoot at aircraft too, with these extruding missile launchers mounted in the sail, there was even more to worry about.

I was hoping our couple of bombing runs, along with some political pressure, might bring the Vietnamese to the bargaining table. It's not like we were out to invade them. All we wanted to know was whether or not they had a nuclear-weapons manufacturing plant, and if so, who they were selling the weapons to. Moreover, we wanted them to stop. Now.

Two major strikes against their airfield ought to get their attention, at least. I knew other things were going on as well, behind the scenes. Diplomatic conferences, exchanges of pointed remarks between envoys, and our own Ambassador Sarah Wexler was raising holy hell in the United Nations about nuclear proliferation, the unprovoked strike attack against our aircraft, and just about anything else that could be force-fed to her by her staff.

Don't get me wrong, Ambassador Wexler is a hell of a lady. She's maybe Tomboy's size, a little on the slight side, but chunkier, older, if you know what I mean.

In the last several years, I'd seen her take on the Chinese toe-to-toe, and after that the Cubans. The way she'd thrashed them up one side of the table and down the other, I'd almost pitied them. She would have made a hell of a fighter pilot.

But so far, Ambassador Wexler wasn't getting too far. The Vietnamese kept pulling out of conferences in a huff, insisting we were the aggressors, that we'd conducted unprovoked bombing attacks against a hospital facility and a children's camp.

Yeah, right. Even Vietnamese children don't get SAM sites for recess breaks. The claims of the Vietnamese were so far from the truth as to be absolute lies, although of course Ambassador Wexler wasn't calling them that. She knew how to play tough, yet still give them some room to save face, and sometimes I thought my job on the carrier might be a hell of a lot easier than hers. We've got a saying—kill them all and let God sort them out. Ambassador Wexler didn't have that luxury.

In addition to dealing with the Vietnamese delegation,

she also had to soothe the worries of myriad other nations
that felt threatened or beleaguered because of the conflict.
Laos, Cambodia, even Japan—all were in an uproar,
desperately trying to decide which side of the fence to sit on.

Add to the mix the silent, ominous presence of China.
They figured prominently in every conflict in that area, and
I had no doubt that they had some delicate, hidden hand to
play in this. Maybe they were the primary customers of the
alleged nuclear plant, although I couldn't see how they'd
need it. Or maybe this had something to do with trade,
expanding China's backyard into a solid phalanx of political
support against the United States. God knows they'd been
flexing their muscles ever since they took over Hong Kong,
becoming increasingly belligerent about everything from
the Spratly Islands to the importation of rice into Japan.

Despite all the factors warring against it, eventually the
overtures came. Not to me at first, although they eventually
trickled down to my level. Instead, underlings at both State
and the United Nations started agreeing with their Vietnamese counterparts that there should at least be a conference—a discussion, if you will—to sort out conflicting
interests in the area. No mention was made of the attack on
Jefferson, nor of the pilots and aircraft I'd lost.

For their part, the Vietnamese refrained from blustering
about the air strikes. Diplomatic notes were exchanged,
arrangements were made. Finally, the beginning of a con-
sensus.

What it all boiled down to was that *Jefferson* was going
to play host to a group of U.S. and Vietnamese officials.
They'd argued for two days about whether the conference
would take place inside or outside Vietnamese territorial
waters, finally settling on giving me rudder orders to

delicately patrol the exact twelve-mile limit off the coast. Thank God for the global positioning system—GPS. It's the only way to get an accurate enough position to make that sort of political statement.

When things start moving, they move fast. The delegations would be arriving soon, alternating Vietnamese and American flights out to *Jefferson,* the pecking order and time of arrival carefully calculated to slight the least number of feelings.

I'd pointed out that receiving a peace delegation on board in the middle of bombing the crap out of their country was a bit inconsistent, to say the least. But State and Defense hardly ever talk, and neither one was backing down from their respective schedules. Maybe they had thought it out and figured they were sending some sort of message.

An aircraft carrier is big, but not so big that you can absorb forty people, all of whom rate high-status quarters, without displacing some permanent residents. We did a quick shuffle, bunking senior officers in with each other, and finally had enough staterooms.

The first aircraft arrived at 1700, a CH-46 ferrying out from Vietnam to *Jefferson,* containing a contingent of U.S. representatives on board. They were mostly underlings, advance men who immediately tried to take command of the ship and rearrange my world to their liking.

It didn't work. I held them off, waiting for the arrival of the heavy hitters.

Finally, they came. First a load of Vietnamese underlings, then the U.S. helo carrying Ambassador Sarah Wexler. I watched the entire evolution from the tower, hoping and praying to God that some dumb fuck wouldn't pick this very moment to do something stupid. Not in front of all these people.

Ambassador Wexler's helicopter settled down onto the deck gracefully, and the plane captains raced out to help secure the aircraft and to escort its esteemed cargo across the flight deck. I watched, my stomach knotted, certain that some young plane captain would choose just this moment in time to try to move an F-14 or turn an engine and suck the ambassador right down the intake.

Minutes later, the Vietnamese VIP helicopter signaled its approach. Its pilot came in gracefully, settling neatly on the deck as though he did it every day of his life. I was somewhat impressed, although the deck of an aircraft carrier is not that tough a target. Still, it does take some getting used to, hovering and sinking down over a moving airfield.

The Vietnamese senior VIP disembarked from the helicopter last, as befitted his status. The plane captains lined up on either side escorted him to the island, where he was greeted by the same side boys that had just welcomed Ambassador Wexler. The 1MC announcement went off smoothly.

So far, so good. Everybody on deck, nobody ingested by an aircraft engine. That had to count for something.

I raced back down the ladder and made it to the wardroom just as Ambassador Wexler and her counterpart were being escorted in. They'd already been relieved of their cranials, helmets that they'd worn during their flights, as well as their flotation devices.

Ambassador Wexler was much as I remembered her, a short, full-figured tiger of a woman who looked deceptively gentle and calm. She tendered me her hand, offered a warm smile, and said, "Thank you for having us, Admiral Wayne."

"Glad to have you aboard, Madam Ambassador," I replied politely. Yeah, like I'd had a choice.

Then I turned to her Vietnamese counterpart. "And you,

sir, welcome aboard USS *Jefferson*. If there is anything I can do to make your stay more comfortable, I do hope you or your staff will contact me personally at your earliest convenience."

The man studied me, his eyes dark and cold. No trace of warmth in his expression, I noted.

Not that I blamed him. He was looking at the son of a bitch who'd just bombed the hell out of his airfield and probably killed a lot of his men. Under the same circumstances, I'm sure I wouldn't have been much more pleasant.

He finally inclined his head, ever so slightly, the minimum sketch of courtesy required in his culture. I bowed slightly, more deeply than he had, determined not to let any inadvertent cultural faux pas muddy up the already turbulent waters of this conference.

"My Chief of Staff," I said to the man, introducing Irwin to both the Vietnamese and Ambassador Wexler.

Then I fell silent. The man's game was getting on my nerves a little bit. The message we'd received from State only gave us the number and approximate ranks of the Vietnamese visitors who would be arriving, not all of their names.

Not this man's name.

"May I notify my superiors of your safe arrival?" I asked finally. "If I could let them know, sir, that Ambassador . . ." I let my voice trail off delicately, waiting for him to fill in the missing name. Seems I had learned something in my D.C. tours after all.

"Than. Bien Than," he said finally.

"Admiral," the Chief of Staff said quietly. "If I could have your attention for a moment?"

I nodded, made my excuses, and stepped away from the

dignitaries. "Jesus, what is it, COS?" I asked. "I'm a little busy right now, buddy."

COS nodded. "I wouldn't have interrupted you, not if it weren't important."

I let out a huge sigh. "Yeah, I know. So what is it?"

He pointed at the overhead. "Another Vietnamese helicopter inbound, Admiral. They say it's been cleared by State."

"Another one?" I hissed. "Jesus, I thought we got them all—"

"We did, Admiral," COS answered, taking a chance on interrupting me. "But I just talked to my liaison on Stan's staff, and they evidently overlooked mentioning this one in their last message. It belongs to the Vietnamese, though. And they want the people on board."

I tamped down my temper, and considered my options. Well, it didn't take long. There weren't any.

"Have the Air Boss get 'em on board then," I said, sighing. "Find out who they are—damn it, we're going to have to rearrange the sleeping arrangements again, aren't we?"

COS nodded. "I'll take care of everything, Admiral. Just wanted to let you know."

COS exited quickly, clearly ahead of me on the details. He was like that, a good man, one who seemed to have developed the uncanny ability to read my mind—or even read my subconscious, knowing what I wanted before I even knew it myself. He was talking about retirement—damned if I'd let him go before I did.

I turned back to my guests and made polite small talk as I heard the ship go to Flight Quarters, then the distinctive whop-whop of a large helicopter approaching my deck. I heard it land roughly, its skids scraping across the deck for far longer than they should have for a controlled landing. I held my breath for a moment, praying that some idiot wasn't going to slam his stupid rotary wing into one of my aircraft.

Finally, the skidding stopped, and I heard the engine start to spool down along with the rotors. My heart started beating again.

"So we'll begin at eight tomorrow morning then?" Ambassador Wexler said calmly. "If, of course, that is agreeable to you, Ambassador Than?"

"Perhaps a little earlier," he said smoothly. "Seven-thirty perhaps?" His voice was perfectly understandable, only the barest trace of an accent in it. Educated abroad, I'd guess—maybe England, judging from an odd emphasis on certain words.

"Seven-thirty then," Ambassador Wexler agreed promptly. She tendered a charming smile, as though the first minor chivying for position had not just been played out right in front of me. "There will, however, be a limited choice of facilities." She waved one hand gracefully as though to take in the whole of *Jefferson*. "As large as this ship is, space is still at a premium." She smiled even more politely now, dimpling one chin. "Under the circumstances, with so much important to discuss, I'm certain the captain's normal rectangular table will be more than adequate for our needs. Don't you agree?"

And counter-serve. I watched the two bandy back and forth, balancing and trading off the small details of the meeting. Unbelievable that there could be a discussion about tea versus coffee when so many of my aviators were dead.

"Dinner will be served at six-thirty," I said finally, not giving either one of them a chance to table the matter for discussion. "I do hope that you, Ambassador"—I nodded to

Sarah Wexler—"and you as well," I added, nodding to Than, "will be able to join me in my cabin for a private meal. Your staffs, of course, are welcome to dine with mine here in the Flag Mess."

"What a kind offer," Ambassador Wexler murmured. She cast a sly glance at me. "Of course, if there are matters that you and I must discuss privately, Admiral—"

"I would be pleased to accept as well," Than broke in smoothly. "An opportunity to get better acquainted with Madame Wexler."

"Fine," I said, trying to sound like a hearty and well-intentioned host. In reality, I'd just as soon have slit the little bastard's throat and thrown him overboard, but again—my options were limited.

Just then there was a clatter at the door leading into the mess. The Chief of Staff stepped in, looking agitated. It's not something I'd often seen from him. "Admiral," he began, and then was interrupted by people crowding into the mess behind him. I took one look at the cameras, the microphones, and the tape recorders now filling my Flag Mess, and started to roar.

Ambassador Wexler saved me. She stepped in front of me, between the Chief of Staff and myself, and said, "A press pool?" She turned back to Than, her face frowning prettily. "There was no discussion of a press pool. Was there?"

Than said nothing. He merely motioned for the rest of the people to come into my Flag Mess.

"Because since there wasn't," Sarah Wexler continued, her voice turning hard and cold, "I think we'd both agree that this would be an unreasonable imposition on Admiral Wayne's resources. These things must be coordinated in advance, you understand. Not simply arranged without consultation."

I recognized those words for what they were—diplomatese for sneaking around behind someone else's back. Sarah Wexler was pissed, almost as much as I was, but for different reasons. I stepped back and let her handle it.

"Admiral! Admiral Wayne?" A familiar voice, one that cut through my anger to knot my stomach back into a complicated tangle. I felt my heart sink as I realized who it was. The one voice I had never, ever wanted to hear on my carrier again.

Pamela Drake stepped out from the pack of reporters. Her hair was cut short now, a bright, shining brown cap above the delicately featured face. The brilliant green eyes were blazing now, alive with excitement and sheer joy at the frustration she knew she was causing me. She walked forward, nodded politely to Ambassador Wexler and Ambassador Than, then extended her hand. "So nice to see you again, Admiral."

Faced with the choice of being publicly rude or following Sarah Wexler's diplomatic lead, I took her hand gingerly. "It's been quite some time, Ms. Drake," I murmured, hoping that would be sufficiently neutral an expression to avoid offending her.

Pamela's smile broadened. "Oh indeed it has, Admiral." She said softly, "Far too long, I think." She stepped forward, hooked her arm in mine, and led me off to a corner before I could even react. Looking back over her shoulder, she said, "The admiral and I are old friends. We have so very much to catch up on."

"Of course, my dear," Sarah Wexler murmured. She turned back to Than and began to speak the doublespeak of confrontation and innuendo that was her natural language at the United Nations.

"What are you doing here?" I demanded of Pamela. "How did you get out here? Don't tell me you've got them bamboozled like you used to do to Tombstone?"

"Bamboozled? Really, Admiral." A look of annoyance shot across her face. "Tombstone is a big boy—he makes his own choices." Something in her voice told me that she had not forgotten those choices, not a single one of them.

"Besides, it's a free world," she continued, tossing her head. "If ACN gets me a billet with the Vietnamese news pool, what business is it of yours? I was the perfect choice, you know. After all," she said, her eyes gleaming maliciously, "I spent an awful lot of time on *Jefferson*. An awful lot."

I groaned inwardly, and cast a glance over at Sarah Wexler, hoping that she was going to be able to work something out with Than about this press deal. The last thing I needed was Pamela Drake on board my ship, the last thing of all. Her very presence had a way of making the most well-planned and smoothly coordinated evolutions disintegrate into a series of sound bites and confrontations, all featuring star reporter Pamela Drake as the winning party. On those rare occasions when she didn't get her way, that portion of the film was simply cut from the story. News at eleven.

"My usual stateroom?" Pamela asked. "As I remember, the last time I was on board, Tombstone had me in there under armed guard. I hope that won't be necessary this time."

I took a deep breath. "Listen, Pamela. I don't know how or where you wangled your way out here, but while you're on my ship, you follow the same rules as everybody else.

No poking around in spaces you're not supposed to be in, no going off on your own and quizzing my crew. I'll make photo opportunities available to you, as well as access to some of my sailors—if you can give me a good reason why I should—but other than that, you're under the same restrictions as everybody else. Fuck with me on this, Pamela, and I'll have your ass off my boat so fast you won't know what hit you."

A look of outrage was beginning to spread over her face, and I continued before she could start to protest. "Remember, I'm not Tombstone. You might have had him pussy-whipped about some things, or maybe it was just out of respect for your prior relationship. Whatever the reason, he cut you some slack on occasion—and you abused that trust, Pamela. Don't think I'll forget that."

"I'm here to do a job, Admiral," she said coldly. "That's all."

I looked at her levelly, ashamed that I was enjoying having gotten to her. "So am I, Ms. Drake. So am I."

NINE
Lieutenant Commander "Bird Dog" Robinson

29 September
Northern Vietnam

Gator had been unconscious for a hell of a long time. I checked his breathing again, then his pulse, though I don't know what I would have done if either wasn't right. And I wasn't sure exactly how many breaths a minute he was supposed to be taking. As long as the chest was moving up and down, I had to be satisfied.

The dark was absolute now. They'd moved a heavy wooden barrier across the entrance, and must have put canvas on top of that, because there were no stray slivers of light creeping past it as there had been yesterday. It looked bad for the Gator and Bird Dog, I had to admit it.

The underground facility was dark and dank, and I had the feeling of being buried alive. I knew from seeing it in the daylight that the ceilings were a good seven feet tall, but it sure as hell didn't feel like it with the lights out. There were small pools of water on the floor, and a steady ominous dripping sound somewhere in the back.

I found Gator a relatively dry spot to lie on, and tried to make him as comfortable as I could. But there was no way to check and see how bad they'd hurt him—they'd even taken away my flashlight during the interrogation. Interrogation—that's what they'd called it. Back where I'm from, we call it something else—beating the shit out of a guy.

Gator had already been hurt when we'd punched out of our aircraft, but at least the drugs had worn off. I'd been glad about that at first—and that was my first mistake.

They'd let us wait for twelve hours, just about ignoring us except for shackling our feet together. Not that we could have gotten far anyway. Gator was in bad shape, still half asleep from the drugs, and I wasn't about to take off without him.

Finally, just as Gator started coming to pretty good, answering my questions and sounding just about like his old self, they came for us.

Both of us.

There were two teams of interrogators. Five guys grabbed me, took me off to one end of the concrete building. I got tied in a chair, was asked a few polite questions by the bigwig, and then it started.

The same number of people had seized Gator and taken him off somewhere else. I'm assuming it was in the same building, but I hadn't had a chance to ask him since we'd been back. He hadn't regained consciousness.

There were the usual questions about what kind of aircraft I was flying, what squadron I was attached to, and what ship I'd come off. Like that was a big mystery— *Jefferson* was just over the horizon, and they damn well knew she was there. They should, after the damage we'd caused them.

I gave them the standard spiel: name, rank, service

number, and branch of service. Then, just like they tell you in all those training flicks, I quit talking.

They try to prepare you for this, just like they try to prepare you for aerial combat. The Navy does a pretty good job with their SERE—Survival Evasion Resistance Escape—School, but there're some things you just can't completely simulate. As bad as SERE School is, you know it'll end eventually. It's always surprising how fast your mind begins to believe it's real, to react to your questioners as though they're really bad guys instead of just other officers playing a part. But even when you start falling into the pattern, some part of your mind knows. Five more days, four more days—you can count it down, know that it's going to end.

What's more, you know they won't kill you. Sure, accidents do happen, even in training, but you figure that's probably against the rules. Killing pilots on purpose, I mean.

I came home from SERE School bloodied and bruised, and a lot smarter about just how little it took to break a man. It can be done—trust me.

The good part was that they also taught us some techniques for surviving it. I started reviewing them in my mind, preparing for the worst. It got bad—and then it got badder.

They started with the easy stuff, knocking my chair off so I hit hard on the concrete floor. I took a hard knock to the head, faded in and out for a moment, and then they jerked me upright. The beating began, starting off with just hard punches to the face and extending from there. By the time they got to my crotch, I was crying—and not ashamed to admit it. Hell, anybody would have been.

Then they brought out the batteries. And the electrodes. I remember how it started, but not how it ended. The pain was simply too great, too much, too hard, too fast, and I blacked out at some point. When I came to, I was lying back on the deck, cold water splashed over my face. I was shaking, couldn't control it, and then started puking.

There had been some more of the light stuff, the kind of torture that hurt really bad but that you could stay conscious through. Quite frankly, I wasn't sure which I longed for more—some degree of control over my mind or the sheer relief of unconsciousness.

Three hours, maybe four—I can't be sure, not with so much time missing in my mind. They never got what they wanted—at least I don't think they did. I can't recall giving them anything other than the allowable information.

They dragged me back to the cave, because I sure as hell couldn't walk. They took me about halfway in, then dropped me down on the dirt floor.

"You have time to think about this," one of them said calmly, as though he hadn't spent the last couple of hours pulping my face. "Think—we will be back."

I sat up, trying to make my vision clear up enough so that I could look around for Gator. Just as the heavy wooden door was slamming shut over the entrance, I saw him.

Gator was further back in the cavern than I was, still and unmoving.

"Gator?" I asked.

No response.

"Oh Jesus, man, don't be dead," I said, talking as much to calm myself down as to reassure him. "C'mon, Gator."

Still no answer.

I crawled on hands and knees over to him, afraid I'd miss him in the dark that was now absolute. I put my face down next to his, felt him breathing against my cheek. I put one hand on his chest, felt it rise, then fall.

At least he was alive. But how badly hurt was he? He'd

gone in in worse shape than I was, and if he'd been through what I had been, there was no telling.

"Sorry, Gator," I said softly, then started running my hands over his body, feeling for damage.

No long bones stuck out from his flight suit, nor had he puked on his quite as much as I had on mine. His breathing sounded relatively even, if a little bit shallow.

I curled up on the floor next to him and tried to come up with some brilliant plan to get us out of this. Surely there was a way—hell, I'd seen every John Wayne movie ever made. The Duke wouldn't be left to die in a stinking, leaky dirt cave with his buddy, no way. There was a way out—there always was.

I pulled myself to my feet, groaning a little, and found I could bear my weight on my own legs now if I leaned against the wall. I walked the perimeter slowly, feeling the outlines of our cave, stumbling once as I slipped in a puddle. I made the entire circuit, still with no good ideas. Finally, I went and sat back down next to Gator.

"They know where we are, Gator," I said, trying to sound confident. I've heard that people can hear you when they're unconscious, and if Gator was in there somewhere fighting, I wanted to let him know he wasn't alone. "Just hang tough, Gator. You're doing fine, you're not hurt bad. We're gonna get out of here soon."

I thought I heard him say something in his sleep, or maybe it was just a groan. My ears weren't working a whole lot better than my eyes. Encouraged, I kept it up for a while, started talking about the squadron and the people we knew, then stopped suddenly. Maybe they were listening—maybe not. That was one of the things they told me to assume, that your conversations were always monitored.

I went back to more general conversation, saying the first

thing that came to mind as long as it wasn't about the Navy, my family, or anything near and dear to me. Finally, I settled on Tennessee-Alabama football games. I retold every one I could recall in detail, focusing on the wins by Alabama. I knew Gator always took Tennessee over Alabama, so I gave them a good buildup too. I talked about the next game we'd see, how many beers we'd have, that sort of thing.

Finally, I guess I drifted off. I sure as hell wasn't awake when the first bomb hit.

If you've ever been on the ground when heavy ammunition starts hitting it, you know the sound. It's something you'll never forget, a noise and fury of vibration that you can recognize instantly. I'm not talking about the light stuff, about handguns and rifles and such. I mean the big motherfuckers I carry slung underneath my Tomcat, the ones I'd dropped around these parts not so long before.

The ground shook like we were in an earthquake, and the noise echoed through our small den. I yelped, dove for Gator, covering his face with my hands. I hunkered over him, trying to protect him from the dirt that was raining down from the ceiling. Dirt and more—rocks, I guess, because something hard hit me in the middle of the back and knocked me flat on top of him. I hung on for dear life.

More bombs hit, real close. Too close. Much more of this and the dirt cave I'd come to despise so quickly was going to be my tomb.

The first major cave-in occurred near the entrance, or so it seemed. I heard the sound, felt my ears pop as dirt collapsed in and compressed the air inside our chamber into a smaller space. Warm, moist ground cascaded across our legs, burying me up to my knees.

I scrambled free, then picked Gator up under the armpits and dragged him back. If we'd been trapped before, we were doubly so now. I didn't know how much dirt there was between me and the wooden door, but I was certain it was too much to dig through right now. Especially since the bombing continued, thundering explosions that deafened you even underground and ripped your world apart.

The earth around me groaned, and shivered. More dirt and rocks rained down from the ceiling, and I dragged Gator even further back. Now we were in the puddle, the water two or three inches deep and covering the tops of my boots.

They must have sent two flights in on a bombing run, because there was about sixty seconds of blessed, absolute silence. Or maybe I'd just gone deaf. At any rate, I thought it was over. Hoped it was over.

Then the second wave struck, even harder than the first. They sounded like they were right overhead, although they couldn't have been. Nothing would have survived in this cave if they had been. More cave-ins, so many more that we were crowded back into a narrow space maybe five feet deep at the very end of the tunnel.

"Hang on, Gator," I screamed, barely able to even hear my own voice over the noise and fury. "Stick with me, buddy. We're gonna get out, we're gonna get out, we're gonna—" A final blast, more powerful than all those that had come before, slammed me down to the dirt on my back, still holding Gator under the armpits. The impact must have been so painful that it woke him, because I could hear him screaming. But between my deafened ears and the noise from the explosions, I could just barely hear him.

A massive, low rumbling, then unexpectedly, light streaming down at me. One thin shaft, hazy and clouded with motes of dirt and dust and God knows what, but sunlight nonetheless. I laid Gator down carefully, propping him up against the back wall, which seemed the most solid of all. I scrabbled up the hard-packed dirt, trying to reach the opening. The wall collapsed under my fingers, cascading down near Gator. I tried again.

This time, I found a small toehold on a wedge of rock, then another. I could reach the opening, barely six inches in diameter, with my hands now. I clawed at it, raining more dirt down, not caring, knowing that this was our only chance for escape.

The loose soil crumbled easily, cascading down in a small anthill on the floor of our cave.

Big enough? It had to be.

I climbed down carefully, not wanting to dislodge the rocks that had served as handholds, and went back over to Gator. He was conscious now, quiet, but with his eyes darting around the cave like crazy. I tried to speak reassuringly. "Stay awake, Gator. We're getting out of here. It's gonna hurt, buddy, but I need you to stay awake. Okay?"

"Okay." His voice was weak but readable, and I breathed a huge sigh of relief. "Let's get going then. Before they find out there's a hole here."

I hoped to God that the Tomcats would hold off for just a little while. Just a few minutes, long enough for me and Gator to get out of this hellhole before they rolled in again with the next wave of bombing. How dangerous that would be, being above ground at ground zero, I didn't want to think about. But anything beat being buried alive.

I grabbed Gator by his collar, helped him stand up. Quickly, I pointed out the handholds, boosted him up to the first one, and shoved him by his butt up to the second. He was moving now, though God knows where he got the strength. I gave him one last shove on his good leg. Then I saw him half sprawl across the opening, his feet still dangling down at me. "Roll out of it, Gator. Roll out."

I heard him say something, but couldn't make out the words. I started on my way up, got halfway there, and turned loose with my hands long enough to lift his legs and heave him up over the opening.

I heard Gator start to scream, then stifle it. I fell back down on the floor of the dirt cave and cracked my head against something. The shaft of light shimmered, seemed to shift and go out, then reappeared.

Gator's pale face was staring down at me from the opening. "Come on, Bird Dog," he said. I damn near cried—now *he* was encouraging *me*? I felt a new burst of energy, and went at the handholds again. This time, with Gator out of the way, I made it.

We lay there for just a second, covered in mud and dirt and panting hard. Then I rolled over and said, "Can you walk?"

Gator grimaced. "Not much," he admitted. "My leg—I don't know if it was from punching out or what."

I shook my head. Better that he not remember, if he didn't. "Probably the ejection. C'mon, I'll help you. We need to get out of here before the third wave rolls in."

I stood up, and started thinking about whether or not the ground under my feet was going to collapse. That gave me more energy. I picked Gator up, slung him over my shoulder, and moved as fast as I could toward the tree line. It sure wasn't a run, more like a staggering walk, but twenty seconds later we were in the jungle.

I lowered Gator back down to his feet. "See if you can stand on one leg."

He tried, and found he was able to put weight on his right leg. I looped his left arm over my neck and said, "C'mon, let's go home."

We got maybe 150 feet away from the camp before the

third wave of bombers rolled in. I could look up and see them, Tomcats on a bombing run, their deadly payloads heavy on the undercarriages. If we ever got out of this, if I ever got back in a Tomcat, I was going to remember how we looked from the ground. That, and how the poor bastards we bombed felt.

There were only four Tomcats on this final run, and they did a damn fine job of it. As they banked away, I caught the squadron insignia on the tail, and realized it was the Black Vipers. My squadron—our squadron.

The last bird rolled in, dropped a couple of five-hundred-pounders on the compound. The last one went dead into the luxurious facility we had just vacated. The entire structure collapsed, blasting a fifty-foot-wide crater in the ground where we'd been.

"Just in time," Gator said. He looked at me with just a flash of the usual Gator expression on his face. "You can't do anything the easy way, can you?"

I laughed a little, then hoisted him back up. "C'mon. We're going south."

The jungle was thicker than I thought it would be, difficult to traverse. Vines on the ground caught at our ankles, and we fell every two hundred feet or so at first. After a while, I got better at it. The sounds of the compound, the bombing and screaming and noise, gradually faded away behind us.

"We need to get some altitude," I said. I pointed at the hill up ahead. "Think we can make it?"

Gator nodded. "I think we need to. I think I know where we are, and if we can get over that hill and head south, there may be some water."

It wasn't until he said that that I realized how thirsty I

was. I hadn't wanted to sample the pools of murky water on the bottom of our cave, and neither had Gator.

And hungry—damn, was I hungry. As the adrenaline started to ebb out of my system, that hit too.

"We can get our bearings," I agreed. "You ready?"

He nodded.

We set out again, now getting better at this traipsing like a three-legged-man relay team through the jungle. I started hearing animals, something moving around in the trees—at least I hoped it was animals. If it was Vietnamese, they sure hadn't figured out that they were supposed to be after us.

Finally, we pressed at the hill, climbing the last hundred feet of it on hands and knees. We broke out into a small clearing, and finally I could get a good visual on the sun.

"South of us is that way," Gator said decisively.

I shook my head. "I don't think so. It's that way." I pointed in a direction ninety degrees off the angle he'd indicated.

"Who's the navigator around here?" Gator demanded. "Bird Dog, you've never been able to find your way home alone. You know that. Now trust me—it's that way." He pointed back in the original direction.

"Okay," I agreed finally. Gator did have a point—I'd always had a lousy sense of direction.

We crossed over the hill and down into the valley beyond it. As Gator had suspected, there was a stream there. We both washed up, and checked each other over to assess the extent of our injuries.

Gator was a good deal worse off than I was. His arm had been hurt in the ejection, but it looked like the damage done to his right kneecap was all courtesy of our late hosts.

At least I hoped they were our late hosts. I'd never wished men dead so badly as I wished they were.

Aside from cuts and bruises, I was basically intact. The question about my testicles I'd leave for later, when I had a chance to check them out more carefully.

The going was a little bit easier nearer the stream, although we didn't dare stay right on the banks. That would have made us entirely too visible from air, and I wasn't certain that just our own guys would be looking for us. However, since we'd heard no signs of pursuit for the last four hours, I was kinda hoping that all the people who should have been looking for us were dead.

We did the nuts-and-bugs routine that they teach you in SERE School, choking down insects and hunting for anything that looked edible. As usual, Gator had studied better in school than I had—we managed to find enough to eat to at least make us feel full, and not kill us right away. Maybe some of it wasn't edible, but at least we didn't feel hungry anymore.

Buoyed up by feeling full, we moved a little faster now. We were still taking it easy, traipsing along in the thinner jungle that crowded the banks of the stream, but I think we both had a little sense of hope that we might actually make it out. Until that point, I had refused to believe it.

Finally, it happened. I heard noise off to my right and up ahead, and Gator and I exchanged a worried look. "We need to take cover."

Gator nodded. "Over there." He pointed to a clump of fallen trees. A natural hollow was carved out beneath them. "There're not a lot of options, Bird Dog," Gator said acerbically when he saw my doubtful look at it. "We cover up with some leaves, maybe drag some brush in front of it—it's the best thing around."

"Okay." We hobbled on over there, and stretched out as best we could. I tossed some leaves over Gator, smeared some mud on his face where the sweat had washed it off, then dragged a loose branch in front of the cover. I added some mud to my own exposed skin, then hunkered down next to him and burrowed into the foliage.

We waited.

TEN
Admiral "Tombstone" Magruder

We hiked through the dead, decimated countryside for at least six hours. The jungle still smoldered in spots. The stench of the fire had long since infiltrated our lungs, and I no longer noticed it. Off on the horizon, I could see a vague glimmer of green, probably marking out the extent of the forest fire that had raged through our part of the countryside. However, as far as I could see to the west, the devastation was complete.

With Than gone, the men were oddly silent. I'd expected some protests as to my request that we continue west. A few of the men spoke English, markedly better than they'd let on earlier. They translated for the rest of them. There appeared to be a little disagreement initially, but the majority of them were so stunned by the fire and our narrow escape from it that they fell back as soldiers always do on the original plan. West it was, whether Than was there to supervise the mission or not.

In part, I think it was due to a loss of confidence in their abilities. They were skilled jungle fighters, adept at sensing danger even as it approached and seeking cover within the lush vegetation. In the earlier raid, they'd moved silently through the brush to seek out the guerrillas who were shooting at us, without sound or any other indication that they were even there. I'd admired those skills then. But here, no longer in their accustomed terrain, they moved more slowly. No matter that the going was easier, if you remembered to check for glowing embers under your feet. No matter that they could see further ahead, detect any hostile approach before it got to us. All those things that reassured me left them at a loss, uncertain and tentative, as they moved through the blasted landscape.

Whether it was that further shattering of their world or simply the knot of command in my own voice, we continued on as a group.

I tried to ask about Than, but the men's English disappeared as suddenly as it had appeared upon his departure. Whether they knew something they didn't want to discuss with me or were equally as ignorant, I could not tell. Questions about the radio, the one I was now certain they must have, also were met with stares of blank incomprehension. Frustrated, I gave up trying to communicate and simply walked.

I suppose it would have been reasonable to abort my mission at that time. Now that it was past, the terror of the firestorm was fast fading. It is like that with most life-threatening situations, at least those you survive.

I was content to proceed along—well, perhaps not content, but at least determined.

It was the second air strike that changed my mind.

I heard them before I saw them, the vague, faint whine that indicates an aircraft at altitude inbound. It gradually grew in strength, and now I was certain that I heard the distinctive rumble of Tomcat engines. It shook me out of the course that I'd charted for us, and brought me back to a realization of what my primary duty was. I was an admiral of the United States Navy, not some New Age truth-seeker at liberty to hike this country for as long as I pleased. Bombing runs, air strikes—there was no justification for me remaining in country. I knew which countries were doing the fighting—and which side I belonged on. Knowledge of my father's fate had waited for thirty-some years— it could wait a bit longer.

The Tomcats broke over the ridge in a tight bombing formation, the noise pounding at us, increasing in intensity, then suddenly dropping down to a lower frequency as they passed overhead. I saw them fitted out with ground-attack weapons, dumb iron bombs, and a couple of Sidewinders slung on wing tips just in case. No fighter pilot ever wants to go anywhere without some antiair weapons in his load-out.

They took no notice of us, proceeding inbound on what I knew was a precision bombing run. They bore in over our firescape, then peeled off one by one as they reached an area of green past the horizon. At that distance, I couldn't see the bombs leave the wings, but I recognized from the maneuvers of the aircraft what had happened.

The dull, muffled thud-thud-whomp that came later was all the confirmation I needed. Bombs going off in the distance—the sound travels for incredible ranges, and there is no mistaking it once you've heard it.

"We have to go back," I announced, absolute certainty in my voice. "Go back—now." I pointed back the way we had come.

The man who had taken over lead of the unit in Than's

absence shook his head. "West," he said carefully, mouthing the word as though it were unfamiliar. "Go west."

"No, not anymore. Those fighters, see?" I pointed up at the place where the Tomcats had been. "I have to get back to my ship. Now."

I was aware that my voice was becoming insistent, demanding, and tried to moderate it slightly. After all, I was dependent upon their guidance and good graces for surviving in this hostile land.

"Go back to town," I repeated.

With a rough gesture, the man summoned the rest of his troops to him. There was a short, hurried exchange, punctuated by harsh exclamations and angry voices. Finally, he looked up at me. "No. We go."

I turned away from them, and made as though to start back down the track by myself, hoping that they would follow.

They did—but not for long. Two seized me roughly by the arms and dragged me back to the rest of the squad. The leader gazed at me impassively. He pointed west.

Unarmed, not particularly skilled in surviving in the wilderness, I had few choices. It appeared that these men would use force to insure my compliance. As much as I needed to arrange transport back to *Jefferson*, it looked like I was going west.

We continued on in silence, the balance of power now subtly shifted back to the men who owned this land. I was in the middle of the pack now, surrounded at all times. Two men stayed close to me, evidently with orders to prevent my leaving again.

Another three hours, and we reached the point at which the fire had evidently burned itself out. The damage was not complete now, and tree trunks still stood erect in places. As we moved further west, there was foliage again, and within a short span of time we were back in the jungle. Only the smell lingered to remind us of what had taken place behind us.

Another clearing, and a camp so similar that it could have been built by the same people that had constructed the first one. I dubbed the earlier camp "Horace Greeley" in my mind, just to have someway to refer to it in my notes.

The physical layout was essentially the same, one main building surrounded by three barracks. The wire fence still stood, along with the guard posts.

But there was one, very significant difference that I noticed immediately. This camp was occupied.

"Who?" I asked, pointing at the camp from the cover of brush.

The leader shook his head. "We go down there," he said. He gestured roughly toward the camp. I heard my two guards move closer, ready to insure that I obeyed.

A prison camp—an occupied one. But from here, I could see no indication of its purpose. Was it still a prison camp of some sort? Surely it couldn't be a POW camp, not after all these years. Every rumor or trace evidence of such camps had been completely and absolutely disproved, and I had no basis for believing that this might indeed be such a facility.

Furthermore, there truly was no possibility that my father was alive and living in it. None at all. Despite my intellectual understanding of that, hope still beat wildly for a few moments in my chest.

Hope that was quickly dispelled once we entered the camp itself. It appeared to be nothing more than a military garrison, not a place of confinement. I saw no one under duress or chained, or in any way constrained in their movements. Instead, men in uniforms, ill-fitting cheap tunics and pants, went about what looked like the normal duties of soldiers in garrison.

"Was my father here?" I asked the leader. I did not know how much Than had briefed him on, but suspected he might know the purpose of my mission in his country. "Here?"

He shook his head, and refused to say anything. Instead, he proceeded to the main building. My two escorts indicated that I should follow.

He knocked once on the door, and stepped into the main building. The door opened onto a large area to the right. To the left, there were a series of other doors, most of them closed. The leader walked in, held a short conversation with a sergeant seated at a desk, then walked back to the last office on the left. He rapped softly on the door and waited.

Finally, the door opened. I strained to hear the words of the conversation, but could make out only the tone. Something in the second voice sounded familiar, very familiar. It was clearly not Vietnamese. The accent was wrong, something else—Slavic.

Seconds later Yuri Kursk stepped out of the room and regarded me across the twenty feet that separated us.

He was just as I remembered him, although it had been several years since we'd last seen each other. He was the Ukrainian admiral who'd been on board *Jefferson* during our attempt to resolve a crisis in the Mediterranean. I remembered him well—it had been he who had set me on this path to find my father. His words were as clear as though they were spoken yesterday: "I knew your father."

"He was here also, you know," Yuri Kursk now said.

"You knew I'd come." It wasn't a question as much as a statement. "And you knew I was in country now. That whole charade—why? Did you do it just to torment me?"

Even as I asked the last question, I knew it was more than

that. It always was, in the intricate game of cat and mouse that passes for politics within the former Soviet Union.

Kursk nodded slowly. "I was not certain, but I suspected you would come." He shrugged, dismissing the matter. "We've studied you for a number of years, you know. While you're not entirely predictable—ah, and I wish that you were—there are some things we know about you. Your attachment to family, your sense of duty. If there were an indication that your father might have survived, I felt relatively certain that you would feel obliged to follow his trail, however cold it might be."

"It was your plan."

He nodded. "There is more tied up in this than you know, Admiral Tombstone Magruder. Your father, problems that have simmered since the last time American armed forces waged war in this country, and even more." His eyes glowed at me, intense and penetrating. "I have some small reputation as a political analyst, Admiral. My own reputation rests on the success of this as well."

"So you win," I said, unable to keep the bitterness out of my voice. "Some intelligence network bet, I guess. Can the great Yuri Kursk get Admiral Magruder on the ground in Vietnam? So what's the big prize? A two-week vacation on the Crimean Peninsula?"

Yuri shook his head. "That may be the result eventually, but the stakes are much higher than that. Much higher than even you know." A faint look of amusement crossed his Slavic features. "As much as I would like to claim that I engineered this entire thing simply as a demonstration of my political acumen, I had other motives. Good motives."

"Shall we play Twenty Questions, or are you going to tell me?" The conviction that I'd been a pawn in a game I neither understood nor wanted to play in grew on me steadily. Halfway around the world, away from Tomboy and everything I loved, threatened by the fire that could have killed us—and for what?

"I will have to show you," Yuri said finally. He motioned to a couple of men, barking out a quick command in Vietnamese. One looked stunned, started to protest, and Yuri dismissed him abruptly. He turned back to me. "We will need a vehicle. At least for the first part of the journey. Then we will proceed on foot."

"I'm not going anywhere until you tell me what this is about."

Yuri sighed. He gestured at a small table with two chairs pulled up to it in the center of the room. "Some coffee, something to eat? It will be a few minutes while they make preparations. I will tell you what I can."

"You'll tell me all of it and answer any questions I have or I'm not going anywhere."

"We'll see."

A sergeant produced two mugs of strong, black coffee, along with a serving set containing sugar and cream. A few moments later, plates heaped with steamy stew were brought to the table as well. "It's not fancy, but it is better than field rations," Yuri remarked as he shoveled up a spoonful of stew. "Go ahead, eat."

I glanced back at my Vietnamese contingent. "Feed them too."

Yuri studied me for a moment, then said, "As you wish" His people scurried around to make sure that it happened.

"This all began immediately following America's withdrawal from Vietnam," Yuri began. He broke off a piece of bread from a basket of rolls placed before us, dipped it in the stew, then bit into it. He chewed carefully, his eyes closed and appearing to think, then continued. "It left a power vacuum, you know. For decades, first the French and then the Americans were here, the primary powers within this country. Neither of you were able to accomplish what you wanted." He shook his head gravely, as though contemplating the mistakes of our respective countries. "This area is simply too alien to you, too foreign. It is my theory that peace was never possible here, not in any shape or form. Vietnam is a small country surrounded by more powerful ones, and she must inevitably ally herself with those more geographically close. But nevertheless, the presence of America here, or, I should say, the withdrawal—worked major changes upon this country."

"How so?" I asked, beginning to eat my own stew. It was a strong, slightly gamy meat, but the rich broth and sustenance were welcome.

"China is the problem, of course," Yuri continued. "She always has been, always will be. At least in this portion of the world. And not just for Vietnam—for Ukraine as well."

"And Russia?" I asked.

A slow, thoughtful smile spread across his face. "Ah, Russia. An entirely different matter, of course. We are bound together with Russia's future, for better or for worse. Ukraine and Russia are so similar, share so many parts of history, that I doubt that either of us will ever be what you would call a truly independent nation. But for better or for worse, there we are. It is something that Americans do not understand, the imperatives of geography."

"What about China?" I pressed.

"China views Vietnam as her own special protectorate. You may not agree, but it is simply a fact. At least from the Chinese perspective. And you must understand one other thing as well—China is very, very protective of her own soil. These two facts inevitably lead to one conclusion—

that any dangerous activities should be conducted in one of her protectorates, not within China's own borders."

"Such as?"

"Such as producing nuclear weapons." Yuri finished that statement and took another bite of stew, giving me time to absorb it.

A Chinese nuclear weapons plan on Vietnam soil. I kept my face expressionless and considered the possibility. It was possible, all too possible.

Since I'd been transferred from South Com and was awaiting a billet at one of the Fleet Commander headquarters, I'd been slightly out of the intelligence loop. It was entirely possible that the U.S. knew about this—and I didn't. Still, it seemed I would have heard at least some rumors about it, perhaps the barest warnings and hints in intelligence summaries. Yet there had been no word, nothing that I'd seen.

Batman? Did CVIC know about this? I hoped so, because it would surely influence whatever plans he was developing now to cope with this latest crisis. And hell, I didn't even know what the crisis was. All I knew was I saw Tomcats dropping bombs in country.

"What kind of weapons?" I asked finally. "Strategic?"

Kursk shook his head. "When you say strategic, I am assuming that you are referring to long-range missiles," he said. "It makes a difference for America—but not so much for us. Most areas in Ukraine and Russia are reachable with a shorter-range tactical missile, particularly if such weapons are transported to the Chinese-Russian border. You see, even when we use terms like strategic and tactical, they have entirely different implications for each of our countries."

"So the shorter-range missiles then?" I asked. "Is that what they're making?"

"That's what our sources indicate," Yuri replied. "Ranges of approximately a thousand miles, maybe fifteen hundred. A little bit more, a little bit less—we're not entirely sure. But we do know that they're making them. And not just for China's use—we anticipate that these weapons will find their way onto the black market soon enough."

"But why?" I said, shoving the bowl away from me. Faced with the prospect of escalating nuclear conflict, I found the stew no longer appealing. "For hard currency?"

"That and more. As I said, China is a major force in this area. However, she is also paranoid about her border to a degree Westerners would find it difficult to imagine. Remember, the Chinese take a rather broader view of what is Chinese territory than we do. Every time some ancient Chinese prince or princess married a member of a foreign royal house, China claimed that land as theirs. They track these things oh, so carefully. And while you and I may acknowledge that their claims are ridiculous, the Chinese believe fervently in them. Thus, in their minds, their own soil has been invaded and taken from them repeatedly. Vietnam, the Philippines, the Spratly Islands, and more. The Chinese all truly believe that those are Chinese possessions, and they are ready to defend their rights."

He laughed harshly, an expression of bitterness on his face. "Who knows what they would be like today had they had our experiences. One out of ten Ukrainians were killed during World War II, at least. Even today, the echoes of that invasion influence almost everything we do politically. To us, China might seem like a mere spoiled child, arguing about possessions that were never really hers. But she is a very large, very powerful spoiled child, and one that does not listen to reason."

"So why me? Why my father?" I asked.

Yuri leaned back in his chair and sighed. "This problem must be dealt with. And dealt with immediately. Already the first shipments are being readied for export. Whether they will be deployed on China's border and aimed at Russia and Ukraine, or sold to nations in the Middle East, I do not know. But it would seem to be in both of our interests to keep them from going anywhere."

"Your interest in world stability is very laudable," I answered, an ugly suspicion finally dawning. "But why is Ukraine involved? Why not Russia?"

"Be assured that we consult our cousins often on this matter," Yuri said. "However, as we work our way to a good relationship with our northern neighbor, there are certain trade-offs that must be made. Russia seems to feel that much of this problem is our responsibility—and that we should solve it. They are a proud people, you know, proud to the point of blindness and arrogance. They would not approach you for help—not in this way. We see it as an opportunity to build closer ties with the United States as well as strengthen our own position with Russia by apparently acceding to their request."

"But why is Ukraine responsible?" I asked, suspecting that I already knew the answer.

"You know why." Yuri's eyes were hard and cold. "Must you make me say it?"

I nodded slowly. "You dragged me halfway around the world to participate in this charade. I think you owe me that much."

"Very well. It seems very probable that the nuclear material contained in those weapons came from Ukraine.

You know what the conditions were like immediately following the dissolution of the Soviet Union. The furor over who was to control nuclear weapons, the seizing of the Crimean Peninsula, and the division of the Black Fleet—all was in disarray. Unfortunately, security of the nuclear weapons located on our soil was compromised. We hold the Russians responsible for this, and they us. As I said, matters are not so clear-cut as our cousins would like."

"So somehow, China obtained weapons-grade nuclear material from Ukraine, and is ferrying that into Vietnam into this production facility. And you want our help in putting a stop to it."

"Exactly."

"Why not do it yourselves?"

Yuri sighed. "As much as I would like to say otherwise, we simply do not have the military force at this time. Our economy is still in shambles, and many of our officers have not even been paid for several months. We have the basis to rebuild a strong, potent military, but it will take time. And time is what we do not have. The only solution, since China's growing strength is something that concerns us both, is to bring the Americans in. Quietly, through round-about channels, through one or two trusted agents."

"Then why did the Vietnamese attack us?" I asked. So far everything he was saying made sense except that.

"Are you so certain that they are Vietnamese?" he asked, watching me closely.

"They were MiGs, of course they—they were your MiGs?"

Yuri nodded. "Most of them, repainted to resemble those belong to Vietnam. We have our friends here as well. Senior men who understand the danger that China poses now. And who are willing to work with us to stop it. The government, of course, knows nothing about this. Or if they do, they refuse to admit it." Yuri sighed, a deep sound breaking loose from somewhere inside him. "So you see the dilemma? This action must be carried out outside normal political channels, with all the conflicting loyalties and problems carefully balanced. And it must be done quickly—another reason to avoid normal political protocol."

"You killed some of my people doing this," I said, cold rage flooding my body. "They died for nothing—for your charade."

"If we destroy that nuclear weapons facility, their deaths will be more important than you can possibly imagine," Yuri shot back. "I sympathize with the loss of your men, but do you have any conception of how much life will be lost if those weapons are made available to Iraq and Iran? Or, for that matter, Turkey?"

"Now wait a minute. Turkey isn't—"

"We had our reasons for wanting to sever your ties with Turkey and the Mediterranean," Yuri continued as though I had not spoken. "Turkey is a growing regional power, one that threatens our very stability. They are the gateway for the Muslim hordes that would rip Ukraine in two."

"And now who's being paranoid about borders?" I asked.

Yuri looked outraged. Finally, his expression relaxed and he gave me a small smile. "I had known that you were very blunt, Admiral Magruder. I should have remembered that."

"What if I do agree to help you?" I asked. "I don't even know if it's possible, but supposing it is?"

Yuri held up two fingers. "First, you will do what you find most honorable in the world—stopping wars before they start. While I cannot promise you that your role will ever be publicly known, you will have the eternal gratitude of Ukraine—and Russia as well. From that new relation-ship, I think you will find a number of benefits flow."

"You want me to spy for you?" I asked incredulously. Surely Yuri wasn't offering me money to be a paid infor-mant? If he knew anything about me, he knew just how utterly ludicrous that would be.

"No, of course not. Well, actually, we would—but I would not insult you by making that offer. No, what I had in mind was something far more personal. The truth about your father?"

I sat back, stunned. Was this the deal? My assistance in arranging for the destruction of a nuclear facility in ex-change for the truth about my father? The utterly bizarre nature of this exchange was beginning to wear on me.

"Tell me everything. Then I will decide."

Yuri shook his head. "I cannot. First, I do not have all the answers. No one person does. It will be a journey, a matter of piecing together small bits of evidence to obtain a complete picture. However, I think you will find our assistance quite helpful in this regard."

His dark eyes studied me for a moment, as though deciding how much I already knew. "There have been rumors," he continued carefully, "about Russian participa-tion in the debriefing of American prisoners of war in Vietnam. Most of them are false. Some of them are true."

"And my father?"

Yuri spread his hands out before him. "I cannot say for certain," he said bluntly, and there was a ring of truth I recognized in his voice. "I suspect he might have been interrogated here—in this very camp. In fact, I am almost certain that he was brought here from the first place you visited and held for quite some time. After that, the trail is not entirely clear."

"There were other rumors as well," I said. "That American POWs were taken to Russia for further interrogation. What do you know about that?"

"It is possible. Again, I cannot offer you complete answers. Only our assurances that we will do everything we can, including opening archives so secret that their existence is barely acknowledged." A small, satisfied expression came over his face. "We have intelligence agencies that are quite capable of tracking down information, even when the trail is very, very cold. The GRU, the KGB—they still exist, although they carry other names now. Their full resources would be placed at your disposal."

"First off," I began, "I have no proof that any of this is true. None at all. Now, I'm not accusing you of lying," I continued, holding up one hand to forestall comment, "but you must admit that this entire scenario is inherently improbable. The story you tell, the promises you make—on the face of it, there's some degree of plausibility, but you haven't shown me any hard proof."

"Second, you would have to understand that I cannot promise to keep any secrets for your country. My superiors will have to be told the true story—not all of them, of course, but the ones that matter. Like my uncle. He deserves to know what happened to his brother. I will leave it up to him to decide who else to tell."

Yuri nodded slowly. "I understand the need for proof," he said. "I can supply that—at least in part measure. The truck they are preparing will take us within surveillance range of this facility I spoke of. You will be able to verify it for yourself, at least to the extent that you can do so while there. I believe if you query your U.S. intelligence assets, you may find that they have other confirmation as well."

He paused for a moment, then continued. "And as to the

need for secrecy, while your position is regrettable, I understand it completely. We know we cannot expect any promises on your part. However, when information you have may endanger private citizens or other sources, we will ask you to use your own discretion in disclosing that information to your people. Fair enough?"

I nodded slowly, still overwhelmed by the strategic problem that Yuri had dumped squarely in my lap.

"What's in it for you?" I asked.

Yuri's face was grim. "My country. These weapons must be eliminated. I have a number of reasons for suspecting that Ukraine may be the first target."

"Such as?"

"You know our country somewhat," Yuri said. "The east and the west sectors of Ukraine are radically different. The eastern has more in common with the Middle East, the western with Europe. Until now, we have had more in common with each other than with the outside world, but that might not always be true. Ukraine would form a perfect staging point for Middle Eastern forces to threaten both Russia and Europe. If there is anything in my power to do so, I will not see foreign troops standing on Ukrainian soil again. Not in my generation, and not in my son's. Can you understand how very important that is to us? I doubt it. America is a bastion, protected from land invasion by the oceans that surround her. You have never felt the pounding of enemy bombs on your cities, seen hordes of enemy soldiers flooding into your country. But for us, the prospect is very real—and not so remote." He eyed me coldly for a moment, then said, "You consider yourself a patriot, Admiral Magruder. I know this about you. Do you find it so unbelievable that a Ukrainian officer would regard himself likewise?"

The question hung in the air, demanding an answer. I knew that there were other men in the world that felt as passionately about their nations as I did about the United States, and often our interests culminated in war. And from my studies in history, I knew what Yuri said was true. Ukraine had every reason to fear tactical nuclear weapons, in a way that America would find hard to understand.

But could I do this? Cooperate with the Ukrainians in order to prevent a war? Or was I trying to rationalize it, a motive born out of the deep-seated need to find out what had happened to my father?

"I'll need to get back to my ship," I said finally. "No promises yet, but I will try to verify what you've told me. And yes, I understand why you've approached me in this way. And you must know how desperately interested I am in the fate of my father. But I can make no promises yet—not until I know what you say is true."

Yuri stood, scraping the chair back across the concrete floor. "That is all I can ask for. Come, let us see if the truck is ready. I will take you as close as we can get to the Chinese facility, and you can see that part for yourself. Then we will arrange transportation so that you may return to your carrier. After that, I will rely on your word as a military officer. And on your sense of honor. Fair enough?"

I nodded and stood as well. "Let's go."

The two rickety old deuce-and-a-half diesel trucks made enough noise to warn everyone for one hundred miles that we were approaching. Or at least I thought so—evidently Yuri and his officers had a different opinion. They explained that the jungle muffled sounds, and that we could actually approach to within five miles of the camp without being detected. I doubted it, but kept my reservations to myself.

Too many unbelievable things had happened in the last week for me to start questioning Providence now.

The road was a one-lane rutted path through the jungle, occasionally blocked by fallen trees or other debris. We moved by starts and fits, stopping to clear the path and drag away dead carcasses when we couldn't go around them. After four hours, every bone in my body ached from the continual jolting. Evidently maintaining shock absorbers was not a priority in Ukrainian maintenance practices.

At the indicated point, the driver pulled to a stop, then maneuvered the truck into deep cover. The silence, after so many hours of angry, sputtering diesel noise, was almost overwhelming.

We each took a pack, a small one this time. I noted that the Ukrainians had no compunctions about having their officers carry their own gear, so I shouldered mine myself without comment. It contained a few days' field rations, some water, and a poncho and blanket.

"You know about the jungle now," Yuri said. He gazed thoughtfully at the expanse of trees and undergrowth around us. "It can be your friend—or your enemy. Stay in the middle, and follow the man in front of you. I have assigned him responsibility for your safekeeping."

I looked at the man he indicated, and saw a broad, Slavic face, high cheekbones topping a surprisingly full mouth, and thin-lidded Asiatic eyes. His hair was coarse, dark, and straight, the same shade as his eyes. A scar disfigured his right cheek.

"He is a Cossack," Yuri continued. "If anybody can keep you alive in rough terrain, it is he."

The Cossacks—I knew how much influence they'd gained inside the Ukrainian military establishment, and how instrumental they'd been in Russia's rise to power over the

Soviet Union. Ukrainians, and in particular Cossacks, had always made up a large portion of the higher echelons of Soviet command, disproportionately so. If they had all returned to Ukraine following the dissolution, I suspected that Russia had another motive in tasking Ukraine with dissolving this problem. Simply put, the Cossacks were one of the most warlike and capable military forces anywhere around.

I could feel the Cossack studying me as well, and wondered what he was thinking. What did he see? A sunburned American, already looking ungainly and out of place in the jungle? Or a new ally, one that he would protect at all costs?

It made no difference, I finally decided. In the long run, we would either make it or we wouldn't. A new fatalism had settled over me since my visit to my father's prison camp.

"We go," Yuri said. He motioned to one grizzled veteran, who took point. We moved off in single file through the brush, making entirely too much noise at first, but then settled into quiet, almost silent progress through the trees.

I watched the man in front of me, marveling at how quietly and quickly he moved. He seemed to anticipate the feel of the ground under his feet, sensing hidden noisemaking traps and rough spots before they even were visible. After a while, I began following in his footsteps—quite literally, having already observed that his choice of path was invariably the best one.

We made good time over the relatively low-rolling hills, and soon Yuri stopped us for a quick, whispered conference. "There are guards from this point on," he explained quietly. He pointed at two of his men. "They will go on ahead— clear the path." He gazed over at me with a concerned expression on his face. "You realize, if we have to use force to get close enough to observe, it will simply make time all the more critical for your decision. Once alerted, they will begin moving the site, perhaps to some location inside China. That would pose an entirely different set of political problems for both of us."

I nodded, acknowledging his concern. "You've gone to an awful lot of trouble, Commander Kursk," I said. "I'm not sure I agree completely with your reasoning, but I'll try to see that it doesn't go to waste. If what you've said is true, then it's in both of our best interests to put an end to this quickly."

Yuri nodded, apparently satisfied. I had promised him nothing, just a hard, honest look at the facts. He seemed convinced that once I understood what was truly at stake, I would do as he wished. The possibility of learning about my father was just an added bonus in the package.

We moved out low to the ground now, crouched and sometimes crawling, seeking the deepest cover the jungle had to offer. We snaked our way up another hill, now moving at virtually a crawl.

Suddenly, I heard noise off to my left. Two men, moving heavily through the brush, not taking any particular precautions against being observed.

A Chinese patrol? I realized that by asking that question to myself I had already acknowledged the probable truth of what Yuri had explained. Chinese had been the first word that flashed in my mind—not Vietnamese.

I saw Yuri motion, and two men peeled away from the column toward the noise. Their guns were still slung across their backs, and each carried a large killing knife in his right hand. They disappeared from view quickly as the jungle absorbed them.

I could hear voices now, faintly discernible. I felt as

though someone had slammed me in the gut, knocking all the air out of me.

I stood up, oblivious to the protest of the Cossack in front of me. "Stop—they're American."

A shot rang out, and I heard a shrill yelp of pain. My blood ran cold.

"Damn it, Gator, I told you—" The voice broke off suddenly, but not before I recognized it.

"Bird Dog?" I shouted. "Damn it all, that can't be you!"

Sudden, deadly silence extended over the jungle. The Cossack soldier was at my side in an instant, his knife out now and gleaming in the sun. We had no language in common, but his intent was unmistakable. He'd arrived at the same conclusion I would have in his position—that the odd American officer he'd been chaperoning through the jungle had betrayed them. That this was a trap, somehow arranged to lead the Ukrainian-Cossack contingent into a deadly, killing cross fire.

He was ready to die, I saw that in his face. But equally clear there was his grim determination that if he was going, so was I.

"Wait," I said, holding up my hands to show that they were bare. "You don't understand. Those are my people. Americans, yes?"

A look of uncertainty crossed his face. The blade did not waver. Nor did he look behind him. I could see Yuri approaching now, moving quickly and altogether too noisily through the brush.

"They're Americans," I repeated. "My people—I know that man."

Yuri hissed, clearly not believing me. I had to admit that it sounded pretty improbable myself. What were the odds that two Americans, and ones that I knew personally at that, would be in this very same spot in the jungle? Astronomical.

"It's Bird Dog Robinson and Gator Cummings," I said rapidly. "They were on my ship, they're F-14 pilots. Maybe they were shot down, something like that. I don't know why they're here, but I do know I recognize that voice."

Yuri was silent, assessing the possibilities. It was clear that he found my story as improbable as I did, but something in my face must have convinced him. Finally, he turned and muttered to the Cossack something low and unintelligible. The man nodded once, then slipped away quietly. Yuri turned back to me. "I told him to bring them to me," he said. He studied me, searching for any sign of uncertainty. "If they are who you say they are, then there will be more explanations. Immediately."

"I have not betrayed you," I said, as calmly as I could. "How could I have arranged this, do you think? We are not nearly as Byzantinely intricate on our plans as your people are. You know that already."

Yuri nodded, still not looking convinced.

"Who was shot?" I asked. "One of my men?"

Yuri shook his head. "I do not know. But we will find out very shortly."

"Let me talk to them," I urged. "They may try to take cover, fight back. If I let them know I'm here, they won't."

Yuri appeared to consider that for a moment, then he nodded. "Call to them," he said. "Tell them to walk toward the sound of your voice. I have ordered my men not to kill them immediately—not until we understand what is happening here. You understand, by doing this, you will lead them to us. If this is a trap, they will both die. Before your eyes."

I nodded, accepting the bargain. I took a deep breath, "Bird Dog, Gator—it's Admiral Magruder. Tombstone."

The silence persisted. I could hear no one moving in the brush, not even my Americans, who were as unskilled as I in the jungle.

Still no answer. "Look, what does it take to convince you?" I shouted. "I'm not under duress—you know I was on *Jefferson,* know I left there with an F-14 for the mainland. Maybe you don't know why I came—maybe that's what's got you worried. They told me there were traces of my father's time in a POW camp here. I've been tracking them down. That's what I'm doing in the jungle, Bird Dog. Gator, talk to him—make him listen to common sense. You always could do that."

Still no answer.

"What do you want me to do, recite the Chargers starting lineup for you? That only works in the movies, Gator. Bird Dog, remember Callie? Remember how you wangled your way out to *Jefferson* while you were supposed to be at the War College? And Gator, I know something about you too—that half the time, you're about ready to strangle that young pilot of yours. He's gotten you into more fixes than anyone else around, and you keep bailing him out. But you love him like a brother, don't you? I know you do—I can see it in your face.

"Bird Dog, you were popcorn officer back when I was in command on *Jefferson.* You remember that? You used to come up with the most god-awful concoctions. Like putting pineapple syrup in the popper. I was so glad when you were promoted—at least we could go back to having decent popcorn in the ready room."

By now, I figured they were convinced that I was who I said I was. The only question remaining in their mind would be whether or not I was under duress, being held under gunpoint by Vietnamese forces simply to lure them out into the open. I turned to Yuri. "I have to go to them," I said. "They're not going to believe that I'm operating under my own free will if I don't. And I need something to convince them." I held out my hand for his rifle.

Yuri scowled. "How do I know this is not a trap?"

I stared back at him levelly. "You don't. All you have is my word—and the fact that I've trusted you so far. Now give me the rifle."

Finally, after an apparent inner struggle, Yuri handed over his AK-47. I took it in both hands, held it out in front of me, and walked toward the place where I'd last heard the noise. "Bird Dog, Gator—look. I'm coming toward you. There are some men moving up quietly on you. And I want them to hold still. Tell them, Yuri."

Back behind me, I heard Yuri shout out some commands in Ukrainian. I could discern no change in the bushes, but I was certain that he had told them to halt their advance.

"Look out, you can see me," I called. "I've got a rifle in my hands. Would I have a weapon if I were under duress? Yeah, it could be unloaded—but it's not." I pointed the weapon up at the sky and pressed the trigger briefly. A small spat of gunfire followed. "See? C'mon out, guys. You have to know that I wouldn't do this, not even if I were under duress, if it meant your lives."

Finally, a noise from ahead, maybe forty feet away. Two figures rose slowly, one propping the other up. I saw the mud-streaked and battered faces of Bird Dog and Gator peering out at me. They were still in their flight suits, but they looked much the worse for wear.

I walked toward them, almost running now. I grabbed both of them in a tight embrace. Gator howled, and I pulled

back abruptly. "He's injured?" A flash of rage—had the
Cossacks done this? Had the bullet found Gator's arm?

Bird Dog nodded. "When we punched out—and his
knee. The Vietnamese did something to it, during the
interrogation. He's in pretty bad shape, Admiral." Bird Dog
looked up at me appealingly, the sheer shock of the circumstances and what he'd been through in the last week on
his face. I reached for Gator more carefully now, working
my way around his injuries. "C'mon—we have some
medical gear."

I led them back out of the bush and toward the troop of
Cossacks. Yuri looked relieved as we approached, although
he still scanned the bush around him nervously. "They are
yours," he said finally. "But we have a very large problem
now, Admiral. That gunfire, it will have alerted the Chinese
in the facility. We must leave—immediately."

"No," I said flatly. "I've come this far, and there's too
much at stake. I must see the facility—I must. Send most of
your men back, and have them take Bird Dog and Gator
with them. See that this man gets medical treatment—you
can see that he's injured. But you and I, and your Cossack
friend, will proceed on. Far enough to at least see this
facility, to give me something that I can take back to my
people."

Yuri started to protest, and I cut him off. "I don't own
weapons on that aircraft carrier now, Yuri," I said. "There
are people I have to convince—a few, at least. Just how
important is this to you, Yuri? Are you willing to go as far
as I am to stop this now?"

Yuri looked subdued. Then finally he nodded. He barked
out a few, harsh, quiet orders in Ukrainian, then motioned to
my Cossack escort. "We will see how good you are,
Admiral Magruder," he said quietly. "The odds are that we

will not return. If so, your men's lives are forfeit, along with those that you have already lost."

I nodded. Bird Dog and Gator held hostage against my good behavior. It was a fair enough trade. "Let's get going then."

Most of Yuri's men formed up around Gator and Bird Dog. One large, massive Cossack swung Gator over his shoulder, the movement oddly gentle. They may not have been from the same nation, they may have been on different sides of too many conflicts in the past, but one-on-one there is something about one fighting man that another recognizes. They moved off into the brush, disappearing, and leaving us alone.

The Cossack grunted, and muttered something sharp. Yuri nodded. "We need to clear out of this area immediately," he said. He pointed off to his right. "There's another path—a hard one, up the mountain, but it will be more secure. And we will be able to see people approaching us as well."

The Cossack took point, I took the middle position, and Yuri brought up the rear. We moved quickly, as quietly as we could, but concentrating on speed at the expense of some noise. I could already hear shouts and cries from somewhere far off floating in the air, and it was evident that my brief burst of gunfire had aroused some interest from the camp.

A harder course this time, sometimes up virtually sheer rock walls and around massive boulders. We threaded our way along animal tracks, ghosts moving through this land that belonged to none of us. Finally we reached the crest of the hill, and Yuri tugged me into position. He handed me a pair of binoculars.

"See—there it is." He moved my head slightly in the direction he'd indicated.

I could see a compound, one markedly different from the prison camps I'd inspected earlier. I tweaked the binoculars, bringing the picture into sharper focus. There were men in uniform there, although not the style I recognized as being either Ukrainian or Vietnamese. No, they were different, looser-fitting and darker in color. Many of them carried weapons at the ready, and there was an air of activity and alarm in their movements.

"Hurry," Yuri murmured. "I do not know how much time we will have."

I stared at them again, looking for some indication that this place was what Yuri claimed it was. The faces were undoubtedly Asiatic, probably Chinese. Still, the facial features were well within the range of physiognomy demonstrated by the Vietnamese people. I could not be certain—not based on their appearance alone.

The sun glinted off something pinned to one man's shirt, and I focused on that, straining to make out the details. It was a badge of some sort, white and plain. There was no lettering visible on it.

Suddenly, it hit me. I dropped the binoculars, handed them back to Yuri, and said, "Let's go. You're right, Yuri. Get us out of here."

Without wasting time for questions, the Cossack led the way. We moved over hills, the sounds of pursuit faintly audible in the jungle behind us. We were running now, crashing through brush as though there were no need for silence, desperately putting distance between us and the weapons behind us.

I panicked, gasping for breath, swearing that I would make this last run if I would do anything in my life. What I had seen was just too vital, of too critical importance for U.S. interests and stability in this region. The knowledge must not die with me, not when so many good men had already sacrificed their lives to get me here.

Finally, we reached the one remaining truck. We jumped into it, fired it up, and were speeding back down the one-lane trail toward Yuri's garrison.

"What did you see?" Yuri asked finally, as he regained control of his breathing. "All my arguments, all my facts—what did you see?"

I closed my eyes for a moment, recalling the brief flash of light on that white badge. It seemed odd, out of place in a jungle camp, and that was what had first caught my attention. After looking at it for a moment, some vague memory came back to me, and I remembered the last time I had seen something similar.

It had been on an inspection tour of the engineering spaces on board USS *Jefferson*. Every engineering technician who works down there is required to have in his or her possession at all times one simple piece of gear. It is their first line of defense, their only indication that something might be going terribly and horribly wrong inside the bowels of the engineering plant.

The *Jefferson* is a nuclear-powered carrier. And what I had seen on my engineering technicians' coveralls, and on the man on guard duty in the compound, was a dosimeter. A small one, the kind a technician clipped to his clothing to monitor his exposure to radiation.

ELEVEN
Lieutenant Commander "Bird Dog" Robinson

30 September
USS Jefferson

I don't think I've ever been as happy to see anyone as I was to see Admiral Magruder. After days and days in the jungle, at first I figured I was starting to hallucinate. You know, like seeing mirages? But I wouldn't have thought that Admiral Magruder's face would have been that high on my list of hallucinations.

By the time I first heard his voice, I was getting seriously worried about Gator. We'd been making progress slowly, but in the last couple of hours he'd started to look like real shit. His face was an odd, green, pasty color and he'd stopped talking. He groaned occasionally, and made it worse by trying not to. I could tell he was hurting, bad, and we needed to do something right damn quick.

All I knew was we were heading south, toward the part of Vietnam that was supposed to be friendly. How much that counted for, I didn't know. Not given the last air strike on *Jefferson*. Still, it was better than heading for the ocean and trying to swim home.

By the time I decided that Admiral Magruder's voice

wasn't some fever dream or nightmare, the possibility that we might not make it was starting to dawn on me. It's not something I'd ever admit willingly, but it was there. But how could I give up with Gator depending on me? I couldn't. So it was one foot in front of the other, stumble, fall, get up, and move on. If we were gonna die, we were gonna do it on our feet.

If it had just been me, I would have stood up as soon as I heard the admiral's voice. But with Gator barely conscious, depending on me to keep him alive, I wasn't going to take the chance.

It was the gunfire that finally convinced me. Not that I needed much more. There is something about Admiral Magruder that is rock solid. It goes through and through to his very core. He can be a nasty bastard if you cross him—just ask the Chinese, or the Ukrainians, or any one of a number of assholes around the world that he's put down recently—but if you're one of his, you know he'll come after you.

As the admiral walked toward me, silent shapes rose out of the bushes around me. Strangers, not Vietnamese—Russians or Asians of some sort, judging by their faces. But their appearance didn't worry me half as much as the knives I saw in their hands.

Before I knew it, Gator and I were hustled into a large diesel truck and headed back out toward civilization. The admiral told us to go, said he had something else to take care of. I didn't try to pump him—by then, I was too worried about Gator to do anything else but be thankful that we were alive.

When they finally drove back into camp, Admiral Magruder's face was as scary as I have ever seen it. Something had pissed him off and bad. All I knew was I wouldn't be on the receiving end of whatever he had planned.

He was traveling with the Russian-looking guy, the one I'd seen on *Jefferson* last time we were in the Med. Not Russian—Ukrainian, I remembered. The details came flooding back in. Hadn't he been the asshole who'd planted the bomb next to Tombstone's cabin? And if so, what was the admiral doing cozied up to him?

And just what were the two of them doing in Vietnam? I knew why the admiral was here. That story had made the mess decks intelligence circuit two seconds after he'd arrived on board. It was a hell of a thing, going after your dad in the jungle, and more than one of us admired him more than we could ever say.

Still, this combination seemed pretty strange. Was there any possibility—?

No. I swore at myself for even thinking it. But stories of the Walker spy scandal kept coming back to haunt me. Now there was a man that the Navy had trusted, had trusted completely. He had access to the most classified material around. He'd had security checks, polygraphs, and every other security measure that the armed forces could dream up to safeguard their classified material.

Yet he'd been a spy. A damned good one, from what I could hear.

Details of other cases nagged me too. The CIA guy that got caught, Lonetree the Marine. What about them? Was there any possibility, however slight, that Admiral Magruder could be involved in something like that? Even unwittingly—hell, it would have to be unwittingly.

But what could possibly have pushed him to those limits? There was only one thing that I knew of—if the bad guys got a hold of Tomboy. Even then, I wasn't certain he would do it.

Could they have Tomboy? It was possible, I guess. We'd all been flying back-to-back missions, the skipper included. She wouldn't have wanted to be left out of that, and if she'd been flying combat missions, there was every chance she'd been shot down. Shot down, captured, and once they realized who she was, turned into the most heinous sort of bargaining chip. Had that happened?

I studied the admiral for a moment, looking at how intense he was. It was possible—what else could bring that look to his face?

Finally, I arrived at a decision. Gator wasn't any help— he was still out cold, although he was getting medical attention now.

I would keep an eye on Admiral Magruder, at least for the time being. At least until we got back to the boat and I was certain that there was no funny business going on. I'd probably have a chat with Lab Rat as well, maybe not tell him directly what worried me, but at least let him know what I'd seen and heard.

Tombstone came in to have a look at Gator. He crouched down next to the cot and put one hand on my backseater's good shoulder. "How you doing, Gator?" he asked softly.

Gator moaned, and his eyelids flickered. "Admiral?" The voice was a weak, hoarse whisper. "I feel like shit, if you want to know the truth."

Tombstone smiled, something I hadn't seen him do very often. "I bet you do. We're headed back to the ship in a couple hours, Gator. You hang on—you're all right now, and you're gonna be fine."

He patted my backseater's shoulder again, then glanced over at me. "Tell me what happened."

I ran back through the parts I could remember, the last battle with the MiG and Gator command-ejecting us. Then General Hue, the guy I thought of as Fred, and the surprisingly easy time we had of it at first. And the dirt cave—what it was like in there, the bombing, and the providential crack in the dirt ceiling that had finally led to freedom.

I glossed over the time in the jungle, not remembering a lot of it. It didn't make any difference anyway—what mattered was that we were here now. I concluded with: "So we're headed back to the boat, Admiral?"

He nodded. His expression had gotten markedly somber when I talked about the cave-ins and the cave, and now he looked angry. "You bet your ass we are," he said softly. "I've got some things to check out." He glanced around, making certain there was no one else in the room with us. I edged a bit closer to him.

"Listen, Bird Dog, pay attention. This is important. On the off chance that one of us doesn't make it out, you've got to get word back to Admiral Wayne. Or to Lab Rat, or to any other senior official you can find. It's important—so important, that if it comes down to sticking with me and Gator or getting off on your own and getting the information out, you've got to go. It's more important than either of our lives. You understand that?"

I started to protest, and Tombstone grabbed me by the shoulder and shook me. "No arguments here, mister. There's more to fighting wars than killing MiGs. If this doesn't get back to the right people, more people are going to die than you ever thought possible in one war."

"What's this about, sir?" I asked. I'd go along with it for now, make my own decision when I heard what the admiral had to say.

So he told me. All of it. Everything from finding his father's Horace Greeley inscription scratched on a prison camp wall to the dosimeter he'd seen pinned to the uniform of the Chinese soldier in the last camp. When he finished, I didn't know what to say.

"Will you promise me, Bird Dog?" he asked. "Swear that you'll do everything you can to get this stuff outta here. Swear it!"

"I swear, Admiral." A heavy, dark feeling settled over my gut. The idea of abandoning Gator anywhere, even in the care of the admiral, was so utterly repulsive that I could barely stand to think about it. We'd been through so much together, almost died together too many times. He counted on me just like I counted on him—it was something that went beyond mere trust.

But this was important—too important. The admiral was right.

If he was telling the truth, one part of my mind said nastily. He could also be part of it, asshole. He's trying to mislead you, use you. There's something going on here that you don't understand.

I ignored the voice. If you couldn't trust your admiral and your backseater, who could you trust then? And without that, then life wasn't worth a whole lot.

Tombstone seemed satisfied by what he saw in my face, so he nodded and looked relieved. "I know I can count on you. Now, let's see how good these people are at keeping their word." He stood, brushed off his jungle garb, and left.

I took his place beside Gator, watching carefully to see how he was doing. His fever seemed to be abating some, and his breathing was slow and steady. The knee was an ugly, swollen mass of purple and red, probably dislocated or permanently injured. Could he make it back to flight status?

I wasn't sure, but his knee looked bad. I'd seen people permanently grounded for less.

The arm was a problem too, although probably it could be fixed easier than the knee. That is, if they got ahead of the angry red infection I saw streaking in his skin now.

All in all, Gator wasn't out of the woods yet.

Or the jungle.

Whatever else you can say for them, the Ukrainians had some decent communications gear. Tombstone later told me that they had a list posted on one wall in the radio shack of the clear circuits—the ones without crypto gear on them—that *Jefferson* used. It was a matter of just a few minutes to go out over military air distress frequencies to them, coordinate a change of frequencies, and then get Admiral Wayne on the other end.

Jefferson's good, as good as they come. An hour and a half later, a CH-46 escorted by two F-14s was overhead, looking anxiously down at the landing zone and checking for wind and rotor clearance. There wasn't much space to spare, but the pilot made it. I know if I'd been in his shoes, nothing in the world would have kept me from getting on the ground.

The admiral helped me carry Gator out to the helo. The Ukrainians had him on a stretcher, but I wasn't willing to trust them with this part of it—Gator was my responsibility, mine alone. The admiral might have felt differently, but I knew he'd understand.

That helo took off like it had afterburners, shooting up out of the trees that surrounded the LZ like sheer speed would compensate for any inadvertent contact with a tree branch. I damned near lost my lunch, what little of it I had left.

Thirty minutes over the countryside, gazing down at it, I

saw a swath of blackened land, evidence of some fire that had raged out of control. The one the admiral had told me about? I glanced over at him, and saw him nodding confirmation. "It was headed west," the admiral said. He pointed out the cave where they'd taken shelter to survive it.

There wasn't much more to say. The admiral had asked me a couple of times about my experiences in the dirt cave where we'd been held, and I found myself markedly disinterested in talking about it. Every time I started to say something, the cloying, dank feeling came back to me. The suffocation, air compressed around us, watching Gator curled in a small pool of water on the deck . . . maybe someday I'd be able to talk about it—but not now.

I finally started breathing easy once we were over the beautiful blue waters off the coast of Vietnam. I stared out at the horizon searching for the one sure thing that constituted safety in my little world—my aircraft carrier.

And there she was finally, stately and serene on the horizon. At first, all I could see was the antennas, that giant air-search-radar mast bristling with electronics. Then as we approached, the rest of her came into view. And finally, gloriously, that beautiful, sacred flight deck that I'd faced so many times myself. After seeing the admiral's face in the jungle, this ranked high on my list of things I'd never forget.

The deck was green, and we were waved in for a quick landing. The pilot took us in hard, slowing at the last moment to feather us back into a gentle landing. Corpsmen were crowding into the helicopter even before the rotors stopped turning, and they immediately took possession of Gator. This time, I gave him up. They could do more for him than I could.

Tombstone turned to me, an exhausted look on his face. Dark circles ringed his eyes, and the lines in his face were deeply etched. He smelled too, though I wasn't about to point that out to him. No doubt my own personal body odor was just as disgusting.

Again, the admiral seemed to be reading my thoughts. He smiled slightly, then said, "You look like shit."

"With all due respect, Admiral, so do you." I tried to muster an answering smile, and found to my surprise that sheer relief let me do it.

He stood, stretching slowly, waving off the corpsmen that were swarming around both of us. "I'm okay," he said. He looked over at me. "How about you?"

"I'm fine," I said, following his lead. The urge to appear just too, too casual for my own good was upon me now. It's something we all do when we've pulled off some incredible hair-raising feat that never should have worked. We cool it, pretend like it was in the bag all the time. "What now, Admiral?" I asked.

He fought off another medic, then shrugged. "We're going to go see Admiral Wayne—both of us," he said as he caught my startled look. "You got a problem with that?"

"Uh, no, sir," I said, hesitating for a moment. I remembered the last time I'd seen Admiral Wayne—God, had it even been this decade? I'd been pissed about the flight schedule, stormed into his office, and demanded to get on it.

Admiral Wayne should have shot me at that point, Hell, *I* would have shot me.

The prospect of seeing him again made my stomach flutter. But after the last week, I could handle a few nerves.

"Let's get going then," the admiral said. "Before these guys and girls decide to nail us with some morphine and kidnap us down to Medical."

"Uh, Admiral?" I asked. "Shouldn't we get cleaned up first? I don't know about you, but I'm pretty dirty." A massive understatement if there ever was one. I was caked in dirt from scalp to toes, even inside my tattered flight suit. Even worse, I felt like things were crawling on me.

Tombstone laughed. "Batman's not going to mind," he said. "And the sooner I tell him what's going on, the sooner we can take care of the problem. C'mon—besides, it'll be good for him. Getting exposed to what a real fighter pilot looks like for a change."

TWELVE

Admiral "Batman" Wayne

30 September
USS Jefferson

The biggest messages sometimes come in curt, oddly accented voices barely audible through the crackle of static. This was one of those. Not only was Tombstone on his way back to the carrier, but he had a "friend" he wanted to bring along.

Tombstone, Bird Dog, a stranger and Gator emerged from the helicopter, Gator on a stretcher. Until I'd actually seen them on my flight deck, I'd hardly dared to believe it was true. Tombstone I hadn't been certain about, but I'd been worried about his safety. And Bird Dog and Gator, as much as I hated to admit it, I'd virtually given up for lost. It was like seeing ghosts walk back across the flight deck. The gongs confirmed it, four of them, followed by the words "Admiral United States Navy." That shook me out of the silent fascination with the camera and brought me to my feet. I waited standing in the middle of my office, barely able to contain myself. I'd wanted to be up on the flight deck, just to see for myself. But with threat indications all over the board, I needed to be here, right next to TFCC.

Tombstone would understand—in my place, he would have done the same thing.

There was no knock, no warning. The door to my office burst open, and I faced two of the dirtiest, filthiest, smilingest aviators I have ever seen in my life.

Tombstone crossed the room in three quick strides and buried me in a bear hug so hard I thought he'd crack ribs. Good thing I was in my old khakis—mud and dirt cascaded down off of him, smearing everything that he touched.

Not that I cared. Hell, I would have let him hug me naked if he'd wanted to at that point.

"You made it back," I finally said as Tombstone pulled back. There was a wholly joyous expression on his face, one of sheer pleasure in being alive.

"Did you let Tomboy know?" he asked immediately. He glanced around the room. "I thought she'd be here."

"She would have, if she'd known you were coming back in like this," I said. "She's flying CAP right now, on a double-cycle mission. Should be back on deck as soon as we get that piece-of-shit helicopter you flew in on out of the way."

Then the stranger came into my office, and now I recognized him. He was Yuri Kursk, and it rankled having him on my ship. Things had a tendency to explode when he was around. I'd never been able to prove it, but I was convinced he was a player in too many dirty tricks on our last cruise. From the look on Kursk's face, Tombstone had already done a good job of convincing him what shallow ice he was on on board my ship.

"But she knows?" Tombstone asked again. "You told her I'm okay, right?"

"Yeah, we told her. She knows. She said to tell you after she hits the tanker, she'll buster back."

Tombstone nodded, relief flooding his face. "It's just as well. Batman, I've got to talk to you." He gestured at Bird Dog, who was maintaining a politely nonchalant expression, pretending he hadn't watched two admirals pound each other on the back like old fools. "He needs to be here too," Tombstone continued. "Both of us have got things you have to know, but I'll go first."

"Just a second," I said. I was used to Tombstone bossing me around, but damn it, this was my ship. And my pilot who'd just come back from the dead.

I crossed over to Bird Dog and stood nose-to-nose with him for a moment, trying to scowl at him. "The next time you want me to put you on the flight schedule, I'm gonna say no," I said finally. "Damn fool—getting yourself shot down."

There was a startled expression on Bird Dog's face for a moment, replaced slowly by a grin. "I guess next time I won't come banging on your door, Admiral."

I threw my arms around him, and gave him the same hard, quick hug that Tombstone had given me. Hell, I was already filthy, and I was so damn glad to see this young idiot back on my boat that it seemed the only right thing to do.

"Welcome back, Bird Dog," I said finally. "Now you two go ahead and sit down—hell, don't mind the couch. I'll replace it if I have to."

With that, the two filthy aviators settled down on the couch in front of my glass table. Tombstone started first.

He cut right to the chase, and confirmed the reports I'd received about a possible nuclear-production facility in Vietnam. He mentioned the dosimeter, then the details that pertained to Yuri Kursk. I knew better than to interrupt him. Tombstone had been in my shoes before, and he knew what would be important to me and what wouldn't. He glossed

over some of the personal details, and I noted pain flitted
through his face. I made a mental note to get him alone later,
to find out what had really happened on his search for his
father.

"You need to hear about Bird Dog's adventure too,"
Tombstone concluded. "Start with General Hue," Tombstone ordered him.

Bird Dog got through his tale just as quickly, albeit with
a few more stumblings and a trace of braggadocio padding
it out. He hadn't had the years of experience that Tombstone
and I had had in debriefing admirals, and it showed. I caught
Tombstone smirking slightly, and shook my head slightly to
let him know I'd seen it. What we saw was us, sitting in
front of us as we had sat in front of other admirals twenty
years earlier.

Finally, Bird Dog concluded his story. He sat quiet,
obviously uncertain about whether we wanted him to
remain here or to leave.

"Go get a shower and some food, Bird Dog," I said
gruffly. "Then get down to Intel—Commander Busby is
going to want to see you right away, I know."

"Thank you, Admiral," he said, and stood. An expression
of relief crossed his face. "I'll do that."

After Bird Dog left, I gazed at Tombstone somberly. "You
want to shower first, or do we go over the plans now?"

"A quick planning session, then I'll shower," Tombstone
said. He reached down, scratched at his crotch, and grimaced. "I'll tell you the rest of it after I'm cleaned up."

I had the Chief of Staff call in my Strike Ops Officer, my
Operations Officer, CAG, and Lab Rat. They all looked
stunned as they walked into the room and took in Tombstone's condition, but they quickly masked their expres-

sions. I cut through the pleasantries, and told them what we had to do.

Strike nodded thoughtfully. "Sure, we can pull that one off. Plenty of weapons on board. The political and international implications, though, that's not in my ballpark. It's up to you, Admiral. How hard do you want to hit them?"

Yuri Kursk spoke up immediately. "There can be no doubt that we have to eliminate this," he announced. "The site must be so completely demolished that there is no hope of extracting usable fissionable material from the debris. You understand that, of course?"

"I understand enough," I said. The bastard had some nerve, sitting in my office and lecturing me after trying to shoot down a couple of my pilots. I ought to turn him over to the squadron and let them teach him a fatal lesson about attacking American forces.

But hell, what Kursk wanted us to do was a good idea—I went along with it completely—but no pissant Ukrainian commander was going to start planning my operational missions for me. Bad enough that they'd had to trick us into doing what we would have done anyway, but like I said before—this was my ship. The little shit needed to start learning that.

"Dumb bombs is all we have left," the Operations Officer said. "We used the penetrating rounds on the revetment. How heavily is this place fortified?"

I glanced over at Lab Rat. "We can expect some concrete shielding, of course. The fact that they're wearing dosimeters means they're at least conscious of and paying attention to the radiation levels. Other nations are usually a lot less picky than we are, but I'd expect to see some degree of shielding."

"How much?" Strike pressed. "Will the five-hundred-pound bombs do the job?"

"You know anything about this, Kursk?" I asked, turning back to the Ukrainian. "Seems your intelligence has been pretty good to date."

"I'd be speculating, Admiral," he said, a new note of respect in his voice. "But I would agree with Commander Busby. The odds are that the shielding is adequate, but just barely. Five-hundred-pound bombs should do it."

"Well, then." I stood, dismissing the group. "Get your plans together—I'd like to roll on this tonight, if we can."

"Gonna be a tougher target at night," Strike said.

"We've got good ground intel, though," Lab Rat answered. "I'm pretty confident on my SAM site locations, and I think you can get around them. We've put a lot of time into this one."

To make up for the stuff that you didn't know last time, I added silently. Over the last week, Lab Rat had been clearly preoccupied by his failure to provide adequate intelligence to his aircrews. I was glad he would have this opportunity to make it up to them.

"Tonight," I said, concluding the discussion. "Let's make it happen, gentlemen."

They all left, except for Tombstone and Yuri Kursk.

"And what about me, Admiral?" Yuri asked. "I wish to be a part of this—it is my right."

I wheeled on him. "Nobody has rights on board my ship unless I give them to them. You got that straight, mister?" While he might not be one of my junior officers, he was very definitely junior around here.

Yuri nodded. "I must go with them," he repeated, as stubborn a man as I've ever seen stand in front of me. "I brought your Admiral Magruder back, I risked much in this plan—I must be in on the final strike."

I sighed. "And just what are you going to do about it if I say no? You're way out of line, mister, and I've got half a mind to just turn you over to Ambassador Wexler and let her deal with you."

The conference between Than and Wexler had not been going well, not as far as I could tell. Of course, I wasn't invited to sit in on the closed meetings, but I could see the tightness around her eyes at the evening meal, hear the polite ice and venom dripping out of her voice every time she addressed Than. This impudent young officer in front of me might just have the key to resolving the entire matter.

"Admiral, please." Now the Ukrainian's voice had taken on a pleading note. "At least consider it, Admiral. I know the country well, every landmark and guidepost in it. If the strike is confused or has problems finding the target, I can get them there. I will do this, Admiral. It is more important to my country than even to yours. You must understand that."

"There is a whole lot I don't understand about this whole situation," I replied slowly. "Starting with why we have to come up with this back-alley solution to resolve this. As Admiral Magruder probably told you, there are ways to deal with this sort of problem that don't involve killing my aviators first."

Yuri nodded, and seemed to draw back inside himself. "I am sorry for that, Admiral. It was necessary."

"Then you write the letters to their families," I shot back. "You tell them how their husbands and wives died in the line of duty, died for something important. Make it meaningful for them, why don't you? Find some way to make it

easier for them in the years to come that they'll be alone,
raising kids, trying to make a go of it."

Yuri straightened, and a new determination was evident
in his eyes. "I cannot make it any easier for them," he said
quietly. "And they may never know why their spouses paid
the ultimate price. But I can tell you one thing—if you do
not do this, if you do not give this mission every chance for
success, you will be the one who has to live with the
consequences. Not I."

An utter, dead silence settled over the room. Tombstone
appeared withdrawn, disengaged from the entire confrontation. I appreciated that, since this was clearly my call, not
his. Yet nonetheless, I figured his advice would be helpful.
I turned to him. "Any thoughts, Admiral?"

Tombstone appeared not to hear me at first, and then his
eyes slowly refocused on me. I noticed how much older he
looked, drawn and drained, as though his time on the ground
had sapped something vital out of him. He shook himself
slightly, as though ridding himself of a bad dream, and some
of the tiredness drained away. I saw the Tombstone I had
known for twenty years, strong and confident, the best damn
stick I'd ever known in my life.

"There's something to what he says," Tombstone began
slowly. "There are a lot of things that can go wrong with a
night mission. You know that." He glanced at Yuri, and
something invisible passed between the two of them. It
bothered me.

"But I can't support putting you in an F-14 for this
mission," Tombstone continued to Yuri, his voice still
thoughtful. "There's no pilot on this ship that I'd risk with
an inexperienced backseater, and I'm not all that sure that I
want a Ukrainian having a close-up and personal look at our
gear from inside the cockpit. No offense, mind you. But

there are times when we haven't been on the same side of the fight. You will remember that."

Yuri nodded, and stayed silent. I gave him points for that.

"However, it might be possible to put him in an E-2," Tombstone added. "Sure, there's a lot of classified gear in there as well, but there's a little bit more space. We can take some precautions, make sure we don't compromise anything." He glanced over at me, saw I was paying attention, and said finally, "There's only one thing that matters to me, old friend, and that's making something good come out of all of this. If having him on scene increases our chances of making that happen, then I'm all for it."

"He could sit in Combat," I argued, aware that my argument was weak. "You can see the entire picture from there."

Tombstone shook his head. "But not the terrain—not the actual radar sweep and raw data. If necessary, we can take that E-2 right in with us, providing fighter coverage for it, and get an eyeballs-on assessment of exactly where we are. It's not something I'd like to do ordinarily, but if we have to do it to get the mission done . . ." Tombstone shrugged, making it clear that while he had his opinions on the matter, the final decision was mine alone.

I sighed. "There are never any easy ones in this office, are there?" I asked him.

Tombstone shook his head, a faint smile on his face. "The easy ones get solved way down below you. Everything that gets up this far is impossible, ugly, and bites. You ought to know that by now."

"I do—but thanks for reminding me."

I turned to Yuri. "I'll think about it, okay? No promises— but I'll think about it."

"I can fly an F-14," Yuri said unexpectedly.

"Off a carrier?" Tombstone demanded.

Yuri appeared to be about to elaborate, then shook his head slowly. "Only once. And I have never landed."

"Not good enough then. I'll think about the E-2, that's all."

A sudden banging on my door distracted all three of us. I saw Tombstone jump; I wondered how long that startled reaction would stick with him.

"Admiral? Admiral Wayne?" The voice was all too familiar. I had taken the precaution of locking the door prior to starting the conference, but I was afraid that might not even be enough given who was on the other side of it.

Tombstone let out a low, involuntary groan. Yuri looked puzzled.

"Admiral, I know you are in there. I've got to see you immediately." The voice would brook no denial.

"In my stateroom," I said quietly to Tombstone. "Go ahead and take a shower—you'll find a spare flight suit in there. Might be a little short on you, but it's better than that filth you're wearing. You too," I said, taking in Yuri with a gesture. "Scoot—go hide."

Yuri's head swiveled back and forth between me and the door. "Who is it?" he asked quietly.

I looked at Tombstone, then grimaced. "A reporter— Pamela Drake, ACN."

Yuri's face lit up. "I have seen her," he breathed. "May I meet her?"

Tombstone shot me a look of disgust, and I shrugged. Such are the consequences of exporting democracy and international news reporting around the globe. "Maybe. But not now. And I know Admiral Magruder sure as hell doesn't want to talk to her. Go on, both of you—in my cabin until I get rid of her."

Tombstone and Yuri walked to the back of my room and slipped into the large bedroom just off it. The door shut, and I heard by the small click that Tombstone had locked it.

I went to the door of my office, unlocked it, and opened it suddenly. Pamela, who'd been about to knock on the door again, stumbled in. She recovered herself, placed her hands on her hips, and glared at me. "Where is he?" she asked.

"Where's who?" I tried for an innocent smile, knowing it wasn't coming off.

"You know who," she snapped. "Tombstone. He's on this ship—I heard the 1MC announcement."

"Oh, that." I swore silently, wishing I'd remembered to tell the bridge to lay off the formalities. "That wasn't Tombstone—it was someone else."

"Who?" Pamela demanded. As I fumbled for a quick answer, an expression of satisfaction crossed her face. "Yes, it was. Don't bother lying to me, Admiral. I know he's here."

"Even if he were, I'm under no obligation to put you in touch with him," I said stiffly. I hate being caught short fumbling for a lie. "I haven't even seen him myself yet. And you will recall, Ms. Drake, that you've agreed to limit your movements around the ship to those I have allowed for you. We clear on that?"

Pamela glanced around the room, and her smile broadened. "Oh boy, this is going to be a hell of a story," she said softly. "Admiral, you've got to let me talk to him. I know he's here."

"He's not," I answered roughly.

"You don't lie very well, Admiral." She pointed at the couch on which Bird Dog and Tombstone had been sitting. I turned, and one look at it told me where I'd made my mistake.

The soft, cream-colored fabric was coated with mud, dirt, and leaves. There were two large filthy patches on it, and a third slightly cleaner spot where Yuri himself had sat. I groaned despite myself.

"Listen, Pamela, for old time's sake—can't you give the man a break?"

She crossed over to my sitting area, plopped her butt down on the one clean chair—mine—and smiled. "If you tell me what's going on and give me an exclusive, I promise to hold up on reporting it. How about that?"

"I could have you thrown in the brig," I offered, now goaded past the point of tolerance. Damn it, why did everybody on this ship feel like they were allowed to give me orders?

"Which worked so well the time that Tombstone tried it," she shot back acidly.

About that she'd been right. Although the confrontation in the Mediterranean had eventually escalated to just that contingency, the resulting furor that Tombstone had faced over tossing Pamela in the brig had only been mitigated by the criminal charges brought against her for interfering with military operations. Both sides counted it a draw, but the controversy that had raged made both sides bitter.

"Or just send you back to the mainland," I continued as though she hadn't spoken. "In fact, I'm inclined to do just that. Ambassador Wexler and Ambassador Than are planning on leaving tonight."

Pamela sucked in a quick breath. "Oh, really?"

"Yes." Although they didn't know it themselves yet. Damn it, the last thing I needed was for them to hear it from her. "At least, I'm pretty certain they will be," I amended, trying to give myself an out.

Pamela settled back in the chair, looking less and less

inclined to leave my quarters voluntarily. "Well, perhaps I'll go with them. Or perhaps I won't. It depends on where the story is, and right now I don't know. I will—by then I'll know."

That wasn't bragging, just plain fact. Pamela had a worldwide reputation for being able to sniff out the story at any locale. She operated on intuition and guts, showing up on scene before any other reporter and getting in the middle of the action faster than even the military forces. I pretty much knew what her choice would be, if things went as I thought they would. She'd want to be on *Jefferson*, trying to get the inside scoop on the attack.

Somewhere in the background, I heard the splashy sound of a shower starting. Pamela's eyes lit up. "And who is in your shower, Admiral?" she asked gently. "Could it be who I think it is?"

She was on her feet in a flash, heading for my bedroom door. I stood and tried to head her off, but she slipped past me.

She tried the knob, and discovered it was locked. She pounded on the door and hollered, "Tombstone! I know you're in there, damn it!"

I grabbed her around the waist and jerked her back. "You will not invade my private quarters," I said angrily. "Of everything you've pulled, Pamela, this is about the—"

The door slowly opened, and a clean, freshly flight-suited figure stepped out. It was Yuri.

He tendered one hand to Pamela Drake, and said in a voice approaching awe, "I'm Yuri Kursk. It is a pleasure to make your acquaintance, Ms. Drake."

I heard Pamela suck in a hard, harsh breath, then transform her face instantly into a winning and sweet expression of welcome. "And a pleasure to meet you, Mr. Kursk," she purred. She took him gently by the elbow, drawing him over to the corner of my room. "We've met before, haven't we? Or at least in passing."

"Met" was probably too strong a word. Pamela had finagled herself on board *Jefferson* during the last Mediterranean conflict, just before Yuri had planted a bomb outside Tombstone's quarters. I wondered what particular version of double-talk enabled her to come up with that interpretation.

"I am a great fan of yours," Yuri began, damn his hide. He was obviously completely taken with her, something I had suspected from the first moment he'd mentioned her name. "Perhaps we could talk."

"I'd like that very much," Pamela said, her teeth delicately nibbling on her lower lip. The smile was genuine now, warm and welcoming. "Could we go somewhere private? My stateroom perhaps?"

"No, you don't," I said. I grabbed Yuri by his elbow and snatched him back from her. "You're not to talk to her—not about any of this. You don't understand what you're getting into, man. She could worm military information out of the Devil himself."

A dawning look of comprehension crossed Yuri's face. He glanced back at Pamela, obviously torn between his admiration as a fan of hers and the need for military secrecy. "I understand," he said finally. He bowed reluctantly to Pamela. "I'm afraid our little talk will have to wait until later."

"Perhaps so," she murmured. "But you've already given me a good deal to think about, your mere presence on this ship." She glanced over at me, then said, "Any concerns about another bomb, Admiral Wayne?"

I saw Yuri stiffen. I made a small motion, dismissing the

incident. "Not at all. Commander Kursk is here at my request."

Pamela took a step toward me. "Oh, really? And just why would that be?"

Fed up, I grabbed her by the shoulder and propelled her toward the office door. She put up a brief struggle, but I was far stronger than she was. Finally, she gave up and went along with it.

"Out," I ordered. I shoved her out into the passageway, being none too careful about it, then slammed the door behind her. I turned back to Yuri. "So much for secrecy— I'll be surprised if she hasn't wormed the story out of you by the time we get the strike under way."

Tombstone's head popped out of the door to my stateroom. "Is she gone?"

Yes." I shot Yuri a disgusted look. "No thanks to your friend here."

Tombstone came out with a fresh flight suit on, one that barely reached down to his ankles. He was barefoot, evidently having decided not to put the filthy ground boots back on his feet.

"We'll have to deal with the publicity sooner or later," he said with a sigh. "Get your PAO up here, along with Lab Rat. We'll have them work out the cover story—then we'll get it down pat. It's gotta be perfect, Batman. At least until we let our people back in the States know what is going on."

"I'll brief Ambassador Wexler," I agreed. "She may have some ideas for us as well."

Tombstone snorted. "Sarah'd probably take lead on the strike herself, if she could."

And that, I reflected, was probably true. Indeed, so would Pamela Drake, for that matter.

"Let's get down to CVIC, if you're up to it," I said finally.

"Lab Rat's probably chewing on his whisper circuits, trying to get his hands on you."

Tombstone nodded. "Got some running shoes I can borrow?"

I sent my Chief of Staff and a Marine guard down to check the corridor between my stateroom and CVIC. It was only a short distance, maybe forty feet, but I wouldn't put it past Pamela to be lurking for us, waiting to pounce along the way.

With the Marine stationed at the only intersecting corridor and the Chief of Staff at the far end, I stepped out into the passageway and motioned Yuri and Tombstone to follow me.

We hurried, almost trotting down the corridor, then slipped into the alcove that was the entrance to CVIC. The watch-stander buzzed the door open immediately. We pushed through the main briefing area and back to SCIF, ignoring the startled and inquiring glances from the rest of the Intelligence Specialists.

Back in Lab Rat's inner sanctum, I finally relaxed. Even Pamela Drake couldn't get past the multiple combination locks and the watch-stander out front, I was pretty sure.

As we stepped into Lab Rat's office, I saw Bird Dog seated in front of him. His head was bowed down, his hands on his knees, and he was speaking in a low tone of voice. He stopped, looked up startled, and quit speaking as soon as we stepped in. "Ready for us?" I asked, although it was obvious that Lab Rat was still debriefing Bird Dog. Still, the matters we had to resolve were far more urgent.

Lab Rat nodded slowly, an uncomfortable look on his face. "Yes, I guess so. Thank you, Lieutenant Commander Robinson."

Bird Dog stood slowly, and scuttled off to the hatch. He kept his eyes fixed on the ground, although he murmured a polite greeting as he slid past us.

I turned to watch him go. Now that puzzled the hell out of me. Just half an hour earlier, that same young man had been standing in my office filthy-dirty and exhausted. I would have thought the first place he would head would be for the shower, maybe to catch some sleep. I'd told him to stop by and let Lab Rat debrief him, but I figured he'd at least shower first.

Evidently, he hadn't. He was still in the filthy, ragged condition he'd been in when he'd inflicted those telltale marks on my couch.

I turned back to Lab Rat. "What was all that about?"

Lab Rat shook his head, and his eyes cut over to Yuri. "Just a debrief, Admiral. That's all."

I nodded, understanding. Lab Rat had something on his mind he didn't want to talk about in front of Yuri.

"Let's get started then," I said, pulling out a chair from around the small briefing table. "Admiral, you want to start?"

Lab Rat stood. "Just a moment, Admiral Wayne," he said, a hard note in his voice. "I'd like to conduct this debriefing with Admiral Magruder alone. And before that, I'd like to speak to you privately."

Lab Rat's face was flushed, but his expression was adamant.

"Anything you have to say to me, you can say in front of Tombstone," I pointed out. "Hell, he had command here before I did. You used to work for him, Lab Rat."

"Admiral, I'm afraid I have to insist. Yes, I've worked for Admiral Magruder and I have the utmost respect for him." Lab Rat's expression softened slightly, then hardened again.

"But you're in command now, sir. If you listen to what I have to say and then want me to brief Admiral Magruder about it, I will. But it's for your ears only at first, sir. I really think that's best."

I started to snap at him, then caught myself. Intelligence work was Lab Rat's area of expertise. I knew how he felt about Tombstone, and if he wanted to talk to me privately, then he had good reasons to. Still, I felt markedly uncomfortable at the idea.

Tombstone stood, scraping his chair away from the table. He motioned to Yuri. "Lab Rat's right, Batman," he said quietly. "It's not my ship anymore."

I started to protest, then fell silent. With a nod, Tombstone steered Yuri gently out of the compartment. Lab Rat waited until they were gone, then shut the heavy steel door behind them.

I turned to him. "So what's all this cloak-and-dagger stuff about, Lab Rat?" My voice was a little bit harsher than I'd like, but the guy had inadvertently been the last in a long line of people who'd pissed me off that afternoon. "What's so damn secret you can't say it in front of Tombstone?"

Lab Rat sighed, and I was surprised to hear a quaver in the exhalation of breath. "I don't know, Admiral," he said quietly. He pointed at a chair. "You might like to sit down—this might take some time."

I planted my old ass in that chair, and sat there and listened to my Intelligence Officer outline his concerns.

"First off, let me say that I believe there's no real cause for concern," Lab Rat began. "But still, until we verify some of this information, I have to treat it as a possible compromise to our national security. Please, Admiral, don't misunderstand me—this is my duty." There was a pleading

quality in Lab Rat's voice that bothered me almost as much
as his words.

I nodded slowly. "Go on."

"Admiral, Admiral Magruder was involved in a series of
almost inexplicable coincidences while he was on the
ground," Lab Rat continued. "In particular, his encounter
with the Ukrainian forces seems almost too coincidental to
believe. How likely is it that they could have tracked him
during his travels in the jungle, that a contingent of renegade
Vietnamese officers agreed to stage an unprovoked attack
on *Jefferson* as a cover story for something they hoped we
would do—mind you, they had no clear indication that
we'd agree to take on that supposed nuclear facility—and
risk taking losses of their own?"

I slumped back in my chair, shocked beyond words.

"Until I know otherwise, I have to view this relationship
between Admiral Magruder and Commander Kursk with
some concern," Lab Rat continued. "Remember, this is the
same man who tried to kill him when he was still on board
Jefferson. And now they are working together?" Lab Rat
shook his head slowly. "Tell me I have a nasty, paranoid
mind, Admiral. Reassure me that there's nothing to this, that
I'm not going to get my ass blasted by D.C. for divulging
classified information to a senior officer who may be
compromised."

"Compromised." I spat the word out, tasting its foulness
in my mouth. "Are you accusing Tombstone Magruder of
being a spy?"

Lab Rat spoke quickly now. "Not intentionally, Admiral.
It's possible that his drive to seek his father has led him to
make arrangements that the United States might view with
some alarm."

"Cut the bullshit, Lab Rat. Do you seriously believe that

Tombstone Magruder would betray his country in any way? That he would release classified information without proper authorization? Particularly to them?"

"He's got you convinced we need to make a bombing run on the interior of Vietnam, based on the same associations," Lab Rat pointed out. "Admiral, please—understand my position. I'm not accusing Admiral Magruder of being a spy. I'm just saying that there's something questionable about this entire association, this sequence of events. Frankly, I don't want to take the chance. Can you honestly say that you do? Putting aside your personal friendship with Admiral Magruder—and remember, Chief Warrant Officer Walker also had personal friends in his command—are you completely and professionally satisfied with this entire situation?"

I was so angry I almost couldn't think straight. I stood, and started to scream at Lab Rat and chew his neck to a bloody, red froth. Then it hit me, the unsettling feeling that circled around the pit of my stomach whenever I was about to make a fool of myself. I sat back down heavily.

Perhaps there was something to what he was saying. No, not that Tombstone would ever betray his country—that I simply could not believe. But the circumstances—yes, there was a lot left to be desired in them. Now that I reviewed them, Tombstone's explanation sounded all the more lame. That the leader of his group had mysteriously disappeared, that he'd fled the fire and had a chance encounter with the one Ukrainian he had reason to hate most of all in the world, then gone with that man voluntarily to conduct surveillance on a secret Chinese weapons-production facility—now that I ran through the facts again, it sounded more and more bizarre.

Bizarre—but true. Had it been anyone else except

Admiral Magruder, who I'd known so long and so well, I would have wondered about it. But coming from him . . .

And that was exactly Lab Rat's point. I couldn't let my personal friendship with Tombstone cloud my judgment in this matter. Not with what we were about to undertake. Really, the only reason I was completely convinced at that point was that both stories backed up Lab Rat's national-asset data about a possible nuclear plant deep in the jungle of Vietnam. Whoever it belonged to—Chinese, Vietnamese, or even Ukrainian—it needed to be put out of business. That they were up to no good was evident by the care they'd taken to conceal their activities.

"Tombstone isn't compromised," I said finally, my voice sounding weak and quiet even to my own ears. "It's not possible."

Lab Rat nodded. "I tend to agree with you, Admiral. But as I said—it's not a matter of what we think or feel. It's a matter of what the facts are—and what our duty requires us to do."

"I don't believe it," I said finally. "I won't."

It was Lab Rat's turn to stand, and he paced angrily in the small confined space. He appeared to be at war with himself, struggling with some decision he knew he must make. Finally he turned to me, a harsh expression on his face. "Admiral, I've reviewed everything I can think of concerning security clearances. Of course, you have the absolute right to grant a clearance to anyone you wish, if you follow the regulations listed in the manual for granting interim ones. I know those rules cold—and so do you, I suspect."

"So what are you saying?" I asked.

"Admiral, Admiral Magruder is a visitor aboard this ship. Technically, you must formally authorize his access to classified material from my shop. As I said, it is your sole decision—but it's normally one made with the concurrence of the top-secret control officer. That would be me."

I felt my jaw drop as I contemplated where this young officer was about to go. He wouldn't dare. He couldn't—

He did.

"I do not concur with any decisions to authorize Admiral Magruder access to classified material," Lab Rat said firmly. "Furthermore—and understand, this is not a threat, I am merely complying with regulations—if you do grant him access to classified material, I will be forced to file a report with the National Security Group in Hawaii, indicating my concern that classified material may be compromised by your actions." A strange, almost pleading look swept over Lab Rat's face. "I don't want to do this, Admiral Wayne. But I don't have any choice."

I sighed heavily, dumbstruck. "If you pull his clearance, you realize he's grounded," I said quietly.

Lab Rat nodded. "I know that. And truly, if I saw any other way, I wouldn't do it."

As much as I hated it, I saw Lab Rat's point. Had it been anyone else, I would have done as he suggested in a heartbeat.

"All right," I said, the words heavy in my throat. "I'm not convinced, for what it's worth. But I agree. I'll tell him myself."

Lab Rat took a step closer to me. "But not until after I've debriefed him thoroughly," he said quietly. "I want a straight story, his first story, Admiral. Not one based on any suspicions that you may raise in him."

"Suspicions?" I was on my feet too now, outraged again. "How dare you—" I bit my words off in mid-sentence as I saw the look on Lab Rat's face.

There are many forms of courage, but one of the most difficult to measure is moral courage. It is that strange conviction that drives a man to do what is right, not what is convenient or attractive. It requires standing up to superior officers when they are in the wrong, taking a moral stand whenever possible. In that instant, I saw those qualities in Lab Rat's face.

"I apologize," I said, my voice quiet now. "You're absolutely right. I won't tell him—not until you tell me to. In the meantime, we'll shield him from all classified material. How is that?"

A vast look of relief washed over Lab Rat's face. "Thank you, sir. I think we can resolve this quickly."

I nodded. "So do I, Lab Rat. So do I."

I opened the outer door, and motioned Tombstone back into the room. I forced a hearty, relaxed expression onto my face. "Your turn, amigo."

Tombstone shot me a quizzical look. "I don't know how long this'll take, but could you have someone hunt me down a bed? I'm about out on my feet—I suspect I need about ten hours in the rack before I even start to sound coherent again." He chuckled, and pointed at Lab Rat. "I pity him, trying to have to piece this story together the way I'm feeling right now."

Inwardly, I winced. Tombstone had no idea of what had transpired, and it would soon be my sad duty to tell him his clearance was pulled. And that he was grounded, since the entire interior of the Tomcat is classified. I wasn't looking forward to it, any more than Lab Rat had wanted to talk to me about it. But it had to be done—and I'd done it.

I left Yuri in the care of two Intelligence Specialists who were obviously chomping at the bit to ask him questions, but were under strict orders from Lab Rat to leave him alone until Lab Rat himself could debrief the Ukrainian. After making sure that he was comfortable and promising to find him a rack as well, I headed back to my cabin. The walk back took far longer than the trip to CVIC had in the first place.

THIRTEEN
Lieutenant Commander "Bird Dog" Robinson

30 September
USS Jefferson

I went down to Medical to see how Gator was doing, but the corpsmen wouldn't even let me in the door until I'd had a shower. They damned near grabbed me and pitched me in one right there, claiming I posed a health hazard to the entire ship. I gave up trying to get in and went back to my stateroom to hunt down a clean pair of skivvies. My roommate was blessedly absent—I didn't feel like doing any explaining. Not after the last week.

I showered quickly, soaping up washing down three times before I finally felt clean. I scratched my head, wondering if anything had taken root in it during my time in the jungle.

I was getting sleepy now that I was clean, but there was one last task I had to perform. Donning clean skivvies and a flight suit, as well as the blessed comfort of clean socks, I headed back down to Medical. The corpsman almost didn't recognize me. He did a double take, then motioned me into the ward.

"How is he?" I asked.

The corpsman nodded with satisfaction. "He's gonna be

just fine, sir. We shot him full of antibiotics and put him to bed. He's out cold now." He gave me an assessing glance. "Something you ought to consider doing yourself."

"I want to see him," I said, ignoring the suggestion that was sounding better and better each minute. "Just for a minute."

The corpsman led me over to the private curtained-off area where Gator was. He had some color back in his face, and he looked better now that he was clean. His shoulder and knee had been bandaged, and I saw an IV line running into his right arm. I patted him on the arm and said, "You're gonna be fine, buddy. These guys are doing a good job. You're gonna be just fine."

As I left, I cornered the first doctor I saw and asked, "How about the knee? Is he going to be able to fly again?"

The doctor's face was guarded. "It's too soon to tell," he finally admitted. He glanced back at the curtain, as though making sure Gator couldn't hear. "There's been a lot of damage. He'll need surgery, obviously. After that, we'll see how it goes."

"He can't fly now, though, right?" I asked. It was a very, very stupid question, given the condition of his knee as I'd last seen it. Another indication that I badly needed sleep and food, not necessarily in that order.

The doctor's face was worried as well. He took me by the arm, leading me over to another treatment cubicle. "You're cleaned up, right?" he asked. "Here, let me check you over."

"No, I just came down to see how Gator was doing," I protested. "I'm fine."

The doctor shook his head. "I doubt it. Let me have a look at you. I'll make it an order, if I have to."

Silently, I shrugged out of my flight suit and stood there

in clean skivvies and socks. "On the examining table," the doctor ordered. "On your back."

I shrugged and complied. Might as well get it over with. Then I could get back to my rack.

The doctor ran his hands over me, asked a few questions about how I felt and when I'd last eaten, then finally nodded. "You're exhausted, of course," he said. "When were you planning on getting some sleep?"

"In a little while," I said. I had been planning on going straight back to my stateroom, but I hated being pushed around by doctors. They seemed to think they had absolute control over everyone's life, and I wasn't about to let him tell me I needed some sleep.

"I see." The doctor looked thoughtful. "Well, I want to run a few lab tests—no, no, I insist. No telling what sort of nasty blood toxins you could have picked up down there." He disappeared out of the treatment cubicle for a moment, then returned with a syringe and a couple of vials. "Make a fist," he ordered.

I started to comply, then felt a sudden sting in my upper arm. I turned my head to look at him. "Hey! Since when do you take blood out of my shoulder?"

The doctor smiled gently. "Ever since I want to make sure a hardheaded pilot gets some sleep before he becomes a danger to himself. Consider yourself grounded for two days—longer, if you don't do what I tell you to do."

The world was fading around me, becoming gray and fuzzy. I protested, I tried to struggle up into a sitting position, but there was no use fighting it. Whatever he jabbed into my shoulder was a lot stronger than I was at that point.

I was still trying to climb off the bed and onto my feet

when darkness washed over me completely. I went down
hard for the count.

This time, the admiral briefed us himself. That wasn't
usually done. Under normal circumstances, you get jammed
into the CVIC briefing room with the other guys flying the
same mission and you get your data dump from Lab Rat or
one of his assistants. But it wasn't every day that we went
to war *without* a full-scale buildup, Air Force tanker
support, and careful testing of the civilian waters by the
politicians back home.

Or that we faced a target that scared the shit out of all
of us.

Nuclear weapons take warfare to a whole new level of
pucker factor. With a target like this, ringed with SAM sites
and shoulder-mounted Stingers, you got to take life seriously. The admiral knew that—down deep, he was still one
of us, even though he was carrying around a hell of a lot of
metal on his collars. He wouldn't be in the air with us—at
least not physically. But from what I'd seen of the J-TARPS,
it was the next best thing to being there.

I expected him to start off with a pep talk. You know, the
God-and-country routine.

Bastard surprised me again. I hate it when that happens.

The lights dimmed and a photo flashed up on the wall. I
sucked in a hard breath. Not something tactical, a copy of
the flight plan, or much of anything else relevant to the
mission. No, this one was a beauty.

It was an aerial view. Burnt jungle surrounded by those
overwhelming patches of green wilderness. Smoke still
curled up from some areas. Down in the lower left-hand
corner, a picture of raw dirt. An excavation, maybe. It
looked like . . .

"No," I said involuntarily. "It can't be."

Even in the dim light, the admiral's eyes seemed to find me. I was staring, feeling like a catfish that someone had started gutting, trying to breathe but feeling panicky.

"Next slide," the admiral said as if he was briefing us on the weather.

A closer view now. I could see figures running away from the excavation, heading toward the sheltering jungle.

Running might have been too strong a word for what we had been doing right then. I had Gator half over one shoulder, and was stumbling along trying to keep him off the ground and moving in the right direction. I remembered the fear, the feeling of dirt caving in on me, the sheer impossibility of thinking about anything else except being out of the cave we'd almost died in.

"You saw us," I said, the words spilling out barely under control. "My God, you *saw* us!"

The admiral nodded. "We didn't know who it was at first. Took a while to get the picture cleaned up enough to make out the details. Once we did, we realized it could be our people. By then, you and Gator had disappeared."

I slumped back down in my chair, reliving the nightmare. A hand clamped down on my arm, startling me.

"Get over it." Two calm, green eyes looked back at me. "You weren't there."

"You *aren't* there. So listen up and pay attention to what you can do something about."

Lieutenant Commander Julie Karnes—the name to match the face popped into my mind. "What the hell are you doing here?" I demanded.

"Paying attention to the brief. Like you ought to be doing," she answered, no more perturbed than a turtle sunning on a rock.

It wasn't an answer, but it was a good suggestion. I turned back to the screen, and tried to concentrate on what the admiral was saying.

"You've all already heard the stories," Admiral Wayne said. "About Bird Dog and Gator. This is where it happened. Next slide, please."

Some damned photo dog had been lying in wait for us when we'd come off that helo from being in country. He must have been using a zoom lens, because what we saw now was a full-face close-up of the three of us straggling off the SAR helo. Hell, I damned near didn't recognize myself, as battered and filthy as I was in that picture.

"I could tell you how important this target is," the admiral continued. "But you already know that. I could tell you what the effects will be if we don't take it out *now,* that we'll be seeing these weapons everywhere in the world in the next year if we don't stop it now. And I could tell you the dirtiest secret of all—that the government wants us to take care of this problem now. Quietly, efficiently, and now. There's no time for foreign policy consultations, for diplomatic dickering and horse trading. And all of that would be true."

He paused for a moment, and I saw him look around the room to take the measure of each one of us. "True, and wouldn't make a whole lot of difference. Not to you right now. Hell, not even to me, for that matter. But what I do care about is my people. And those bastards tried to kill some of them. Succeeded, in a couple of cases. Shot down the E-2, the helo, and a couple of fighters. As nasty as that was, it's sort of one of the risks of military life. You hate it, but it's there."

"But this"—Admiral Wayne pointed at the photo—"is something different. Something more brutal than anything we can conceive. Torture, pain, and trying to bury a pilot and his RIO alive. Now *that* is something to get pissed about. You got any questions about it, you just take a good look at Bird Dog. Or go down to sick bay and see Gator. Remember what happened to them and watch out for the SAM sites. Remember, and make them pay."

With that, the admiral stepped away from the briefing podium and handed the slide clicker over to Lab Rat. Lab Rat flashed up a smaller-scale aerial photo that encompassed the entire missions area. The burnt jungle was still visible, but took up less of the picture now.

Julie Karnes. Now just what the hell was she doing on *Jefferson*?

Back a couple of years ago, I'd spent a year at the Naval War College in Newport, Rhode Island. It was the first time I'd had shore duty since my earliest days of pilot training, and I'd run amok.

Well, sort of amok. At least until I'd met Callie Lazier, a surface warfare officer in my class. I'd fallen for her hard—hell, I'd even proposed. What's worse, she'd accepted.

Then, when the opportunity came up to scoot back out to *Jefferson* to do a little flying during a real crisis, it had all fallen apart. Callie was pissed at me for going. Started making this mumbo-jumbo touchy-feely crap about fear of commitment and all that stuff.

I'd pointed out that she knew I was a pilot when she got hooked up with me. Just where the hell did she think I would be after War College?

She hadn't understood—but then, those surface pukes never do. It's a whole different Navy, steaming around at the hair-raising speeds of thirty knots.

We'd made up for a while, but it hadn't lasted. She'd Dear-John'd me on the next cruise.

And Julie Karnes—she'd been Callie's roommate through it all. I knew her, of course, but not well. She was an F-14 RIO, which should have given us a lot in common. Except there were other things I was interested in when I was over at their place, things that had nothing to do with radar, ESM, or even flying.

Plus, I'd gotten the feeling she didn't like me too much. I'd figured it was because I took off to go fly missions over Cuba while I was supposed to be making like a student and keeping good ol' Callie happy. Those women—they stick together.

So aside from Callie, the last person I really wanted to run into was Julie Karnes.

The female in question shot me another nasty look, as if she knew I wasn't paying attention. I looked back up at the front of the room.

Lab Rat was running through the estimated SAM locations, warning us in every other sentence that the damn things were mobile and could be anywhere. Our ingress and egress routes were planned to avoid their detection envelopes, but there he went again. "They could be anywhere, people. And the range is—"

I tuned it out, and concentrated on the routes inked out in blue marker on the screen, picking out landmarks and drop points.

"Is he boring you?" The whisper was so quiet I almost missed it.

"Gator will—I mean, my RIO will take care of it," I whispered back, annoyed at her for breaking my concentration.

That cool green stare again, clearly pissed now. Like I cared.

But I wasn't flying with Gator this time, was I? What

about the RIO I *would* get? Would he be as good as Gator? I'd been spoiled a little by flying with a solid, experienced backseater for so long. Hell, by all rights, I should have had a nugget in the backseat—the Skipper tries to put a seasoned guy with a newbie to increase the chances of survival. It was just that a lot of people didn't want to fly with me. I had no idea why.

So maybe I would have to worry about SAM site planning, more than I would have before. Shit—all I wanted to do was fly.

"Maybe I will, maybe I won't," she replied. "There're two of us up there." She said the words casually, like it was no big deal.

"I pity your pilot," I answered.

I swear to God, she smiled. I hadn't meant it as a joke.

"So, now I know two things about you that Callie never told me. First, you don't pay attention at briefings. And second—you don't read the flight schedule."

She was right about the last one. I hadn't wanted to see it, to see my name on there without Gator's right below. But I had this weird sinking feeling that I was missing the point.

Now she was turned full-face to me, paying as little attention to the brief as I was. "You *didn't* read it, did you." A statement, not a question. "You're flying with me, Bird Dog. And I swear to God, you're leaving command-eject selected."

We trooped out of the ready room and headed for the paraloft to pick up our gear. Karnes was already carrying her brain bucket and knee pad, but I wasn't suited up yet.

"This isn't a good idea," I said as we let the parariggers help us adjust our ejection harnesses. Mine was brand-

new—the last one had already done what it was supposed
to. "Flying together, I mean."

"Why not?" she asked, reaching down to adjust her crotch
straps. I watched, still slightly bewildered at the machina-
tions women go through with them. Like what do they have
to adjust has always been my question. "Not that I'm
disagreeing with you," she continued, evidently satisfied
with the fit.

"Because! We've never flown together. I don't think
hostile SAM country is a good place to begin our relationship."

"Ah. So unless it's a nice peacetime hop—or War
College—you don't believe in new relationships. Is that it?"

"That's *not* it, and if you were any kind of a RIO, you'd
agree with me," I shot back. There was something in that
oh-so-cool voice that really pissed me off.

Truth be said, the last crack was below the belt. And not
true. The Tomcat community isn't all that big, and the
chicks had gotten a lot of attention from the press and from
everyone else. I knew what kind of aviators they were, more
from their squadron mates than from the media, and I knew
more about them than I would have known about a guy in
the same position.

An oddly erotic memory of Callie popped into mind at
that word—*position*. Ah, the things we'd tried . . .

I shoved the thought away. You don't let stuff like that
distract you when you're getting ready to fly a combat
mission.

The point of the whole matter was that everything I'd
heard about Julie Karnes was good. Not too good to be true,
not that sort of bullshit. The golden-halo effect, you can
pick it out after a while in the canoe club. No, it all had the
ring of an honest assessment. So maybe she didn't have as

much time in an ejection seat as Gator did, but she was supposed to be a damned competent RIO.

"I *am* a kind of RIO. But I'm not Gator's kind." She turned around to face me, hands on hips, her helmet dangling from one hand. "I gave up babysitting after junior high school. It didn't pay enough. It doesn't now either. So get this concept through that overblown ego of yours, amigo. We go out there as a team, not as hotshot young pilot with Daddy in the backseat. You have a problem with that concept, you speak up."

"I have a problem with your attitude, lady."

She sighed, then put her helmet down on the long table that the riggers use for packing parachutes. "Then try to find someone else who's willing to fly with you, Bird Dog."

The tone set me back. I'd expected her to be pissed, to come back with some smart-ass remark. Instead, the voice she'd used was gentle, almost kind.

"You won't, you know," she said, turning her back slightly to me as she fussed with the crotch strap again. *Damn,* I wished she'd stop that. "Everyone in the squadron knows you. Knows how you are. And after this last stunt, where Gator finally had to put your ass in the drink to put out the flames, they're all spooked."

"They are not."

"They are *too*." She shot me a look of pure exasperation. "Go ask your skipper if you don't believe me. I talked with her when I checked in—they stashed me with VF-95 since I was only on board flying in with Admiral Magruder. She came looking for me earlier today, asked how I felt about flying with you. She was going to take you herself, just to prove something to the rest of the squadron, but she's got some nugget to look out for. So I told her *I'd* do it."

This little revelation left me speechless. Sure, I knew

some of the wimps in the squadron were worried about flying with me. But Gator'd always been there to defend me. It'd never come down to the point of having to cram someone else in the backseat, and even if it had, Gator would have made them go. *Made* them, as one of the senior RIOs in the squadron. He'd personally vouch for the fact that I'd behave.

But like I said—Gator wasn't here. Only this skinny broad with the green eyes and the mouth.

"So what if I say no?" I asked.

She sighed again. "Then either the skipper flies with you or you're off the schedule. I don't know whether she'd put up with another temper tantrum from you right now, and I don't want to find out."

Off the schedule. No way. Not during this strike. This one was personal.

She evidently read minds. "So you think you can get over your attitude problem long enough to go kill some dirt?"

"Why did you? Agree to it, I mean." It mattered to me, if not to her.

That cool, long look again. Like seawater, but warmer. "I've been around you a little more when you weren't playing hotshot," she said finally. "I don't think you'll get me killed in the air, and that's really my only criteria for flying with a pilot. If anything, after your little trip downtown, you'll be a little more cautious."

"Scared, you mean."

This time she laughed. "Oh, no, not that. Not in a Tomcat. Bird Dog, listen—let's come to an understanding. I'll agree that you're the best pilot in the world, absolutely invulnerable in the air."

"Okay."

"And you admit that while you're immortal, maybe the

guy in the back isn't. So it's not a matter of whether or not you're afraid, okay? It's a matter of having to fly with us lesser beings, ones that get killed when the aircraft is hit. That suit you?"

Oddly enough, it did.

"Let's go check out a bird and preflight," I said finally. "I got a mission to fly."

"*We* do, amigo. Learn the word—*we*."

I signed our bird out from Maintenance, and Julie followed me up to the flight deck. The noise was overwhelming—engines turning, aircraft taxiing, all under the watchful eyes of the yellow shirts and the flight deck handler.

We preflighted, doing together the things I would normally have relied on Gator to do alone, the brown-shirted plane captain tagging along with us. He had a worried look on his face. Evidently the RIOs weren't the only ones worried about my flying.

"I'll bring it back," I told the youngster. "In one piece."

He nodded doubtfully. "Good hunting, sir." We climbed up into our seats, and he helped us secure the ejection harness. The whole routine had a new significance to me now that I'd had to trust my ass to one.

More checklist, then finally we were ready. I kicked over the engines, immediately relaxing as I heard their pure, throaty growl. The noise enveloped me, holding me safe in the middle, protecting me against anything bad. I felt safe.

"You ready?" I asked over the ICS.

"Ready," she said shortly.

Okay, so she wasn't a talkative one. I'd already figured that part out from remembering her at War College.

I taxied slowly across the deck, following the yellow shirt's signals. We were a little slow off the spot, delayed by that touching little heart-to-heart in the riggers' shop. Women—just what had she accomplished with all that crap? Why do they always want to *talk*? Okay, so maybe I'd started it by not wanting to fly with her, but still . . .

The rest of our flight was already off the deck, forming up and cutting slow patterns in the air while they waited on me and a straggler still sitting on the waist cat. Some mechanical problem. Green shirts, the enlisted technicians who know how the guts of this beast work, were popping open panels and swarming all over the bird.

We rolled slowly past them. They scattered, evidently flushed off the deck by the Air Boss, and then we had a green deck.

I cycled the control surfaces one last time for the catapult officer. The retaining pin that anchored my nose wheel to the catapult shuttle was already in place. I got the full-power signal, and slammed the throttles forward into full military power. One last check of the control surfaces, then the yellow shirt popped off a sharp, theatrical salute at me. I returned it. I owned the aircraft now, and anything that went wrong was my complete responsibility.

A few seconds later, that sudden jolt that says the shuttle was moving. Then that sickening, exhilarating buildup of speed, blasting us forward to 140 knots in just over that many feet. Just barely enough airspeed to get airborne, with more thrust than lift.

The first seconds off the cat are critical. You're in free fall for a moment, waiting for the aircraft to decide to fly. When the seas are rough, the waves are so close you think you'll never get airborne.

But you do. Unless you have a soft cat, a launch with insufficient airspeed, a Tomcat on afterburners has enough forward speed to stay up. But you always hold your breath a little, waiting for that to happen.

"Yee-haw!" A cheer from the backseat came over the ICS. It startled me. I'd heard other pilots say that their RIOs enjoyed the cat shot—I love 'em myself—but Gator always hated them. In landings, he was steadier than I was, but something about the launch just got to him. I'd hear him quit breathing, then give a long gasp after we were airborne for sure.

"Nice to have an appreciative audience," I said. Maybe this flight wasn't going to be as bad as I'd thought.

We climbed quickly, joined on the rest of the formation, and slid into position. We were flying in the last spot in the V, to lead's right. I glanced over at the other side of the formation and saw the distinctive face of Skeeter Harmon. He shot me a short, quick wave, then got back to the business of flying welded wing.

There were nine of us in the wing, all Tomcats fully loaded with ground-attack weapons and two little Sidewinders on wing tips. We were surrounded by Hornets with full antiair loads, flying in loose-deuce pairs and covering all angles of approach. The Hornets, thirsty little bastards that they are, had launched first so they'd have time to hit the tanker before the real firepower showed up. There wasn't a lot of chatter on tactical, although I heard Thor's distinctive drawl rap out the punch line to a rude joke.

Hornets versus Tomcats. It was a good mix this time. I'd rather fly antiair than ground-attack roles, but those damned little lawn darts were better at maneuvering against the MiGs. And we could carry a lot more firepower to the dirt than they could. I just didn't want them to get too used to it.

We were only fifty miles off the coast, well within Vietnam's coastal radar range, so it wasn't like this was going to be a complete surprise. They must have been on some sort of alert schedule. As soon as we reached the twenty-mile point, they were coming out to meet us.

Four pairs of Hornets peeled off to deal with the first wave. It chapped my butt to continue on inbound and let somebody else fight the air war, but there it was. You fly the mission you draw. Safe—or relatively so—inside a cocoon of Hornets, I pressed on and got to watch the air battle from the outside.

Ten MiG-29s against eight Hornets. Hardly seemed like a fair fight, our Hornets were so quick. They were fighting in the loose-deuce formation, one guy high covering the one down below fighting. The high position had the advantage of being able to trade altitude for speed almost instantaneously, and of having a little longer radar range.

The first MiG made an immediate, deadly mistake. He took on our lead Hornet without waiting for backup. Think of it as a cop walking into a bad neighborhood late at night alone. He should have known better. The pilot in the high slot nailed him with a Phoenix while the MiG was boring in, fixated on that lonely little Hornet out in front of the pack.

They started smartening up after that, although I'd wondered that it'd taken them that long to do it. You'd think the first engagement would have taught them better.

Never underestimate the value of training. You fight the way you train, and it was clear that these pilots had been thoroughly brought up in the Ground Control school of air combat. The interceptors on the deck, the GCIs, were trying to run the air battle, in typical Soviet fashion. It doesn't work against a flexible, fluid force like a Hornet pack.

I saw one Vietnamese missile brush by a Hornet with what looked like only inches to spare. The Hornet driver jinked, and flew right into the second missile. Not a direct hit—the missile clipped the tail assembly. A huge, bright chunk of Hornet took off for the ocean, and the rest of the aircraft flew by sheer momentum alone before starting spiraling toward the water. Just as the spin went flat and deadly, a chute popped out of the canopy. I flashed on that, remembering how it'd been.

Still we pressed on, leaving the first waves battling behind us. The MiGs just couldn't get around those Hornets at us, the fat, high-value targets they were after.

More MiGs, more Hornet interceptors. Another wave peeled off to take on the new flight.

"How're they doing back there?" I asked over ICS.

"Looks good—only two MiGs left in the first wave, four in the second. Those Hornets are kicking some ass." Karnes sounded cheerful.

"Yeah, well, we're the ones who'll have to live with the bragging when we get back," I grumbled. "Hate landing with 'Winders on the wing."

"Five minutes to feet dry," she answered, reminding me that we weren't all that far from starting our bombing run.

I kept track of the air battle over tactical, listening to the Fox calls and yells. A few of my Hornet brethren and sistren got into trouble. I heard another call of "I got a chute," a pilot reporting seeing another one punch out successfully, and the gleeful cry of the woman that took that particular MiG out of play forever.

"Feeeeeet dry," Karnes sang out. The further we got into the mission, the more cheerful she sounded. I started to wonder why I ever thought she seemed such a straitlaced little priss.

Jungle beneath us now, smooth and unscarred miles of tangled trees and foliage. Pines on the higher slows, the vegetation still thick and luxurious. Way far to the north, smog and smoke clotted the horizon, indications of city life. Not our problem. We were headed deep into the jungle to the secret facility hidden there. It could hide too much.

"SAMs," Karnes said, interrupting the mood I'd been drifting into, watching the jungle and remembering. "Search mode now—no indication it's got us."

"Won't be long, though." The RIO's counter-ESM gear could detect hostile emissions long before the bad guys could see us. One of the standard problems of any piece of gear that spits out energy into the air is that it's detectable long before it's useful. "We're not doing much to avoid detection, unless you've got a cloaking device installed back there that I don't know about."

"'Fraid not. Just the Prowlers."

The EA6-B Prowlers were tucked in just below us, under both our limited antiair capability and that of our remaining Hornets. They were equipped with HARM missiles and a variety of jamming gear. We were about to play a delicate game of timing with the bad boys on the ground.

As soon as we started jamming, they'd know we were inbound. Their radar screen would turn into broad spikes and circles of noise, overloaded by the massive amounts of electromagnetic energy the Prowlers would be putting out. The trick was to get the HARM missiles off the rails at the antennae *before* we were actually detected, let them do their work, then jam the hell out of the remaining antennae. And it all had to happen before they knew we were inbound, which should be—

"They got us," Karnes announced. "Snoopy's got them too. Solid lock—they're going to targeting mode, Bird Dog," she warned.

No noise, just bright light streaking away from below me as the Prowlers shot their load. Too late? Maybe—if the

Vietnamese detected the missiles inbound, they'd shut down all electromagnetic radiation. That tactic had worked well on older HARM missiles, which had to hold the radiating source all the way into impact point.

Not so with the newer variants. They could lock on and hold the position in their tiny little computer brains long enough to blow the shit out of a recently shut-down antenna. But not while the Prowler was jamming—that was the tricky part.

Of course, they already knew in a general sense that we were coming in. Their fighters would have been relaying position reports back to their GCIs. But like they say—the devil's in the details. Where and when we'd be going feet dry and where we'd go after that were still up for grabs.

"Vampires *inbound*!" The E-2 Hawkeye removed all doubt from my military mind. The SAM sites had us—and cold.

Two Hornets vectored off to intercept, dropping our escort service down to six. What the hell was the point of having them fly CAP if they weren't going to stick around?

The high-spot Hornet held back a bit, waiting for his wingman to take the first shot. He'd retain a measure of altitude and maneuverability, waiting for a second shot if the first Hornet missed.

"Two more. Bird Dog, *three* missiles inbound." Karnes was starting to sound a little shaken now.

"Slow movers, honey," I said reassuringly. "Don't forget—they're strictly subsonic. I have to, I can outrun them."

"I know that."

"I know you do," I said, still trying for the cool and casual tone. "I'm just talking aloud to convince myself. Just think about how bad it's going to be when we get back to the boat, listening to those Hornet drivers boast. First thing you know, they'll be claiming there were thirty missiles instead of three and that they took them all out with guns."

Shit, I was starting to sound like Gator. How many times had he pulled that routine on me, trying to get me to settle down and fly the aircraft? He'd talk, just as if we were out on a normal training hopping, making these little observations about how slow the missile was, how good a shot I was, anything he could think of to keep me focused and confident. And here I was doing the same thing to a RIO.

Still, everything I said was true. Just like Gator would have done it. The missiles *were* a lot slower than we were, and the Hornet pilots *would* be boasting.

"Yeah." Silence from the backseat after that.

I let her think about it for a while, then asked, "So, you know any good jokes? I'm getting bored up here, and Gator always had a couple of new ones."

"Bored?"

"Yeah, bored. How do you feel about aerobatics?"

"Love 'em."

Another surprise. Gator always puked unless I gave him plenty of warning. "Maybe on the way back then."

"Sure."

A small puff of smoke off on the horizon, then another. Some too cool, too casual boasting from the Hornet pilot— two missiles scratched.

"Where's the other one?" I asked, just to keep her head in the game.

"Still inbound—five miles and closing." Good, she sounded steady and cool like she ought to. Maybe I'd learned something from Gator after all.

"High guy will get him," I said. I made sure my position

in formation was solid, then turned my head to the right to watch.

I could see it now, arcing up and spewing a trail of white smoke behind it. I hoped Karnes wasn't looking at it. Every time I see one, I get this cold crawling in the pit of my belly. She sounded okay now, but I didn't want to be nursing her back to health every five minutes. "Any other contacts in the area? How long till IP?"

She spouted off the answers, and I knew from the sounds of her voice that her head was buried in the black plastic hood fitted around her radarscope. It keeps the sun off the screen, makes for better visibility. "Four minutes—on profile, on time. Starting descent and approach in two minutes, ten seconds."

"Okay."

While her head was down, I reached up to the switch overhead in front of me and switched us out of command-eject. If she pulled the plug, she'd be the only one going. Not that I didn't trust her, mind you—I just didn't want her deciding when I ought to depart the aircraft.

The Hornet overhead was moving now, streaking down toward the remaining missile and vectoring off dead on so he could improve the angle on the target. Head-on shots are hard to make—worse, because of the rate of closures, you might not have time to get a second shot off. He turned back in toward it, giving me a classic quarter-stern view of him. A nice bird—if you like Hornets.

Another missile off the rails, then a second one. He was getting a little antsy, just the way I would be if I had missiles inbound on the back of my attack aircraft. Still, he should have waited a little on the second shot, given himself some time to look at it.

"Thirty seconds," Karnes announced, her voice still

slightly muffled. I knew she could see the Hornet, his missiles, and the incoming SAM playing out on her scope. There, though, it was controllable. Not like having to watch real aircraft and real missiles against the cloudless sky.

I knew it before she did. And before the E-2C and the other Hornets. The geometry was wrong, all wrong. It would be close—but not close enough.

"Incoming! Break formation!" Even as I started shouting over tactical, I rolled the Tomcat into a tight right turn, barrel-looping down toward the water. I flashed by the two Prowlers, saw the startled look as the guy in the right-hand seat turned toward me, heard the beginning of a curse over tactical.

Karnes yelped once, then settled down into feeding me a steady stream of information. "Okay, Okay, there's no lock, no lock . . . still heading for the formation . . . Hornet's taking another shot. . . ."

What the hell was wrong with them? Gaggled up together there, they were a missile sump. I stared up at the formation as it flashed by, passed out of view, then steadied up overhead as I pulled out of the dive.

Finally, they were starting to react. Skeeter was ahead of the rest of them, peeling out of formation in a hard left break, electing for a straight dive for the deck instead of a rolling descent. The Prowlers were accelerating and descending as well, on a straight line that pulled out ahead of the formation. One went high once they steadied up, the other low.

The rest of the airspace was cluttered with Hornets and Tomcats, some breaking high, others opting for distance separation. Like I said, we could outrun this sucker—but only if we tried to.

It was a mile away now, streaking toward the last spot its

nose-cone radar had spotted large patches of metal in the sky. It wavered a little, like a hunting dog scenting the air, then picked out one of the Prowlers. They were slower than we were—I wasn't so certain about their chances.

"You've got the angle," Karnes announced, breaking her normal monotone for an insistent suggestion. "Bird Dog, you're the only one within range who's out of their evasive maneuvers."

"All I've got is Sidewinders. IR-seeking."

"It's hot—look at that exhaust. The 'Winder will see it."

I toggled one on, and sure enough got the signal. A signal—who could be certain in the mass of metal and aircraft all going in different directions just then.

"There's a Prowler on the same bearing," I said. "I can't—"

"You have to. He hasn't got the speed."

"If I miss, the Sidewinder will get the Prowler."

"Then don't miss. You're the only chance he's got."

She was right. I knew it the moment she spoke.

I selected the Sidewinder, waited for the growl, then toggled it off. "Break down and right, Prowler," I shouted over tactical as the missile leaped off my wing tip.

The Prowler was listening and paying attention. It broke hard, straining the ancient airframe past any G-tolerance ever built into it. Too close, too close.

For one second, I was certain I'd missed.

I hadn't. The Sidewinder caught the SAM at an angle on the tail and sent both of them tumbling end-over-end through the air. Something hit, something cooked off—a brilliant fireball erupted where the second before there'd been flashing metal and sun.

"Thanks, Bird Dog." Jake "Snake" Allen, the Prowler pilot, sounded like he meant it.

"Got one left—you stick close on me, Jake. I'll take care of you."

We formed back up loosely, more loosely now. We were on final approach to the drop point. There was every reason in the world to abort the mission. We'd just screwed up every detail of the carefully planned bombing run, the precision timing between our aircraft, the spacing, everything. But no one said a word. We were there to put metal on target, and that's exactly what was going to happen.

Back before global positioning systems, before precision avionics and high-tech black boxes, aircraft dropped ground ordnance. They did it the old-fashioned way, with eyeballs and sheer judgment. We still practice it some, but not as much as we should. Not as much as we were going to right now.

"Looking good, Bird Dog. Twenty seconds out—ease back off Runner now, you're crowding up his tailpipe. Piece of cake, piece of cake . . ." Karnes continued as though nothing of importance had happened. Whatever nerves she'd experienced early on were gone now, replaced by precision guidance and ice water in her veins. I listened, double-checked her suggestions against ground truth as I saw it, and slid back slightly to give Runner in the aircraft ahead some clearance.

"Ten seconds . . . nine . . . eight . . . a little to the right, that's good . . ." she said, continuing the countdown methodically along with a running commentary on our orientation to the IP—impact point. It was working with us now, smooth and telepathic, almost as solid as with Gator. "You're in, you're in—*now*!"

I dropped the bombs and peeled off at a right angle, following the egress plan we'd briefed on board the ship.

Karnes pulled herself off the radar and twisted to stare back over her shoulder at the IP while I flew the aircraft.

She didn't need to. I could have told her how they'd hit. A little to the left of center, about thirty feet or so. But well within the lethal circle of death we'd designated on the chart earlier that day.

"Oh, yes," she said quietly. "Yeah, they're dead on."

"Not a little to the right?"

She was silent for a second, then said, "Well, maybe. Still good, though."

"I know."

"How?"

I shrugged. "Don't know. I always do, though. You believe it too, or you wouldn't have told me to shoot that Sidewinder."

"Maybe I do," she said thoughtfully. "It was just something Gator told me—about your flying nap of the earth in the Arctic in zero visibility. I figured if Gator was willing to go up with you, it must be true."

"Just remember—hell, you admitted it earlier. I'm immortal. The guy in the backseat is the one I have to worry about."

"It's beautiful back there," she continued. I took a quick glance back at her—she was still craned around in the seat watching the IP. "I can't see anything anymore. Just smoke and flames."

"That's the way we like it."

We had about five seconds of peace and quiet to contemplate the pleasures of a good, hard-hitting bombing run. Then her ESM detector went off.

"Crap. More SAMs." She was back in the hood now. "That Prowler—where *is* he?"

"Cut out before we did. You got his squawk?" I suggested, referring to his IFF signal.

"Yeah, I got him. Carrier's keeping him under close control. I think he's out of range of the site now. Uh-oh."

It always worries me when RIOs say that. "Uh-oh what?"

She sighed. "The Hornets—they took out most of the MiGs, but then they started getting low on fuel. They're cutting out one by one to hit the tanker."

"And the MiGs?" I prompted.

"Headed toward us, but bearing to the north some. I can't tell if they're running an intercept or not. The geometry doesn't work for it, but . . ."

"But they could if they wanted to," I finished for her. "Wouldn't take a whole lot of fuel, not with us each carrying one or two Sidewinders."

"Yeah. I'm watching them. If they're going to turn into us, it'll have to be—shit, they just did. Six of them, Bird Dog, about eleven o'clock and high."

I gave the sky a quick once-over and had them. They were there, just barely visible.

"Viper 201, Snoopy. Be advised, six bogies inbound." The E-2C bubba sounded alarmed. He rapped out a quick series of vectors to open the gap between the MiGs and us, then added, "We're buster back into the inner air zone. Say your state?"

I glanced over at the fuel gauge. "Enough for a shot at the deck without tanking. Hold one—we're vectoring in to provide CAP for you."

"Me too," another voice chimed in on tactical. "We got enough fuel."

Skeeter. How did I know he would be in on this?

"No, Skeeter," I said firmly. "You go—"

"Not this time, Bird Dog." There was a cold note in my wingman's voice I couldn't quite place. "No, not again."

"Just what the hell does that mean? Skeeter, you get your ass out of here!"

"No way. You think you can shake me off, go ahead and try."

I groaned. "Listen, we're almost back inside the cruiser's missile coverage. It's not like this guy's going to need CAP for long. He'll be back on the deck before you can get over here."

"Nope."

"Umm—Bird Dog? Two thousand yards back and forty-five degrees down—it's a little late to be sending him home, don't you think?" Karnes's voice had the first note of amusement I'd heard in it since we'd gotten airborne.

And just why *didn't* I want Skeeter around? I tried to convince myself that it wasn't necessary, that I could handle taking care of the E-2C by myself.

Sure. Like I did last time. There was a reason we fought in pairs.

Then what was it? I could only think of one possibility, one that pissed me off right down to my boots.

Skeeter was a hell of a stick. So was I. Something about that bothered me.

He didn't have any judgment, no sense of when to call it quits and back off for another shot. I couldn't depend on him the way—

The way Gator depended on me? Look what had happened to my RIO.

"All right," I said finally. "Take high station on me." Two clicks on the circuit acknowledged my order.

Skeeter made a smooth transition to his new station. I

reached up and switched the eject-select switch back to command-eject.

The MiGs were definitely inbound now, balls to the walls for us. The Hawkeye was going buster back to the boat, but it was going to be close.

"Pull off. Stay between the E-2C and the MiGs," I said.

"Roger."

Now we were orbiting, letting the Hawkeye make his dash back to the boat while we loitered high waiting for the MiGs.

"First Hornet's off the tanker," Karnes reported. "But he's Winchester—out of weapons."

"Who's got anything left on their wings?" I asked over tactical. A few Hornets answered up. Altogether, we had eight Tomcats with two Sidewinders each, me with one, two Hornets with two Sparrows and two Sidewinders, and three Hornets with one of each. Not a lot of firepower, but it was all we had airborne.

Six MiGs versus fourteen U.S. fighters—nine Tomcats and five Hornets. Twenty-two Sidewinders and four Sparrows on our side, God knows how many air-to-air missiles on the MiGs. I liked the odds.

"Carrier's launching the reserve Hornets, but it's going to be about ten minutes," I heard over tactical.

"We don't have the time or the space," Karnes said. "It's us, guys."

"More MiGs," the Hawkeye chimed in. "We got them just launching to the north. Getting too hot for us here, shipmates. We're out of here."

"Roger, Snoopy. See you back on the deck. Break— Viper Flight. There's not going to be an E-2 overhead giving us the big picture," I added. "Wait for them, call out your targets, and kill them. No excuses, no wasted shots. We hold on until the cavalry arrives, you got it?"

A chorus of clicks on the circuit acknowledged my transmission.

Like I said—good odds. The MiGs had more missiles, but we had something they didn't have.

Each other.

It didn't take long. Within five minutes, all that was left of the MiGs was smoking craters in the sky and oil and debris floating on the ocean. We were all Winchester and low on fuel. A quick plug and suck at the tanker, and we formed back up in a starboard marshal pattern to wait for our look at the deck.

They were waiting for us just inside the island, crowding around the metal hatch that let out onto the flight deck. I pushed past most of them, too exhausted to pay any attention to them. I just wanted to go pee and get something to drink. Then maybe shoot some pool—yeah, that'd be good. That's what the carrier needed most of all—a pool table. Make it mandatory, just like the popcorn machines.

I looked up just as this was all starting to make sense to see Admiral Wayne blocking my way down to the ladder. "Hi," I said, aware that it wasn't probably the most appropriate greeting I could manage to the senior officer on board the ship, but still preoccupied with the desire for a pool table.

The admiral looked at me with an odd expression. "Hi yourself, mister. Medical's looking for you. Want to explain to me how you managed to slip out of there? And what you're doing flying when you're not medically cleared for it?"

"Ummm . . . not exactly, Admiral."

"To which part?" Now the admiral looked truly disgusted. "Oh, never mind. I should know better by now. But if you're not too busy, would it be too much trouble for you and your RIO to get your butts down to CVIC for a debrief?"

"No, sir." I glanced back, and saw Karnes moving toward me. Odd, I'd never realized she was so short.

"We were just heading down there, Admiral," Karnes said smoothly, sliding in between me and the admiral. "Just on our way, sir."

I nodded, trying to look like that had indeed been my intention. I wondered if Karnes played pool.

We slithered down the ladders and passageways to CVIC, Karnes practically dragging me by the scruff of my neck. "And the next time you get some bright idea about skating out of sick bay without permission to go flying with me," she hissed, giving another jerk on my collar, "I'm gong to kick that little stud ass of yours up and down about twenty ladders until you come to your senses."

"It seemed like the right thing to do at the time," I offered, aware that it wasn't much of an excuse.

"You don't think. You fly. Thinking is my job," she answered. "Now, just shut up and let me handle the debrief."

I waited until the admiral and Lab Rat left the room. "So how's Callie?"

Karnes looked up at me, grime streaking that pretty little face of hers. "Same bitch as always, Bird Dog. What the hell did you ever see in her anyway? The boobs?"

I felt my jaw drop. "But you two were *roommates* at War College! I thought—then what was all that flack about me being a stud?"

Karnes shrugged. "Had nothing to do with what Callie said about you, shipmate. Just a personal assessment."

And I'd thought MiGs were hard to read. This woman had them all beat to hell.

"So maybe when we get back to the States—or the next liberty port," I started, not sure where I was going with the idea, but getting reeled in as surely as a trout on a fly line.

"When we get back, we're going to dinner," she answered immediately. "And more. Think you're up to it? Or did that MiG shoot down something I didn't see?"

"Oh, I'm up to it," I said, fumbling for answers. "But trust me—that's the *only* time you're getting in the front seat. The rest of the time we're out here, you're the guy in back. Got it?"

FOURTEEN

Admiral "Tombstone" Magruder

30 September
USS Jefferson

Batman pulled out a cigar from the depths of his desk. Only his Chief of Staff knows that he keeps a collection of Dunhills and Punches for special moments. The small humidor he's been carefully tending as long as I've known him holds one layer of his precious weed. He checks the distilled water in the small humidifying canister every night, right before he racks out.

"You want one?" he asked.

"A Punch, I guess." I knew Batman preferred the Dunhills, and I've always had a soft spot for Punches, ever since I found the molded and wormy remains of one in my father's footlocker. I don't normally smoke, but there are occasions that can only truly be celebrated with a good cigar.

Batman tossed me the clipping tool, then waited for me to use it. This was like him also, the punctiliously good manners, even among old friends, as we were.

I guess we had a fair amount to celebrate. The nuclear facility in the jungle was a dark, smoking hole in the ground. At least for now, that danger was past. More likely, just postponed temporarily.

And Batman had his ship back. The ambassadorial contingent had departed earlier that day, hard pressed to find anything further to debate now that we'd resolved the problem with bombs. Peace through superior firepower—I know Ambassador Wexler's a believer. Than was too, by now.

"They let you smoke in your cabin?" I asked. Even during my days on board *Jefferson,* smoking had been strictly limited to areas away from everyone else. I'd designated one of the areas on the O-10 deck, seven flights above my cabin. We had more men quit that cruise than ever—it just wasn't worth the climb.

"They'd be disappointed if I didn't. After what we went through today." Batman clipped the end of his Dunhill, lit it, and puffed thoughtfully to get it going. Finally, he let out a deep, self-satisfied sigh. "That'll do it."

We were silent for a few moments, enjoying the cigars made slightly even more pleasurable by the fact that they were forbidden. Like sneaking into the bathroom to smoke as a high school kid, I guess. "That was something," I said. "I wouldn't have believed it."

Batman nodded. He knew I meant the J-TARPS systems. It was my first exposure to an operational test, and it gave me an eerie feeling to be flying missions slung below a Tomcat. "Takes some getting used to, though," he said. "Knowing when to jump in, knowing when to shut up. You try to micromanage them in the air, you'll get their balls shot off for them."

"I figured that out. Saw your hand itching a couple of times to pick up the mike, though."

"That it was. But I stayed out of it—at least until the very end. When I thought Bird Dog was going to send that kid home again, I almost choked." Batman scowled as he remembered it. We'd both listened in as Bird Dog had tried to order the persistent Skeeter back to the boat, and finally changed his mind.

"Hell of a pilot," I said.

"Which one?"

"Both of them, I guess. What're you going to do to keep them in line from now on? I think they're going to be a little hard to live with for a while."

Batman snorted. "Tell me something I don't know. Bird Dog's been a pain in the ass since Cuba."

"Good stick, though."

"I'll give him that. But that's not always enough—you know that."

I did indeed. There is a quality that sets apart the finest aviators from the pack, an almost uncanny ability to meld with their aircraft, to run the time-distance-weapon problems in their head without any other decision-making tools. Bird Dog had it, and so did Skeeter.

But it wasn't enough. We fight as teams in this Navy, and not only in combat pairs. It was all a team, from the cruiser that provided long-range air-combat support to the helos that fished pilots out of the drink. It's not enough to be a solo star—you must be a team player as well.

"I think Bird Dog's catching on," I said finally. "Takes some of us longer than others."

Batman laughed. "I wondered if you noticed that. Every time that guy gets himself in the middle of trouble, it reminds me of you."

"If you were a shade darker, you could be Skeeter's father too," I pointed out, not unreasonably. There was something about the way Skeeter performed, the sheer persistence and superb flying abilities, that reminded me of having Batman on my wing.

Batman looked startled, then slightly pleased. "Like I said—the kid's a good stick. Still young, though."

I tapped the ash off my cigar. From the Flag Mess on the other side of the bulkhead, I could hear some officer complain about the smell. A few other voices spoke up and hushed him. I gathered smelling the cigar smoke was the final, unspoken proof that the wardroom relied on as a sign that all was well.

"You didn't find him." Batman's voice was oddly gentle.

"I got close. But there wasn't enough time."

"You coming back?"

I thought for a moment, then shook my head. "Whatever was in that last camp vanished in the fire. If there was anything there to start with."

"So the trail ends here," Batman said. He fiddled with his cigar for a moment. "Doesn't it?"

I smiled a bit. He always could read my mind. "Not entirely. Aside from the issue of my father, there are other questions to answer. The big ones, like what are we going to do about China and Vietnam? And the smaller ones, equally as puzzling. Who was the man that we killed in the jungle—the white guy? A mercenary? Or something else? And Than—what kind of game is he playing? No, there aren't any dead ends here—just more questions."

Batman sighed. "I'd hoped this would be the end of it. The final answer. For you, at least."

"Oh, but there *are* answers. Just not in Vietnam. Not the final ones anyway."

A look of deep concern passed over Batman's face. He leaned forward, planted both elbows on his desk, and pointed the cigar at me. "You're not serious."

I nodded. "I'm very serious. It won't be right away, I suspect. I'm slated to take over Seventh Fleet next month. There's no time, and they're just now starting to declassify some of the records I need."

"What records? Surely with your clearance you can get into anything in D.C. that you need, right?"

I took another long draw on the cigar. "Not in D.C. In Russia."

SOMETHING EXPLODED IN THE SKY...

...something metallic, something swirling, something from hell. Four dark beasts filled the southeastern horizon like the lions of the apocalypse. The reflection of morning light off the sand splayed like blood across their wings...

Startled from the half-daze of the monotonous watch, the sentry grabbed his rifle and flung himself against the sand-filled bags at the front of the trench. It took a moment for his brain to register the fact that the planes were coming from the south and not the north—they were friends, not foes. The thick canisters of death slung beneath their wings were not meant for him.

"What the hell are those," he asked his companion as the planes roared over their positions.

The other soldier laughed. "You never saw A-10 Warthogs before?"

"They're on our side?"

"You better pray to God they are."

A New Series by James Ferro

HOGS

GOING DEEP

Coming in May 1999